NOWHERE IN SIGHT

Elaine Braman

Margarete Johl

Whimsical Publications, LLC

Florida

To purchase the authorized electronic edition of *Nowhere In Sight*, visit www.whimsicalpublications.com

Cover art by Traci Markou
Editing by Brieanna Robertson

ISBN-13: 978-1-940707-26-6

Published by
Whimsical Publications, LLC
Florida

I pressed the garage door opener, and the sensor lights pinged two-sixty watts of light off the white walls. The hinges whined, and the door staggered open. I made a mental note to spray the hinges with WD-40, and hoped the noise had scattered the cat, but Calico hadn't moved.

When I rushed toward the Lexus in my bare feet, waving my arms like a football coach to the end zone, Calico leapt to the trunk and ran off toward the bushes. I set the alarm again and waited for the dome light to fade out, but after what seemed like an hour's worth of minutes, it stayed lit.

"Dammit, Matt." I looked up toward Emma's window to see if by chance he was laughing at me. The window shade was at half-mast like an eyelid, and the blackened window glared down at me.

I unlocked the car, turned the interior light switch on-and-off, grabbed the rifle off the back seat, and stuffed it in the Red Rider sleeve. The interior light faded, leaving me in total darkness when I shut the door. A shiver ran across my shoulders even though it was near eighty degrees. A car across the street started up. I flinched. It coasted away down the hill. I ran on tiptoes to the end of the driveway with the rifle hitched up under my arm. The car coasted to the stop sign, turned on its lights, and sped off toward town. Probably one of the neighbor's one-night-stands. But I still wondered if it was the car that I thought followed me.

The bushes behind me rustled, and I spun around, aiming the car remote at the bushes.

Calico was back, meowing at me and weaving back and forth across the driveway. It stopped and looked into the open garage.

"Oh no you don't."

Calico snapped its tail at me and skittered in under my Jeep.

"Oh no you're not!" I ran up the drive after the cat and stepped on a pebble I'd swear was the size of a golf ball. It flicked out from under my foot and my foot went out from under me.

The rifle flung from my hand, along with Matt's car keys. Both hit the garage floor at the back of my Jeep and slid under the car. I fell to my hands and knees and my teeth slammed together. After several hammer-slamming-thumb cuss words and knee cradling moans, I crawled far enough under the Jeep to retrieve the keys and rifle.

The cat hissed at me, but didn't move.

"Oh come on, cat, go, get out. I'm missing *Dancing with the Stars*."

I didn't mind cats. I liked cats, just not my neighbor's cats. And didn't figure they'd appreciate me locking their cat in my garage all night. I limped around to the driver's side and lay down on the cement floor.

With the rifle stock in hand, I swept the barrel back and forth as if it were a broom. "Go, go on, get out, cat!" I crawled further under the Jeep.

Calico cowered up against my right front tire. He hunched low, his ears swiveled sideways like a swing-wing fighter and his tail swished in wide arcs. Shit, he was ready to attack. He hissed and raked his front paws at the rifle sleeve like a boxer delivering a one-two punch. His right paw caught hold and he tugged. "No, no, kitty. Let go." He pulled back, flipped over sideways and inside out, I'd swear, before his claw released. I yanked the rifle back before he could attack again. And when I did, a click and a whoosh vibrated my hand. A bang like a rock bouncing across a cobblestone road echoed through the garage.

"Shit!" I screamed, and jerked my head back, but not in time to miss the rifle's recoil. The butt end slammed into my brow, and my head bounced against the undercarriage. My heart lobbed into my throat, and the gunshot rang in my ears. My vision blurred, my nose stung, and my right front tire hissed stale air in my face from the huge grin in the rubber. But Calico had screamed his way out of the garage unscarred. I lay there dazed and stared at my flat tire. All I could think about was the hole in Matt's Red Ryder sleeve. At least until a warm tickle ran down my nose to my lips and I tasted blood. Shit, I shot myself.

I began to wiggle my way out from the Jeep just as a pair of feet entered the garage. I froze.

Whoever was attached to the bare feet said nothing and stood still with his toes curled against the cement. Another click jolted me, and I was doused into darkness when the garage sensor light clicked off.

"Where are you?" a man's voice yelled.

ACKNOWLEDGEMENTS

We shout THANK YOU to our publisher Janet Durbin, at Whimsical Publications, for recognizing our potential. Thanks to Brieanna Robertson for her editorial skills and keeping us honest with our punctuation. Thanks to Traci Markou for working with us and designing our book cover – love it!

A special thanks to our friend Sharon—with a standing O—for inspiring us with her oven fire story, which we twisted into Nowhere in Sight, heating up Kate's date night.

A special thank you to MaryAnn de Stefano at MAD About Words (madaboutwords.com) for her professional manuscript evaluation, story and structure guidance and detailed critique. It was a pleasure working with MaryAnn.

"It was a great read with intriguing mysteries—you deftly handle two mysteries—surprising twists and turns, and a skillful and playful writing style. It doesn't get much better than this!" MAD.

BOOKS BY ELAINE BRAMAN
AND MARGARETE JOHL

Right in Sight
Nowhere in Sight

CHAPTER 1

He was staring at me.

I had looked away and dared a peek back in his direction, but he continued his blazing scowl. I hated when people stared; it made me nervous and made me check for missing buttons on my blouse or smudged mascara beneath my eyes. I looked up and right, and down and left before locking eyes with him again. I kept waiting for him to holler across the terminal, "Hey, aren't you that Kate Lambrose who writes that *In Sight* column for *City Scope News*?" Not that I was that well known, and certainly not at the Phoenix Sky Harbor airport.

I turned a slow 360, taking in all the sights. Five elderly women lined up in wheelchairs and sat with their hands clasped in their laps. I smiled and nodded a silent hello to all of them. They all had that frightful lost look in their eyes as if they were orphans. Next to them, a young mother juggled her two toddlers while their father talked on his cell. Classic.

I continued my rotation and paused when I reached Lu-anne Hamilton's nose. My new friend towered over me. Even in her pale pink sneakers, the waistband on her jeans neared bib height on me. She teetered from foot to foot while reading *Right in Sight*, a new novel she picked up at the newsstand. How she could concentrate on a plot while some robotic voice announced the next arrival or delayed departure was beyond me. I admired her ability to be oblivious to the world around her and her self-confidence to wear pink sneakers at the age of 42. I was six months older than her and hadn't worn pink sneakers a day in my life.

My full circle brought me right back to Mr. Scowl. He had moved closer and stopped when I turned. The game 1, 2, 3 Red Light buzzed in my brain. And something was familiar about him. His black-rimmed glasses posed against his forehead and magnified his frown wrinkles. I could never keep my glasses perched on my forehead. It was a guy thing like arching spittle. Mr. Scowl looked to be in his late sixties with a full head of white hair and thick black brows.

"Jeez," I said.

"You talking to me?" Luanne nudged me.

I half turned and cupped my hand from my nose to my chin in case Scowl could read lips. "That man"—I pointed into my open palm—"is staring at me."

"Where? Who?" Luanne stretched up on her toes.

"Stop that." I gripped her shoulder and pulled her down from her giraffe stance.

"Do you have any idea how many men are in that one line? Which guy are you talking about?"

I faced her full on. "The one with the black glasses, white hair, and blue shirt. The gruesome one."

"Oh, he almost looks like the attorney from the bank."

I sighed and shook my head. She wasn't seeing straight. Luanne's vision was blurred with dollar signs from claiming her inheritance. I doubted either of us took more than a three-second glance at the attorney. Our attention had been on the yellow-tinged document; Luanne's grandmother's last will and testament.

"No." I shook my head and pointed my thumb over my shoulder. "That man doesn't look anything like your attorney. Well, except maybe the white hair and blue shirt. But I'd swear I've seen him before."

Luanne shrugged and looked back at her book. "He was probably on the same flight with us from Boston to here." She closed her book and stuffed it under her arm.

"I don't know, maybe." I returned her shrug.

"Sure, that's why he looks familiar, but from a distance, he could almost be my infamous father, Mack." She sucked in a long breath. "Maybe that's why he's gruesome to you."

"And that idea doesn't bother you?" I slammed my fists on my hips.

"He's dead," she said.

"Did you see a dead body? I didn't. And what if his death was just a ploy for revenge?" After all, Mack was conniving enough to let Luanne's mother drown, and he tried to fry us in a dumbwaiter when we learned the truth.

"Oh my God, Kate!" Luanne laughed. "You need to write fiction, not a newspaper column. Or go with Emma to her creative writing class."

"Huh. Maybe I should." I laughed. Or at least consider writing a memoir. But fiction would give me the outlet to play the character dressed in black. A rogue private eye or an investigator of the underworld. I always wanted to join the ranks with Woodward and Bernstein.

"So when does Emma return from California?" Luanne asked.

A sigh threatened to escape my lips. I missed my daughter already, and she had only been gone four days. Somehow, the planned two-week vacation with her father had turned into four weeks instead. I had 28 more days to stumble through without Emma.

"They return to Boston on August 2nd, unless of course she gets homesick and calls."

"Seriously, Kate. She's fourteen and with her father. How is she going to get homesick?"

"Wishful thinking?"

"I know, but you need to embrace your freedom while she's away. Kick up your heels, find a man, have sex, and help me spend my inheritance."

"Jeez." I looked over my shoulder toward Mr. Scowl, but he was gone from his post. "Luanne, you need to whisper about inheritance, not announce it to the whole airport."

The inheritance was originally left to Rosalyn, Luanne's mother, by Lydia, Rosalyn's mother. It was confusing even for us who understood the fallen leaves from Luanne's family tree. Anyway, Luanne was now the proud owner of a yellowed, frayed land deed listing a parcel of land at the corner of 34th street in New York City. To be exact, a parcel where Macy's stood, or some part of Macy's back door. Along with the deed, she had the original signed land lease between Lydia and Macy's. The best part of the lease, according to the attorney who translated the fancy-dance lingo, was that Luanne's estate was now worth over ten million dollars. The other items in the deposit box were unique and memorable. A pair of diamond earrings, which dangled brilliantly against Luanne's dark hair, a purple rabbit's foot, and a brittle turtle shell. The significance of those last two items would forever remain a mystery, because there was no one to ask. Luanne was the last leaf on her family tree.

She patted her belt buckle. "No worries, Kate. No one can get to my inheritance unless they strip off my clothes." She laughed.

"What?" I stepped back and eyed her. Luanne wore her stylish clothes tighter than wallpaper. Someone would need a putty knife to strip them off. "What did you do?"

She flipped her long, dark hair over her shoulder. "I'm wearing it," she whispered, and fluffed her blouse.

She always had a color theme with her tops and shoes. Her pale pink lace blouse skimmed her hot pink camisole. I, on the other hand, owned black, brown, navy, beige, and white, and preferred comfort and stretch.

"I don't think I want to know where you stuffed that document."

She smiled. "Only the Queen's guard can get ya there," she squealed in her faux British accent. She habitually conjured up different dialects for entertainment, or to hide her thick Boston accent. I didn't know which, but it was fun.

I slapped my hand over my mouth to muffle my laughter and turned a 180.

My giggle jumped right out of my skin as Mr. Scowl faced me head-on less than ten feet away. My heart bubbled in my chest. A stench of after-shave strayed up my nose. It stirred a familiarity that zoomed in and out of my mind before I could clasp onto the memory. I pretended to sneeze into my elbow and shuffled backwards behind Luanne.

I spun around and looked for some elbow room to stand, but better than that, I spotted two men giving up their seats along the back wall.

I grabbed Luanne's arm and scurried through the cluster of people. Luanne made a crinkling sound as she sat down, and I frowned at her.

"Never mind," she said. "Tell me, did you get any more information from your dramatist, Perry?" Luanne asked.

"Terri Wolf, not Perry, and no, not yet. I left her a message about the strange caller, but then you and I left for Arizona, so maybe I'll hear from her tomorrow."

Here I was in pursuit of a missing heirloom for one of my avid readers and providing emotional support to my BFF while she claimed her inheritance. Huh. I could add, *inheritance hunter* to my resumé.

"Why do you suppose your mystery caller referred to her as a dramatist?"

"I don't know."

"It's odd. Don't you think?"

"It's all odd. Maybe he meant drama queen," I said.

"I'd bet my purple bunny paw one of them is lying to you."

"I don't think it's Terri. She doesn't seem like the type."

Luanne batted her pink-tinted lashes at me and shook her head. Her way of telling me that my wishful thinking was naïve.

Luanne didn't know Terri like I did. After I received Terri Wolf's letter asking me to help find her family heirloom, I met with her over brewed tea. In her late sixties, with a hair-do left over from Carol Brady, Terri stood maybe four-foot, ten inches tall. If a puff of wind caught her skirt, she'd soar off like a kite. And she had more wrinkles in her cheeks than my pillow slip had. Terri hadn't meant to stuff the portrait in the box headed to Goodwill, but her husband had walked in just as she was trying to remove the portrait from the frame. The portrait had no sentimental value to her. She had her eye on the frame, and being an antique dealer, she knew its worth.

"If he wants to file for divorce after thirty years of marriage, then I deserve the frame. I figured I'd leave him the portrait. After all, it is his grandmother, not mine," she had said. "But of course I wasn't going to tell him that. I don't want another confrontation about what belongs to who. And I'm just telling you. You won't tell, will you, Kate?"

For God's sake. I was a CSN reporter, not FBI, CIA, or Homeland Security. I took my oath seriously and never revealed my source. And I didn't need my sources confessing their personal business. I didn't like gossipy secrets, especially when I was the one left holding the lies.

"I, uhm, I can't imagine when I'd have the opportunity to tell him." I looked toward the front door and prayed Albert Wolf wouldn't rush in huffing and puffing and demand the truth. The little piggy in me would squeal for sure.

"Well, I'm just saying, you don't need to tell him," she said. "Oh, by the way, there is a handwritten phrase on the backing board that reads, '*Your future is in the past.*'"

When I asked her what that meant, she just laughed and said she didn't have a clue. To me, it sounded like a curse. She then handed me a snapshot of Poppy, her poodle, sitting on the couch with the portrait hanging on the wall in the background. I was surprised. I expected Grandma Moses, not a young woman no more than twenty-five years old. Terri explained that the portrait was painted back in 1907 and then handed me a post-it note with a detailed description of the 10" x 13" frame.

The frame was handcrafted in Germany in the 1800s, with swirls of stylized leaves and waves. It had deeply hand-carved undercuts, pigeonholes, and hand applied genuine 22-karat gold leaf. To Terri, the frame was a priceless antique. To me, it was God-awful. She made me promise not to mention in my column that the frame was an antique and just refer to the portrait as a family heirloom. I promised her I would do my best and wrote my copy titled *Ornate Treasure Chase.* I used Terri's detailed description and a cropped photo showing the top half of the frame and Grandmother's face.

Two days after the *City Scope* edition hit the newsstand, I received my first reader-response about the portrait. My mystery caller was either a woman with a near tenor voice or a man with a near soprano voice who refused to give up *his or her* name. Mys Caller was excited to see the portrait of Grandmother alive and well in my column. But Mys Caller was adamant that the framed portrait was indeed *his or her* grandmother stolen from *his or her* home after a house fire forty-five years ago.

"Seriously?" I asked. After all, I had just dealt with a hair-raising fire because of a forty-year-old murder. How co-incidental my newest caper would be so closely significant to my last.

"Of course I'm serious, Ms. Lambrose. And I demand to know the name of your dramatist," Mys Caller said.

"Dramatist?" I asked.

Mys Caller yelled into my ear. "Yes, dammit. What is the name of this person claiming to be *my* grandmother Petra's grandchild! Look Ms. Lambrose...my family died in that house fire. I was away on a scout camping trip. I have no siblings left."

Girl Scouts? Boy Scouts? I thought, hoping to identify the gender of my caller. But I didn't think it appropriate to ask at that moment. "I'm happy to take your name and number and when and if I recover the frame and or portrait, I'll invite you to come view it."

"The frame? Are you fucking kidding me?" Mys said. "I want the portrait, for crying out loud. The frame is worthless, nothing but sticks glued together."

I had considered asking Mys Caller if they knew the phrase handwritten on the backing board, but after the profanity blasted in my ear, why divulge any information when Mys Caller refused to offer his or her name?

"Look, like I said, I'll take your name and number, but I cannot reveal my source and—"

"And your column is a joke, Ms. Lambrose, and you and your newspaper have not heard the last of me!" Mys hung up loudly.

A joke? And then I had my a-ha moment. Mys Caller was probably none other than Terri's husband. It all made sense with what Terri had said. Her husband would be upset with her if he knew she had misplaced their family heirloom. When I questioned her about the possibility of him reading my column, she said that he didn't read anything but the sports page and that he thought my column was a joke.

"Huh, a joke my ass," I said aloud, and turned to Luanne who had her nose back in her book. "Do you think my column is a joke?"

"Well, isn't it supposed to be entertaining and funny?"

"Yes, but I mean is it a joke as in worthless words?"

"Who said that to you?" Luanne asked.

"Yes or no?"

"No. And obviously your editor doesn't think so either or you wouldn't be still writing it." She smirked. "You need to learn to trust your gut, Kate."

I stuttered to defend my confidence, but the robotic voice announced the boarding of our flight number 2021 home to Boston.

"Hold that thought." I gathered up my belongings, and we shuffled down the ramp.

CHAPTER 2

We hoofed down the middle aisle like cattle off to market. I pulled up the rear with my elbows tucked against my udders. The stop-and-go shuffle gave me time to look over my shoulder for Mr. Scowl. I hadn't seen him in line in front of us as we passed through the gate, which meant he was following me.

Luanne stopped and whispered over her shoulder, "Ten-A."

"What?"

"Ten-A, Ten-A," she said.

The boarding pass in my hand was seven rows beyond 10A. "No." I nudged her. "We're in seventeen B and C."

"I know." She chuckled and shuffled along. "Fourteen-F," she called over her shoulder.

"What game are you playing now?" I stretched my neck to look for 10A, expecting to see Mr. Scowl. But a man wearing a western hat occupied 10A. His biceps stressed his black tee, and he was ruggedly handsome.

"Bingo," I whispered at Luanne's back.

"See what I'm talking about?"

Ahead of Luanne, the young mother with the two toddlers ducked into their seats, and I peered around her searching out seat 14F. He wore a business suit, freshly pressed and ready for serious cross-examination. Not a hair out of place with side burns trimmed straighter than my bangs.

Luanne's taste in men varied from boot-kicking bull riders to lethal, legal liars. At least her current love interest, a well-mannered, macho medic, shocked Luanne's heart into a steady rhythm. But I had no room to tease her about her choices. First, I had dated so-and-so back in college, who was arrested for B&E. Second was my daughter's father, who decided after fifteen years of marriage he preferred a male partner over me. And then there was my friend, the therapist, who was fun and safe. Not that any of them were poor choices at the time. But none of them could jolt me out of my panties like Michael Earl could. Not that we were an item, but I wouldn't mind seeing him in his cop uniform and nightstick. *Uhm, Michael Earl*. My heart purred.

Luanne stowed her carry-on in the overhead above our seats. "Are you sure you don't want the window seat?"

"Not unless you can open it." I fanned my face, waving away thoughts of Michael Earl.

She shook her head and settled in. After scanning the occupied seats around us for heads of milk-white hair, I plopped into the middle seat. Either Mr. Scowl was far up front, or in the lavatory, or not on this flight. I shrugged, dropped my tote under the seat in front of me, and begged karma that no one would sit next to me.

"You're not going to get all crazy again like on the flight out, are you?" Luanne asked.

"Nope." I lifted my sleeve and tapped the Dramamine patch.

On the flight out, we had been seated by the emergency exit row until the flight attendant instructed us on what our job was in the event of an emergency. "You what? You want me to help everyone else off the plane first?" I said. "Are you freaking kidding me? I've got a daughter. I will get off this flight when I want." After we were re-seated one row behind the emergency exit row, and Luanne ordered wine, I calmed down.

"I'm self-medicated and should be sedated enough by the time we hit the runway." I winked.

"Uh huh, sure." Luanne nodded.

I clicked my seat belt, tugged it tight, closed my eyes, and searched for my inner peace.

"So, finish telling me about Terri," Luanne said. "Convince me that she isn't the one lying to you."

"Not much more to tell."

"Just talk, it'll keep your mind off trying to fly the plane."

"Haa Haa."

One flight attendant walked down the aisle, checking laps

and tapping seatbacks that needed to be returned to their upright position. The forward attendant stood mid-aisle and prepared her what-the-hell-to-do-if-we-crash speech. I swallowed hard and glanced at Luanne, who was once again oblivious with her nose back in her book.

"All right, all right," I said. "After I received Terri's note, I had to check facts, you know? I don't want a run-in with the police again or end up with a stolen portrait that once hung on the walls of the Louvre or something."

Luanne snickered. "Right. From the Louvre to Yardman? Bit of a stretch, don't you think?"

"You never know."

The plane lurched forward and the engines throttled up.

"So, when I met with Terri, she divulged all the down and dirty details, even some dirty laundry about her pending divorce."

The tires thumped over the tarmac in opposing rhythm to my pounding heart. We picked up speed, rocketing down the runway. I clenched my eyes closed and grabbed hold of the armrests. I was ready to help lift this plane off the ground.

"So, then," I continued, hoping to keep my focus on our conversation and away from the shuddering plane. "I got that call from Mys Caller and still don't know if it was a he or she."

"No caller ID?"

I shook my head. "All zeroes."

"I don't answer for all zeroes."

"Neither do I at home, but at work, it's a different story. I might miss out on a good scoop."

"True."

The front of the plane heaved up and I was pushed back into my seat. I grabbed Luanne's hand when the landing gear clunked in place under my feet. The pilot dipped the plane right, made a turn, and kept climbing. The pressure built up in the cabin, in my ears, and in my chest. I half expected to explode.

Luanne patted my hand and mumbled something. I opened my eyes so I could hear her better. "What?" I asked.

"I said, you have control issues."

"And you don't?" I laughed.

Her right eyebrow climbed centimeters up her forehead

in a perfect tweezed arch. She was the only person I knew who could convey a dozen emotions with one brow.

Even though Luanne and I met by chance on the night her surrogate mother, Abby, died, we became fast friends. In less than two months, Luanne had dragged me out of my solitary life and done more for me than two years of therapy. And she claimed that her newfound wealth was my fault and that made us even. My now wealthy friend absently stroked the purple rabbit's foot. She had attached it to a chain and used it as a bookmarker—an eccentric keepsake that suited her mystic nature. After all, reclaiming a piece of her missing past would give her closure and help her gather her fallen family leaves.

The angled thrust leveled off, and chimes dinged overhead.

"Welcome, folks." The flight attendant keyed her mic. "The captain has turned off the seatbelt sign and—" The rest of her spiel was gobbled up by the crying baby up front.

I yawned to snap the altitude cotton from my ears. Luanne leaned her head back and closed her eyes, which meant I could get a head start writing next week's column. I pulled my tote from under the seat and bent forward at the exact moment the guy in front of me reclined his seat. I folded up like an omelet and dragged my head sideways from under the seat back. After I yanked my hair free from the tray clip, I slipped my work folder from my bag.

I flicked the wrinkles out of my newspaper, snapped it open, and studied my column layout. The *Ornate Treasure Chase* was the top story in my column last week, and would be at the bottom this week. I had nothing more to say about it, at least not yet.

My column, *In Sight*, had gained notoriety since I received the cryptic poem asking me to locate a missing person. Come to find out the missing person was Luanne's birth mother, Rosalyn, who long ago died. But I didn't know that then. And the poem was written to expose the truth about Luanne's stepmother and Mack's role in the death of Rosalyn. It was a sad, tragic, and twisted story that went up in flames along with the newspaper office. Since then, my editor warned me to stay clear of requests from readers asking me to search for missing people. Good thing only a portrait of Grandmother was missing; she wasn't a living, breathing victim.

The plane shuddered and dipped. A hairy-knuckled hand grabbed the seat back in front of me. My eyes slid from the manly hand across to his waist and traveled up the length of his blue button-down shirt.

Mr. Scowl towered over me and reached into the overhead bin directly above our seats. Holy crap. Where had he come from? And that smell—bug spray or something. The sugary stench stung my nostrils. I swallowed hard and tried not to stare up his nostrils or at the sweat stains darkening his armpits.

"Luanne." I nudged her arm off the armrest.

"What? And what is that smell? Did something break in—" She stopped mid-sentence when she looked up. "It's him."

The plane bounced again, and Mr. Scowl braced his hands on the bin. His glasses slid off his forehead and plopped in the seat next to me. One of the lenses popped free and leapfrogged into my lap, landing smack dab on my by-line photo.

"Eeww," Luanne said.

I squeezed her wrist to cut off whatever insult hung on her tongue, but I was too late.

"Greasy too," she added.

"Oh Jesus, I'm sorry," Mr. Scowl said. His hand hovered above my lap, ready to pick up his lens.

I stared at it, amazed at how it had landed. It perfectly circled my picture and magnified my toothy smile.

Luanne plucked the piece of glass from my lap and handed it over. "Here. You'd have to take her to dinner first. No free grabs."

"Oh my God. Don't listen to her," I said. "No dinner necessary."

He frowned at me, and Luanne whispered that she didn't think that's what I meant.

"Thanks, I think." He took the lens from Luanne's fingertips. "Hey, that's a picture of you, right?" He squinted his left eye and used the lens as a magnifier. He looked like a German field marshal, but I was surprised by the sweet tone of his voice. It wasn't as threatening as his scowl looked. And up close, with his lopsided one-dimpled grin, he didn't look anything like Mack.

"Hey yourself," Luanne said. "Do we know you?"

"I, uhum, don't think so, why?"

Luanne elbowed me. "Then why were you staring at us?" I asked, picking up where she left off.

His lips creased together. "I didn't know I was. When?"

I looked at Luanne. She shrugged and said, "Maybe you were just in his line of sight."

That made sense to me. After all, I wouldn't have seen him looking at me if he hadn't been in my line of sight. Luanne and I looked back at him with nothing more to say.

"So what did you do to get in the paper?" he asked.

"I wrote the column." My chest puffed out as I sat a little straighter.

"Oh, so you're a journalist, eh? You know, I've done some writing once or twice in my life. What do you write? You look like an outdoorsy type. You write sports?" He plunked down in the seat next to me.

I fidgeted closer to Luanne.

"Nah, you wouldn't write about sports. Maybe a bunch of house-wifey anecdotes." He bounced his head back against the seat and cackled.

I whipped my head toward Luanne, who had a wide grin plastered on her face, but her teeth were clenched. I frowned at her with my lips firmly squeezed between my teeth. Mr. Scowl literally cackled like a chicken. At any moment, we would burst out laughing.

I exhaled a long breath. "Uhm, no not sports and no household hints," I said. "I write the *In Sight* column for *City Scope News*. It's a new age, humorous lost and found piece with a twist of advice," I explained.

"Oh like a Dear Abby column?"

Luanne groaned. Abby wasn't a name either of us cared to hear or reminisce about, for awhile at least.

"Yeah, I hear ya over there." He leaned across me and waved his hand in Luanne's face. "I'd rather read about sports too," he said.

I could almost feel the heat radiating from Luanne's face as her rude-person-temper smoldered.

"Advice, huh? So what kind of advice?" He settled back in the seat and fussed with his lens, squeezing it back in the frame. I handed him the *City Scope* newspaper. "Here, read for yourself."

Luanne whispered into my shoulder, "Your new best friend, Kate?"

I shrugged. "No harm," I said. Besides, as a journalist for *City Scope,* it was my job to solicit readers. After Scowl finished scanning my column, he handed it back to me.

"So let me get this straight. People write you letters asking you to find shit for them?" He didn't wait for an answer. "That doesn't seem odd to you? I mean, can't people find their own stuff? I mean, after all, there *is* the Internet and all that jazz."

"True," I said, "but sometimes it's all about how the item went missing to begin with that tells the story."

He frowned. "Yeah, yeah, so are those the requests you get?" He nodded at the stack of mail I had on my lap.

I always carried my requests with me for inspiration. Some weren't even opened yet, and others, like Terri's note, were paper clipped at the bottom of my pile.

"Yes." I patted my pile.

"Let me see'em," he said.

Faster than I could think of a polite way to tell Scowl that my lap was none of his business, he grabbed the stack of mail. It happened so fast I didn't see where his Jekyll ran to hide.

At least Luanne had the good sense to push the call button. I ripped my mail from Mr. Scowl's sticky fingers and hoped I caused some paper cuts along his lifeline. By the time the flight attendant pushed past the drink cart, Luanne had beaten him back into the aisle with a scowl of her own.

"He's jumping seats and helping himself to my belongings. Right off my lap." I squinted at the flight attendant as if she'd caused his behavior.

"It's not like I groped you, for God's sake, just picked up your stupid letters. But maybe next time you're in my sights, I'll take you out," Mr. Scowl said.

"Did he just threaten to shoot you?" Luanne asked.

I shook my head. I wanted to believe he was just hinting for a date, the dirty old man.

CHAPTER 3

After I picked up my Jeep from Luanne's house, I had a 45-minute drive to ponder Mr. Scowl's last words. Every thought ended with the same questions—why did he grab my mail? What was his ulterior motive? And now—why was a large silver sedan mimicking every turn I made.

Never had I noticed how many silver cars traveled the roadways—behind me, beside me, and in front of me. By the time I exited Route 2, I'd come full circle in my ramblings and lost sight of the silver car.

I turned left on Winter Street and barreled up the hill. Just as I was about to turn the corner, a pair of headlights flashed in my rear view mirror. I sped around the corner and repeatedly jabbed my thumb on my garage remote button. The door bobbed in place, wide open, and I skidded to a stop, hitting the tennis ball strung from the rafters. It bounced frantically against my windshield and mimicked my pulse.

Pressing the remote, I yelled, "Close, close." As I ran around to the front of my Jeep, the door whined down painfully slow. So slow that the headlights from a car pulling into my driveway lit up my garage floor for one second.

I stood in the doorway to my kitchen with one foot still in the garage. The house creaked and groaned with old growing pains. The refrigerator icemaker spit out a cube and I jumped. But no other sounds from outside echoed in the dark.

I patted my chest to revive my heart out of a-fib and sucked in a long, cleansing breath. Nothing more than my imagination and someone borrowing the driveway to turn around.

As I hauled my belongings from the Jeep, a car door slammed shut, and it wasn't mine. Shit! Another door slammed, followed by rustling. Holy crap, how many people were outside?

I beat feet back into the house, locked the door behind me, ran upstairs in the dark, and groped my way into my daughter's bedroom.

I peeked out Emma's bedroom window to the yard below. A two-ton gray Cadillac hogged my driveway. Downstairs, the doorknob rattled and the stalker punched my doorbell like a pedestrian waiting at a crosswalk.

A female voice yelled, "I know ya home!"

I knew the voice, but couldn't give it a name. A hulky figure wearing a straw sombrero stepped off the porch landing and onto the driveway. The dark complexion made the person look like a shadow under an umbrella.

The stranger's head dipped back and scanned up toward me. I sidestepped from the window and stumbled into the bedside table. My hand steadied the touch lamp to keep it from falling and it lit up, framing me in the window like a Christmas tree.

"Hey, Katie, there ya are!" Sadie Arnold waved like a drowning swimmer.

I slid open the window. "Are you following me?"

"Not following. I saw ya at the Burger King. Come on down and open up the door so I can talk at ya."

"Wait. I wasn't at Burger King."

"Ya, I know. Did ya know they got two for one jumbo drinks?"

I shook my head and slammed the window shut.

"Come on down, honey, and open up ya door. Ya can't be leaving ya biggest fan on ya doorstep, would ya? Please."

Yes, I would at this time of night. Nevertheless, I was relieved it was just Sadie. She had scared whatever lulling effects the Dramamine had right out of my system. My fear turned into irritation. And what the heck did she mean, she saw me at the Burger King?

She dinged the doorbell again just as I reached the front door. "Okay, okay." I slid the chain free and swung open the door.

She plowed on through, dropping a Market Rite grocery sack filled with newspapers at my feet.

"Oh thank ya, Lord, I was afraid I wasn't gonna make it. I got to use ya facilities." She sashayed her hips from side to side. The giraffe print muumuu she wore swirled around her girth like a weatherman's windy day graphic.

"Are you alone?" I asked. "I heard two doors close."

"Oh. I was getting my articles out of my back seat file box." She pointed at the grocery sack filled with tabloids. "I figured we could dish some scoops."

Ice cream? I thought, but then connected scoops with tabloids. Sadie had her own expressions and lingo that baffled me much of the time.

"But first I have to take care of business, if ya know what I mean." She handed me her bladder buster-sized drink. "That there is my twofer."

"Twofer?" I frowned.

"Uh-huh. Buy one get one free. Which way, Katie?" For a large woman, she was light on her feet as she did the tinkle dance.

"Through the kitchen on the left." I pointed.

Sadie slammed the door and kept chatting. "I can't wait to hear if ya found any new leads, Katie. I love it when ya run ya column and have these unsolved mysteries that require the public's help. 'Cause ya know, I am the public, and I'd do anything to help."

When she emerged from the bathroom, I headed toward the door to show her out. She followed me far enough to retrieve her grocery sack then circled back to the couch.

"You're very helpful, Sadie." My palm cradled the doorknob, ready to whisk it open. "But it's late."

"Oh hon, it's only eight p.m. and y'all still on Arizona time. Come sit."

"Wait. How do you know I was in Arizona?" I planted my hands on my hips.

Sadie smiled so wide her cheeks hiked her harlequin frames out of sync with her eyes. "I got me some sleuthing abilities too, ya know."

"Tell the truth." I frowned, pressing wrinkles into my forehead that would never fade.

"Oh all right. One of them gals at CSN office told me where ya went."

I bet I knew which one, too. "And how did you know I was home now?"

"Well, I told ya that, weren't ya listening?" Her eyes did a slow roll. "'Cause I saw ya at Burger King. I was in the drive-thru. Ya know how that faces the interstate off ramp? It was pure luck. I spotted your Jeep and followed ya home from there."

That made sense. It didn't explain the silver sedans, but my paranoia and imagination would.

"Sadie, I'm really tired and have to unpack. Can we do this another time?" Although, I still didn't know what *this* was or why she was here.

She snuggled deeper into the couch and patted the space next to her. "Come sit. I wanted to discuss the Ornate Treasure Chase." She pulled the straw hat off her head and tossed it on the coffee table. Beneath her hat, her dyed blonde hair was pressed flat by a do-rag with only her curly bangs springing from its confines.

My shoulders slumped and I tossed my head back, wondering why I ever opened the door.

"Oh I can see y'all wondering what I got to say. Asking the Lord above ain't gonna get ya the answer. But I'll tell ya. I don't think that portrait is missing at all."

"Why do you say that?" She had my attention despite my vow to not dish. I sat on the opposite side of the couch from her. "Why write to me to find something that isn't missing?"

"I'll tell ya why." She dug into her grocery sack and flitted through the tabloids like a postal worker processing mail. "I read a story in one of these here papers about a similar thing. 'Cept it wasn't a portrait, it was a diamond necklace. And it wasn't lost, but reported stolen."

"Yeah, but that's not anything like my story."

"Now wait, don't go jumping ahead of me. What I'm telling ya is it was *reported* stolen, but it wasn't. Maybe the portrait is just reported missing, but not."

"Why would someone do that?"

"Here!" Sadie held up the rag mag and jabbed at one of the headline hooks. *Bogus Claim Harms Family Name.* "Read it."

I gently pushed her extended arm back out of my bubble space. "You read it. I'm tired."

"Oh sure, I understand. I'll just tell ya about it. It's because of insurance."

"Insurance?"

"Exactly. If that portrait is an ornate treasure, why not just pretend it was missing and collect on the insurance?"

"I really don't think that's the case. It's a family heirloom, not tagged as any inheritance with extraordinary value." At least I didn't think so.

Sadie grabbed her bladder buster soft drink and slurped. "No?"

I shook my head.

"How about this then?" She pawed the stack of papers again and showed me another headline. *Aliens Snatch Art to Get Inside Perspective of Humanoid Life.*

I shook my head again.

"Ya don't believe in aliens?"

"Uh uh."

She turned her nose toward me and stared at me head on through her reading glasses. Her eyes were magnified two times larger than normal and widened in soft dismay. "But I saw lights in the sky. I sent ya an email 'cause I figured ya missed it being out of town."

"I'll look into it for you." I yawned and stretched my arms. I didn't want to be rude. I liked Sadie, but not after a very long, strange day. "I really do have lots of stuff to do, and have to be back at work early tomorrow." I slid off the couch, hoping she'd follow.

"Oh go on and do what ya have to do. I don't mind. I'll sit here and do research for us."

"Really, Sadie, you don't have to—" My home phone rang, cutting my direct approach off before the words left my lips.

Sadie looked to the ringing phone and back at me. She smiled so wide I saw every tooth in her mouth. "Well aren't ya popular? Looks like ya got messages on the machine there too. Ya want me to get that?"

"No, no." I grabbed the handset and grumbled, "Hello."

"Jeez Kate. You were supposed to call me when you got home," Luanne said. "Then you don't answer your cell." Her voice raised an octave. "I don't think you want to know what I thought after that run-in with that freak on the plane."

"I'm sorry, sorry," I said. "I got a little sidetracked."

Sadie rattled papers behind me. "Lookie here at this one." She swatted me with a tabloid. "Oh, I think I have it now."

"You have company?" Luanne asked.

"You could say that."

"Do you need me to call a cop for you?"

I rolled my eyes. Luanne would never give up pushing me toward Michael Earl. "No, nothing like that." I giggled.

"Who's there?"

"Sadie Arnold is visiting," I said with a forced smile.

"Your favorite groupie?" Luanne laughed.

"Yup."

"Okay then. Au revoir."

"French?"

"I like variety," she said, and hung up.

Sadie wasted no time filling the sudden silence and spouted off another three headlines. I left her on the couch rooting through her papers and headed to the kitchen. She talked loud enough that I'd swear she followed me. I poured myself a glass of wine and dug a frozen leftover slice of cheesecake from the freezer. I'd indulge later, alone.

I sauntered back into the living room and plopped back down on the couch. "You're not going to find where that portrait went by reading any of that," I said.

Sadie sighed. "Well, I suppose. Although, says here an alien Bible was found and they worship Oprah. I believe that, 'cause I love that woman too. I'm gonna get me some tickets to her show one day."

I smiled into my drink. Sadie was a woman with dreams, and I liked that about her. But right about now, I'd offer to buy her a ticket if she'd take to the road.

"Hey, ya wanna watch some TV? Maybe that'd loosen our minds a little, ya know, help figure out your puzzle."

I snatched the remote out of her hand before she could turn on the TV.

"How about these here messages?" Her hand hit play before she finished her sentence. "Maybe ya got a lead on here we need to hear."

"Hi Kate, Call me...please. I have an important question to ask you." George, my ex-husband's, voice bounced from the speaker. I jumped up and hit pause.

"Oh my? Who's that?" Sadie asked. "What do ya suppose he wants?" She shimmed her shoulders and winked at me.

If she only knew. I had nothing George wanted. But it tickled my curiosity as much as it did Sadie's. What would be important but not important? Because surely, if George needed an immediate answer, he would have called me on my cell.

I gathered up Sadie's rag mags and dumped them back into her grocery sack. Sharing, or rather listening to her theories about the portrait was something I could tolerate. I wasn't prepared to let her into my personal life. "I'm sorry, Sadie. I really am tired. Reverse jet lag, you know."

"Right. I understand." She clamped her straw hat back onto her head. She spared a longing look at my answering machine as she glided past it, but I whisked ahead to open the door.

"Drive safe. I'll check out your email," I said.

"Emails," she corrected. "Are ya sure ya don't want to go over some other items? I have a list of things for ya to investigate. And we haven't figured out where the portrait is yet."

I had the door just inches away from her backside, trying to propel her forward without actually hitting her. "Later, okay?"

"But the stars and stripes, what about them missing from the flag?"

"Optical illusion. Must be how the wind blows."

"Oh, Katie, that's a good answer! Maybe I'll take a trip and check it out. Do a little scoop snoop."

"Uh huh, goodnight." I shut the door and leaned against it.

When her engine started, I settled back on the couch and resumed play on the answering machine.

"Emma and I are having a wonderful time, and guess who won first place for his nightscape oil and acrylic entry?" George said.

Oh, that was nice. I rolled my eyes. He probably wanted me to announce his partner's accolades in the paper. He was barking up the wrong tree on that one, but he'd been barking up the wrong tree for years during our marriage. I erased George's message, and dialed him back. His voicemail picked up, so I left him a brief message that I was back in town, offered congratulations to his partner, and love, hugs, and miss yous for Emma, then signed off with, "Tag. You're it." I pressed play for the next message.

"Hey, Kate, I know you and Luanne are in Arizona. Sorry I missed you."

I purred. The timbre of Michael Earl's voice melted me into the cushions, and I propped my feet across the coffee table. I thought about him a lot, but couldn't get past the awkward phase to call him and chat. Huh, now I'd have an excuse to call him.

My brain immediately hop-scotched off into the future. "I missed you too," I would say. But of course, that future didn't exist beyond the figment of my imagination.

I focused back on Michael's message still droning from the answering machine.

"You know, I'm really curious what was inside that box," he said. "And if it was worth the trip."

Oh my. I sighed, even though I knew he was talking about the safety deposit box. I could replay this message all night. I curled my toes and cooled my forehead with my wine glass.

"Anyway..." Papers rustled in the background and he cleared his throat.

Although my fantasy was one-sided, I imagined that he was clearing his head of the same sultry thoughts. Because heaven help me, my brain stoked a fire that threatened to melt me into a puddle.

"I wanted to let you know the forensics are back and the identity of the two bodies found were positively confirmed as the Malecks."

That was a definite mood killer, and I pressed pause. Three weeks ago, Luanne and I had learned that Mack and Nora Maleck's Impala was found alongside a frontage road off Interstate 10 between El Paso and San Antonio, Texas. The vehicle had been abandoned, out of fuel with a radiator drier than the desert. The local authorities assumed the occupants had set off on foot for assistance or hitched a ride.

"Karma delivered some Texas-sized judgment," Luanne had said when she learned that her father, Mack, and his wife were left to wander in the shimmering heat waves radiating from the desert floor. I, on the other hand, had worried they had escaped over the border to Mexico.

I pressed play. "Anyway, I hope that gives you some closure and relief," Michael said.

Closure? Yes. But relief? Not exactly the type of relief I expected.

CHAPTER 4

At 7:15, my alarm finally pulled me out of my jet lag nightmare. I bolted upright, snatched straight from dreamland and dropped into my real reality. I sniffed the air for smoke. None. Slamming my palm on my clock, I quieted the blaring fire alarm that had been in my dream.

Shaking and bathed in a cold sweat, I sat stranded on the edge of my bed. Jeez, it had been nearly two months since fire chased me out of the basement of *City Scope*. I hadn't had a nightmare all weekend, but now on home turf, my subconscious ante upped all its chips. Definitely no more rich cheesecake before lights out.

My dream-self chose a seat in first class. Mr. Cowboy, Luanne's 10A bingo score, saddled up in the seat next to me. And in the next minute, it was Michael Earl, and then not. I chatted him up one side of his well-worn denim, straight down the other side like a blind woman reading Braille.

Mr. Cowboy draped a red bandana across my lap when sizzling rib eyes appeared on our seat back trays. Yippee ki-yay. I sizzled.

His lips brushed mine, and it was Michael again. I hurled the plate into the air. Molotov cocktails splattered around me and burst into flames. Luanne disappeared along with Mr. Cowboy. Hell, all the passengers were missing. I had dreamed myself into a Stephen King novel.

White puffs of clouds rolled past the windows and seeped through the plane's seams, filling it with smoke. Finger curls of smoke reached toward me and burst into flaming walls, pushing me further back into Coach. Like a fighter pilot pulling an emergency chute, I ejected from my seat.

I landed feet first in the middle of the tarmac. Matchbox-sized silver sedans revved their engines, and a pistol fired in the distance. They raced toward me, coming faster and growing larger. I kicked them left and right until hundreds of tiny cars laid abandoned along the runway.

I ducked inside the closest airplane hangar where row after row of portraits hung on the walls. All my family and friends' faces stared back at me, even Sadie and Mr. Scowl, but no Grandmother. Mr. Scowl cackled, "I told ya I'd keep you in sight. Now I'll just take you out."

The floor became a treadmill, and I huffed, running in place while a voice whispered, "Brosy, Brosy I'm keeping you right in sight."

Wow. I needed a new bed or a Feng Shui furniture arrangement, or a sleeping partner to curb my feral imagination.

On rubbery legs, I made my way to the bathroom. After I splashed water on my face, I clomped downstairs to the kitchen and started my coffee. I could pee faster than my coffee maker could drip caffeine and I sailed back upstairs to shower.

I had just flung my damp t-shirt and bed shorts in the hamper when my cell played the chorus of "Just the Girl" by Click Five, my ringtone for my loving daughter, Emma.

Holy crap, it wasn't even 4:30 in the morning for her. In my dive back to the bedroom, I sideswiped my shoulder against the doorjamb and bounced into the chair, stubbing my toe. "Shit, that hurts." I flung my half-naked body across the bed and snatched the cell. "Emma, what's wrong?"

"Hi, Mom. Guess where we are?" She giggled.

"California," I said. Emma's giggle slowed my heartbeat back to a normal rhythm that now pulsed in my big toe. "Do you know what time it is?"

"Four thirty-five, but Dad says you can't always trust the clocks in rental cars."

"What are you doing driving around in the dead of night?"

"We're going to breakfast at IHOP. But Mom, I searched online for any update on your portrait mystery and don't see any, what's up?"

Emma's interest in my column made me smile. I missed her input this time around. She loved a good puzzle as much as I did, and keeping her involved kept us close.

"Nothing new with it yet, honey, but I'm thinking there is more to it than just a misplaced picture." I think that was wishful thinking on my part, but it sounded good.

"Oh yeah? Like what? Like the mystery caller? Did you

find out who that was yet?"

Secretly, in the depths of my mind, I had connected Terri's husband, Albert, to the mystery caller. Or was it Mr. Scowl?

"I just got back from my trip to Arizona with Luanne, so maybe I'll dig something up today or this week."

"Oh yeah. How was your trip?"

"Good, I'll tell you all about it when you get home."

"Cool. And Dad is taking us on a cruise. We're headed to Long Beach after breakfast."

Long Beach. Cruise. Catalina Island. My breath caught in my throat. Images of Luanne's late mother, Rosalyn Kohler, out at sea, and specters of skeletal hands emerging from waves flashed before me. I shook the worries out of my head. Mack was dead. He wouldn't be tossing anyone overboard ever again.

But still..."Put your father on the phone," I said.

"He's driving," Emma said. "Do you think it's too early to call my BFF, Dad? I want to tell her what I'm doing."

Emma left me in eavesdrop mode, listening to George's jolly chuckle.

It wasn't the first time I wished the slogan reach out and touch someone was literal. I wanted to stuff that merry right back down his throat. He'd never been that jolly when we were together.

"Emma," I shouted. "Put your dad on the phone, now!" He was not taking our daughter out into the black, heaving ocean.

"But you said not to drive and talk—"

"Fine." I rolled my eyes so far up under my lids that pain seared my pupils. "Hold the phone up to his ear."

"She wants to talk to you."

"Put it on speaker," George said.

"No, don't." How dare he box me in. I had a few words I wanted to say to him. But not the vocabulary I wanted Emma to hear. Static tickled my ear while the phone jostled around. I growled and choked my phone.

"Good morning, sunshine." He laughed.

"I doubt the sun has risen," I said through clenched teeth. "I don't remember discussing this."

"She sounds grumpy, Dad."

My ears heated and tingled. Three thousand miles away

and two years of divorce and he still pushed my buttons.

"You're right. We didn't discuss a cruise," he said. "What's the big deal, Kate?"

I knew that tone oh so well. And when he attached my name to the end of the sentence, he was saying, "to hell with how you feel." God, I hated his self-righteousness. And I hated the green monster descending upon me, pushing me into the outfield. But damned if I'd let those fly balls sail on by.

And why didn't he comprehend the big deal? People end up missing. It had been only six weeks since I exposed the drowning of Rosalyn. I doubted he'd forgotten, and it irked me he didn't have the same level of concern that I had. Didn't he watch 20/20? People went overboard all the time.

"Hello? I shouldn't have to spell it out for you George. I never agreed to a cruise. It's just not a good idea."

"Sure it is. It's a wonderful opportunity. Where's your sense of adventure?"

"It ended in a dumb waiter."

"Oh brother, I get it now. You're not still stuck on...look, it's a cruise ship, not a rowboat or a yacht. You worry too much, Kate."

That may be true or not, but my biggest worry was how Emma was feeling about all this tit for tat at the moment. I did my best never to pit Emma against her father. I never wanted her to feel strung in the middle, and I knew she didn't, but I couldn't say the same for me right now. For years, I had been so in love with George that I never noticed his condescending edge. The only good ideas were his while my achievements were always dismissed with a chuckle. Or my triumphs were merely the effect of what someone else did before me.

But I didn't notice any of that until the day he told me he was gay. His pompous attitude rushed at me and slapped me square in the face. He tried to be different, he had said, and thought a wife and child would make that happen for him.

Not that I was just realizing it, but...no wonder I had relationshipitis, as Luanne called it. Her advice echoed in my mind. *Kick up your heels. Enjoy your freedom. Find a man and have sex.*

Huh, do what George did. Find a man and have sex. I laughed out loud and wondered if his man Ethan was in the car with them.

"What's funny, Mom?" Emma asked.

"Oh just a thought. Are you having fun?" I asked.

"Lots, but I miss you."

Hearing that pulled me in from the outfield. "I miss you too, and I'm having fun too." Liar, liar. "So, Ethan, are you there? And are you joining them on the cruise?"

"Hi Kate, and yes, I'm going too."

"Glad to hear that." I hoped George was scowling over that comment.

Ethan and I had come to terms with each other. To me, he was the *other,* and I scared him. It wouldn't hurt to pull him into the infield with me and shove George to the outfield.

"I even have a new swimsuit," Emma said. "Did you know the boat has three pools?"

"You promise to pay attention to the lifeboat drills?" I said.

"They have those?"

"I'll make sure she does," George answered.

"Yes. And George...you make sure that you follow our agreement. And in case you forgot what it is..." I rustled the newspaper lying on my bed, as if I were turning pages looking for the clause. I knew it by heart and was prepared to remind him that both parents agreed to discuss any and all major changes and events with each other before presenting the idea to Emma.

"I haven't forgotten," he said.

"Really? I think you have."

"What agreement?" Emma asked.

"Ask your dad, and when you come home, you can read it if you want."

It was my turn to chuckle. I was pretty sure I had just caught all the fly balls. The connection hiccupped with dead air.

"I'll call you...we...get...ack," Emma said. "...ov you."

"I love you too. And stay away from the railings." I clutched the phone, waiting for an answer. The connection fizzled, but I hung on. When the signal bounced back, I heard Emma say, "Does the agreement have anything to do with parasailing?"

CHAPTER 5

My drive to the new *City Scope* office was an extra ten minutes north on Brown Avenue on the outskirts of Yardman. Unfortunately, my new route took me in the opposite direction of Hot Joe's coffee shop. And after my conversation with Emma and George, I needed a chocolate latte to soothe my woes. I headed straight for Hot Joe's.

I missed being able to walk down the street for a latte from the old office, still in ruins, especially at this time of year. It had been over a week since I last stopped in, and at that time, my story about the lost portrait was fresh print. The coffee klatch groupies hanging around the counter had brewed more suggestions about how to find it than I could listen to, but it was all fun.

Last week, Hot Joe's had an eclectic collection of high top tables and stools along the storefront sidewalk. But those had been replaced with small, matching rounds and fringed umbrellas. The uniformity surprised me, and I wondered if the inside had a facelift also. Not that it mattered, as Hot Joe's patrons would have stood all day for a cup of coffee. Not one seat was vacant, and the line was out the door, as usual.

The breeze circled the smell of warm coffee and vanilla scones. Heaven. I stood in line an arm's length behind a man with an oval patch sewn to the back of his shirt. It read, Tire Tread Shoppe, and he oozed grease from his baseball cap to his boots. The smaller oval patch on his shirtsleeve read Cheekie, which forced me to snap my eyes shut to keep from ogling his butt. I turned toward the groupies huddled under the umbrellas.

A woman wearing a paisley nightdress and lime-green slippers sat at one of tables. Her permed hair peeked beneath her hairnet. I tried to slide my gaze past her, but she caught me, eyes wide. I made a mental note to write her fashion statement on my don't-let-me-get-old-list, which Emma promised to read to me when I forgot about it.

"Kate, Kate Lambrose," she hollered, her arms crisscrossing above her head as if she were signaling for a jet landing.

"Hi, how are you?" I waved back and smiled. I hadn't a clue who she was.

"Did you get my email?" she asked. "I sent it to you yesterday."

"Oh, no, not yet. I'm on my way into the office now. But thank you. I'll look for it first thing." I feared it would be about finding her missing shoes and signed, "Homeless Housewife."

Then three other people sitting around other tables waved and said, "Me too. Me too. Me too." They started discussing whatever it was about with each other, congregating around one table and dragging their chairs in close. Their heads bobbed up and down in agreement with each other. Hands and arms waved about, and two men high-fived. To say the least, I was more than curious and teetered back and forth like a runner waiting for the gun to fire. The line moved into the coffee shop, making my decision for me, and I shuffled along. I wanted to know what their emails were about, but I wasn't about to give up my spot in line. I'd sit down with them on my way out after I had my latte fix in hand.

But by the time I snaked my way out the door, only one elderly gentleman remained at the tables. And he wasn't among the group that said they had sent me an email. I shrugged and headed off to my Jeep, now in a hurry to get to the office and read all about it.

After I buckled my seatbelt, I snapped the sun visor down. The elderly man was square in my line of sight and framed perfectly in the center of my windshield. What I saw sparked a half-finished memory, but I was on the outside of it looking in.

I hadn't seen him before today, but the scene had me snatching at stray straws as to why it stirred a familiar thought. He sat with his back to the window and stared off into space. His coffee mug rested on top of his neatly folded newspaper. One leg rested atop his knee and he swayed his foot to his inner rhythm. His sunglasses perched, not across the few strands of hair left on his head, but against his fore-head. Just like Mr. Scowl.

"Oh my God," I said out loud, and shifted into drive before I had even started the engine.

I was right! I had seen Mr. Scowl before. Right here. The day before Luanne and I flew out to Arizona. The memory of sweet-smelling aftershave rushed at me. I had smelled it then, when I rushed out the door that day and I had just quickly glanced in his direction.

I started my Jeep and left rubber as I peeled away from the curb. My thoughts zigzagged all over the place. I should go to the police station and report it, but report what? I saw the same man twice within a week in all the same locations as me? No, that didn't sound right.

I bypassed the police station, zoomed up Brown Avenue, and dug in my tote for my cell phone. I couldn't wait to tell Luanne. But both her cell and office line rang to voicemail.

"Dammit, call me." I slapped my cell back into my tote.

I whirled into the driveway to *City Scope* and screeched to a stop just before the speed bump. Pulling my latte from the cup holder, I downed the last few drops and coasted over the bump.

The contemporary cement office building hid in a cloud of transplanted old oak and maple trees, like an elephant in the city jungle. The entrance to the underground parking garage on the left side protruded like a flaring elephant ear with a matching exit on the right side. *City Scope* occupied the first, second, and third floors in the right front quad of the building, just as it had in our old building, but it didn't feel like home yet.

An eerie, stale quiet greeted me when I swung open the Newsroom door. Although we now had a reception area up front, we didn't have a receptionist. I doubted we would ever see one sitting at the front desk. *City Scope* just didn't warrant a greeter, but we named our missing receptionist M.I.A.

I raced passed Mia's desk and the six-foot partition that split the reception area from our new tic-tac-toe cubicle layout. In our old office, we were arranged in rows of three and our floors were old barn boards, but those had melted like butter in the fire. Here we had a burgundy carpet speckled with tan and mauve dots. It was either the pattern or the flame retardant stench that made me dizzy on day one.

At the top left tic-tac-toe square, Joyce Hendrix was up-dating her white board schedule for the day.

"Hi, Joyce," I said.

"Oh, Kate...you're back." Her dozen or so bangles jingled as she reached to hug me.

I got a nose full of stiff Aqua Net sprayed hair. Her pen-ciled-in blonde brows matched her hair color perfectly and painted her face with constant surprise. So much so that I wasn't sure if she was actually surprised I had returned.

Joyce had been with *City Scope* for ten years. She was our research extraordinaire who also wrote the obituary col-umn. She was one of the smart people who could play Trivial Pursuit. I was always telling her to try out for Jeopardy. And if any of the categories were Woodstock or political move-ments of the 1960s, she'd win the round hands down.

"Did I miss anything?" I asked.

"Are you kidding?" She laughed. "How was your trip? What did Luanne find in the bank vault?" She looked at her watch. "No, wait. Hold that thought. Tell me later. I have to run. Oh, and I emailed you a bunch of crap about antique frames." She gathered up her leather satchel and waved bye.

"Where is everybody?" I hollered after her.

"I'm here." Simon Rutter rolled back from his desk. His ear buds hung from his ears.

"What are you listening to?"

"Was listening to a motivational CD about sales and ad-vertisement." He pulled the buds from his ears.

"Sounds boring, if you ask me." I crinkled up my nose.

"Yup, but the word came down"—he thumbed toward the ceiling, second floor, where the boss's office was—"that I needed to up my ante for advertising sales."

I think that was the most Simon said to any of us in days. But if he was getting pressure from upstairs, I understood his need to buckle down and get to it. I had no doubt his little study session would boost his numbers. After a few replays of his CD, he'd be able to parrot back whatever he heard. He was an ace at copying whatever most of us said, and I appropri-ately named him, at least in my mind, Simon Says.

I headed to my bottom left square. Our middle tic-tac-toe square had a circular podium that held an assortment of cactus plants, some with waxy red flowers. I chose my corner cube for two reasons. One, for the window view, and two, it placed me at the opposing corner to my nemesis, Ondrea Franklin. I hoped for a cat's game in our verbal tic-tac-toe battles.

At my desk, I stabbed the on button to my PC, waking it from its limbo, and wiggled the mouse as if I could kick-start the machine. The fan whirred and the monitor blinked, but no connection.

"Oh come on." I snagged my cell and dialed Luanne. Voicemail again. I dialed again. If she had her phone on vibrate, I was giving her a thrill. By the third redial and no, "'*ello, Kate,*" with a faux accent, I left a message.

"I told you I'd seen Scowl before!" I rambled on, leaving a detailed message. "Call me."

I wasn't crazy after all. And to celebrate, I grabbed the baggie of peanut M&M's out of my desk drawer. I'd diet later. I tapped the spacebar when icons appeared on my monitor. The PC responded with its *please wait* hourglass figure. "Sheesh, I said I'd diet later."

My email icon came into focus, and I clicked it open. It would take at least five minutes to sync up, and I headed to the kitchen.

The lights were on in our Copy Editor's office. Eugene Keenan reclined in his desk chair, his back to the door and his feet propped on his desk. A stack of papers lay across his bulging belly, and he puffed air in a quiet snore. I giggled and back stepped into the hall. A pot of hot, fresh coffee sat waiting on the warmer. "Thank you, Eugene," I said. Obviously, he hadn't had his first cup yet.

When I returned to my desk, I stood and stared in disbelief at my inbox. One hundred and twenty-three unread emails stared back at me. My usual Monday morning was spent sorting through mail, but never had I seen more than fifty emails. I plopped into my chair, grabbed my mouse, and scrolled through them. I recognized many of the names. The list was endless and they had similar subject lines—"strange smell," "stinky air," "awful stench." One said, "yuck smell and loud drumming." I stopped scrolling when I landed on an email from Jonathan Dohe, my therapist friend I dated at arm's length. The subject read, "Weekend." I clicked it open and the body read, "How was your weekend in Arizona?" That was it. I sighed, rolled my eyes, and caught view of Jonathan's business card wedged in the corner of my two-by-two foot corkboard. I pulled it free from under the wood frame and flipped it around between my fingers.

Shortly after the fire, he moved back to Connecticut to open a new practice near his parents. They were suffering from old age and needed his attention. He and I talked about maintaining a long-distance relationship and had kept in touch daily for about two weeks. After that, our phone calls dwindled to every other day, then once a week. Last week, we agreed neither one of us could sustain a long-distance relationship. So much for absence makes the heart grow fonder. In our case, absence made the heart abandon each other. We promised to call, but email was easier without floundering to fill the awkward pauses.

I tossed his outdated business card in the trash bucket. It floated to the bottom, out of sight. I leaned over and looked down into the bucket. The card lay face up. His thumbnail picture smiled at me, and my heart clenched. *I'm sorry*, I thought, and swept last week's *City Scope* edition off my desk into the bucket, cloaking Jonathan's smile. We were just too busy on separate paths of life to endure a long-distance relationship, but if we had ever reached that point of deeply loving each other, we might have survived.

I clicked reply and wrote, "Fun, exciting, and restful." Some of that was the truth, but I didn't go into detail about Mr. Scowl. That would only spur him on to suggest safety and all that jazz. I then listed the items found in Luanne's grandmother's safe deposit box, because that's what he really wanted to know. Ever since my search for Rosalyn Kohler had uncovered an inheritance for Luanne, everyone close to us wanted to know what was in the bank vault.

After signing my email with XOXO, I backspaced, deleting my faulty affection, wrote, "Hugs, Kate," and clicked send.

CHAPTER 6

I scrolled to find the first email that had the subject line "Stench in Yardman." Honestly, it annoyed me that the last email received couldn't make its way to the bottom of unread emails and have the first one stay at the top. But I diligently made my way through every last one of them. The emails indicated that all these people were residents of Yardman. And they all wrote about a smell similar to rotten tequila, burnt turpentine, spoiled eggs, or rubbing alcohol. Also, the drumming sound was described as a train off its tracks or heavy hip-hop bass cranked from speakers in some kid's car trunk. The car trunk bass I understood, but no train had rolled through Yardman since the 1970s. And I would swear my M&M's now reeked of rotten eggs cooked in turpentine and smothered with tequila.

The smells and noise mostly occurred during the weekend. The last two weekends to be exact, and these residents were sure I could solve this mystery for them.

"Oh boy," I said. "Who do they think I am, Sherlock Holmes?"

However, I loved the idea of how I could turn my *In Sight* column into a true investigative piece if I solved this mystery. I rubbed my hands together like a fly on the wall ready to pounce on a crumb. Although helping the locals find their misplaced treasures resulted in some funny stories, this one demanded ironclad ninja black instead of comfort and stretch.

I made a list of all those who included their names in the email, minus Jonathan, minus the three new *In Sight* requests for my column, minus the eight who wrote about the portrait, minus the six from Joyce and from my biggest fan, Sadie Arnold. Next, I banged around in Mia's desk for a local phone book, which I knew had a Yardman street map. Let the circles begin.

I could've searched the World Wide Web for a street map, but my Internet search skills always led me on a scenic tour. Huh, so did looking for the phone book as I ended up in the kitchen to warm up my cold coffee.

Eugene sat at the round lunch table with his coffee and the same stack of papers that he had used as a blanket.

"Good Morning, Eugene." I made my way to the coffeepot.

"Hi, Kate."

"You live in Yardman, right?" I asked.

"All my life. Why?"

"Where? I mean, what neighborhood?"

He frowned at me. "Sunset Avenue, why?"

"Is that near the high school, the Creamery, Winter Haven, or here?" I picked locations in the four corners of Yardman.

"Oh, I guess I'd say the Creamery. Why?"

"Did you happen to notice any rotten egg smell in your neighborhood over the weekend?"

He shook his head. "No. Why?"

"Oh. I just heard from a few people complaining about a stench in the air over the weekend."

"Where?"

At least he had moved from "why" to "where," but I wasn't going to stick around for the who, what, and when.

"Don't know yet, but if I find out, I'll let you know," I said, and walked out.

By midmorning, I had finished mapping my address listings and determined that they all lived in an L-shaped area that butted up to the Glenwood Cemetery. I sent a blind copy, group email to all letting them know I'd update them when I had something to report.

After filling in all circles of the sixes, eights, nines, and zeroes on my desk calendar, I put the *Stench in Yardman* aside, believing I would come up with a starting point if I stopped thinking about it. Although, tracking down a smell might prove easier than hunting for Terri Wolf's antique frame showcasing her husband's grandmother's portrait.

The eight emails with comments about the portrait didn't offer any helpful information.

I had followed the links Joyce sent me, leading to antique shops and pictures of similar frames—not at all what I needed. My eyes blurred, and the next thing I knew, my whole body jolted sideways, waking me from my boredom-induced nap. Antiquing wasn't a high for me. And if any of this information was pertinent, I'd rather discuss it with Joyce face-to-face and then weed through looking for relevance. Joyce was entertaining. With her animated features, she had a unique way of explaining even the most boring reading material in Technicolor.

I opened my notepad on my PC and added some notes to my *Ornate Treasure Chase* list.

Terri Wolf had said the frame was an antique. Mys Caller claimed the frame was four sticks glued together. Terri claimed the portrait was her husband's grandmother. Mys Caller said the portrait was his grandmother. Mys Caller also said he or she had no living relatives, so Terri's husband couldn't be related to Mys Caller. On the other hand, Mys Caller could be Terri's husband, and in that case, Terri was already in hot water for accidentally donating the portrait.

According to what Joyce found, a frame like Terri's could be a hundred years old. As I considered the conundrum, my pinkie beat against the enter key, advancing me further into blank space. The shilly-shally zone, as my mother referred to the act of procrastination.

The room sighed around me, and the acoustic tiles over my head flopped back into place, my personal alert that the front door opened. I stood up, craned my neck over the cubicle wall, and spied Dan Suenowski. Dan stood near six feet, five inches and his shoulders were probably as wide as he was tall. Once the quarterback for the Yardman's football team back in high school, he still lurched instead of walked.

"Hey, Kate, how was your trip? Did Lulu finally get her inheritance?"

"Exciting, and yes, but don't ever call her Lulu."

Dan's hulk and biker braid wouldn't deter Luanne from choking the life out of him if she heard him call her "Lulu." She hated nicknames as much as I hated being called Katie.

"Trust me. It's Luanne."

Dan shrugged as he sat down and powered up his PC. "So, gonna fill me in?"

In our new office space, his cubicle was to my right and not behind me like it was in our old office. The configuration meant we were no longer bumping chairs. Huh. That must have been the goal with the tic-tac-toe layout.

"You first," I whispered. "Where is Ondrea?"

Her absence concerned me. That old cliché popped to mind—keep your friends close, but your enemies closer. She wasn't exactly friend or enemy, just the office diva with a capital "D." And my brother fawned over her. I'd slit my wrists if she became my sister-in-law.

Dan snickered. "Oh hell, I didn't even miss her. But she took a personal day and went hunting or fishing for the weekend."

I swallowed the sip of coffee in my mouth with a loud gulp, slid my chair back to my desk, and grabbed my phone to call my brother Matthew. If he had taken her away for a weekend, that meant serious business. That was too close to home for me, but he'd say it was none of my business. I had no choice but to grit my teeth and accept his choices. I slammed the handset down before I reinvented Julius Cesar's quote to "I think, I speak, I regret."

"So? Are you going to share?" Dan rolled into my square.

"Huh?"

"How rich is Lulu?" He waggled his brows.

"I'm not really sure." I lied, as it wasn't my business to tell.

"Well, are we talking Donald Trump or Bill Gates rich?"

"Why?" I frowned at his pick of the two men to compare Luanne with. Why not Martha Stewart or Leona Helmsley?

"Just curious."

I narrowed my eyes. "Dan Suenowski! Are you a gold digger?"

"What? Me? No, no, no. I just thought, well, uhm, that Lulu could use a friend."

I socked him in his arm. "Stop calling her Lulu." We laughed and my phone joined in, chirping. I grabbed the handset off the cradle. "She'll cut your tongue out," I said to Dan.

"Hello? Hello, Kate? Who is cutting whose tongue?" Luanne had finally returned my call. "Don't make me come down there."

"No one, never mind that. Where have you been, Lu-anne?" I made sure I enunciated her name for Dan's benefit. He smiled wide, and I jabbed my index finger at him, sending him back to his own square.

"What's going on?"

"Just giving Dan advice on word choice."

"Okay. So how do you feel about dinner?" Luanne asked.

"I generally enjoy it."

"Good. We'll pick you up at seven on Friday. See ya then."

"What? Wait. Don't you dare hang up on me." Dammit, she did. I dialed her right back at her office. The moment the ringing stopped, and before she even said hello, I fired off my questions. "What do you mean we'll pick you up? Who is we? What are you up to? And didn't you listen to my voicemail message?"

"I have a date and wanted you to come along, and no, I didn't listen to your message."

"Luanne Hamilton. I am not your training wheels." She hadn't been serious about a man in almost two years, not since her husband passed away. But with her macho medic on the scene, she was now determined to resuscitate my love life.

"It's not like that."

"Since when do you need a chaperone, anyway?"

"I don't. My date is bringing his buddy. Well, his buddy asked to come along." She laughed.

"A blind date? Are you serious?"

"Why not?" I could literally hear her lips smack into that stubborn thin line.

"Who?" I asked.

She didn't answer, and I could hear the echo of my own voice as she listened to the message I left on her cell phone.

"You saw Mr. Scowl again this morning?" Her voice hit that octave only dogs could hear, and I pulled the phone from my ear.

"Nooooooo. Not this morning. I just remembered it this morning. Remember I said he looked familiar. Well, it was at Hot Joe's."

"You need to report a stalker," she said. "Call Michael Earl."

"And say what? I've already gone through this in my

mind. It's ridiculous. Excuse me, Officer Earl, but some guy who drinks coffee at Hot Joe's, stares at people in airports, wears too much aftershave, and snatches mail for a living while on planes is creepy. Hell, we don't even know his name."

"Mr. Scowl." Luanne laughed. "Oh dammit, Kate. I have to run, but you can tell Michael all about it on Friday."

"On Friday? What?" I asked. I bolted to my feet. Michael Earl wanted me to come? No, that's not what she said. She said he asked to come. Oh!

"Wait just a minute."

"Ciao," Luanne said, and hung up on me again.

Ciao? I rolled my eyes. She had moved again. This time from France to Italy. I made a mental note to strangle the international faux accent right out of her. But that would have to wait. I had more important challenges to tackle first, like where was Terri Wolf's family heirloom? Did Terri's husband know it was missing, and was he my mystery caller? And what stunk in Yardman besides me thinking someone was following me?

CHAPTER 7

I was home by seven after loitering through the grocery store. With Mr. Scowl on my mind, my shopping spree turned into a hit-and-miss zigzag though the aisles, avoiding the path of any white-haired male. Never had I noticed how many senior citizens shopped at Yardman's Market Rite before now. The hair at the nape of my neck flinched at every corner, and I spent half my time looking over my shoulder. I felt like the mouse set loose in a maze searching for a meal before the snake caught me.

It didn't help that I was missing Emma, drowning in my aloneness, and feared she'd never come home because she suddenly loved her father more than me. Not that I thought she loved me more than she loved George, but why not have the green monster follow me around too?

With Emma away, I had no motivation to cook a nutritious meal. I opted for comfort food and a couple of staples. A block of cheddar cheese, crackers, Milano cookies, a jar of peanut butter, bread, a pint of milk, tuna fish, five apples, and two bottles of a white wine.

But I should have bought some hamburger, now that I saw my brother's car parked in my driveway. I doubted Matthew would share my cravings for junk food.

I squeezed my Jeep past his mud-covered Lexus, punched the garage door remote, and drove in until the tennis ball rested against my windshield. After popping the hatchback open, I walked back to Matt's car and looked inside. He wasn't reclining, snoozing, or anywhere in the car.

His orange hunting vest lay across his .22 rifle in the backseat, and his Red Rider gun sleeve lay crumpled on the floorboards. It tickled me that he still carried his .22 around in that sleeve. He had others to choose from, but our father had given Matt the Red Ryder sleeve on his tenth birthday.

My grin flipped upside down when I spotted a round hair-brush filled with long brunette strands. It rested in a hot pink cap on the dashboard. Ondrea evidence for sure. I pressed my forehead against the window. Ondrea's three-ounce bottle of Light Blue perfume and her tube of lipstick littered the open ashtray. Wow. She was making herself right at home, and I prayed he hadn't brought her to my home.

I looped my four grocery bags on my arm and opened the door to my kitchen. "Hello!" I dropped my bags on the table. "Matt, you here?" I didn't expect an answer, unless of course I had left a door unlocked. He didn't have a key. Maybe my kinky neighbor, the divorcee across the street, pulled him into her house for a cold beer. She always brought home strays. The two-legged kind.

I walked into the living room, hollered up the stairs, and rounded the corner through the dining room back to the kitchen in less than a minute flat. My condominium was small, but perfect for Emma and me. Together, we could clean the two bedrooms and two baths upstairs and the three rooms downstairs from top to bottom in less than three hours. By the looks of my kitchen, I needed to at least drag the mop around the floor.

A soft *tap-tap-tap* like water dripping stopped me from hollering again for Matt. I frowned and opened my mouth as if that would help me listen better. *Tap-tap-tap* again, and I hugged the refrigerator with my ear pressed to the side of it. No melting ice. The tapping picked up speed, and my heart thumped to the rhythm. The sound spun me in circles until I narrowed in on its direction. The slider door rattled. I grabbed the Windex bottle from the counter and whirled around like one of Charlie's lethal angels. Yanking the curtains aside, I fired a blue streak and jumped back from the glass before realizing it was Matt staring back at me.

Had the glass not separated us, Matt would have taken a shot of multipurpose cleaner straight to the head—and he needed it. His forest-green camouflage fatigues were battered with cakes of mud on the knees, and splatters across his chest.

"What are you doing out there?" I hollered through the glass, and wiped away my Windex ammo.

He pressed his palms against the glass. "Open up."

"Stop it. You're mucking up my window." I unlatched the slider and he yanked it open.

"Where the hell have you been, Kate, for Christ's sake?" He stormed in, closed the slider behind him, and tossed his backpack on the floor.

"Wait, whoa." I held up my hand. "Don't yell at me. Why are you in my backyard? Was I expecting you?"

"No, but it's late," he continued to yell, "and there are muddy footprints on your back deck!"

I frowned at the dry mud on the deck. My postage-size backyard was blanketed with healthy green grass, except for the path that lead along the back of the condominium at-tached to my left. Someone, even Matt, had to walk that path to get to my back door.

Still, a burp of panic bubbled in my chest. Whose foot-prints? When had it last rained to make mud? When had ei-ther Emma or I been out there last?

"Huh. Those are probably yours." I pointed to Matt's un-laced boots.

"They're not." He walked a wide circle around me. "See? No footprints. I'll need a chisel to knock the crud out of these treads."

"Then the grounds maintenance man. I don't know. What does it matter?" But it did matter, and I flipped the latch on the slider, locking the footprints out. It couldn't have been footprints left behind by the person following me, because I was here first. And Sadie had come in the front door.

"Where were you?" he asked.

"At the grocery store." I rolled my eyes. "Who are you, my father?"

He cocked his head at me and shrugged. When our father died, Matt became the voice of reason for my sister and me. Allison was thirteen then, and I was sixteen. Matt jumped from eighteen into father figure overnight and still wore that hat even though I was closing in on forty-three years old.

"You could have told someone," he said.

"Told who?" I planted my fists on my hips. "And if I did, how would you know who I told so you could ask *who* where I was anyway?" I burst out laughing.

Matt tried to hide his crooked grin under his frown, but

failed.

"Okay, fine." He laughed. "But you might want to check with maintenance about the footprints."

I knew what he was thinking, and I might have thought the same. But Mack was confirmed dead. "You can stop thinking that," I said.

"What am I thinking?" He turned the kitchen faucets on full force. After dousing his hands and arms with double squirts of dish soap, he scrubbed his arms with my sponge.

"Mack is dead, and it's confirmed, so those aren't his muddy footprints." I yanked the slider curtain closed and shrugged, still not convinced the mud prints didn't belong to Matt. He loved feeding my paranoia until I scared the hell out of myself.

"Good to hear."

I had been thinking the same thing, but hearing Matt say it out loud pinged sympathy in my heart for Luanne. After all, good and dead, Mack was still her father, and his death had to hurt on some level.

"And where have you been, by the way?" I asked. Not that I couldn't tell. He left a trail of evidence in plain sight. I knew the "what" of "what" he was doing. The "who" involved with the "what" and the "why" was obvious, but the "where" was missing.

Matt hitched his shoulders and shook his head.

"Oh no, you don't get to brush me off," I said, "not after all that." I waved my hand toward the sliders. "And how did you happen to end up in my backyard anyway?"

"I was looking for a way in." He handed me the sopping wet dishtowel and swung open the refrigerator. "Kate, there's nothing in here but a bottle of wine." He turned and frowned at me with the bottle in hand.

"I've been away and Emma is away, so what do I need a full fridge for anyway?" I unpacked my groceries and snuck my Milano cookies in the cupboard while he poured two glasses of wine.

"So, I can use Emma's bed for the night?" he asked. "Where is she, by the way?" He took his wallet and keys out of his back pocket and placed them on the kitchen table.

"She's in California with George and Ethan sightseeing. Why?" I grabbed a cutting board, a slab of cheese, opened a sleeve of crackers, and sat down at the table.

"Nice. When's she coming home?" he asked.

"August second. Why?"

"Wow, that's a long time to be alone." He looked at me over the rim of his wine glass. "Aren't you worried about being alone in this big house?"

"Oh my God, Matt. It's not a big house, it's a condo and I have attached neighbors."

"Yeah, way over on the other side of your garage," he said.

"Stop it." I looked toward the slider and vowed I'd call maintenance in the morning about the muddy prints. After double-checking the lock, I pulled the curtain aside and shoved my two-by-four into the groves. "Did you show up here just to make me paranoid or what?"

Matt's silent snicker shook his entire body, and I slugged him in the shoulder.

"No. I just dropped Ondrea off at her house, and I'm too tired to drive home."

Aw, so I was right. They were away together. "So, where did the two of you go?"

"Hunting."

"Hunting? Hunting what?" Shooting at defenseless animals was not something I supported, even though Dad dragged us all out pheasant hunting. Nor could I think of what hunting season was open in the middle of July.

"Crow," he said.

"Crow? As in *caw-caw*?"

He nodded.

"Are you kidding me? There's a crow hunting season?"

He nodded again. My brother, the lawyer, wasn't in the habit of sparing words, so when he said nothing, it clearly indicated avoidance.

"Yeah, sort of, yes." He swirled the wine in his glass and sniffed it.

"What does that mean? Sort of? What are you hiding?"

"Well, crow season isn't officially open yet, but we were on private land."

Private land? Like sacred ground? Like Glenwood Cemetery? "Oh my God. You weren't in a cemetery, were you?"

"No, Jeez, Kate. How does your mind go from private

land to a cemetery anyway?"

"Never mind." I waved at him. I wasn't about to tell him about the stench in Yardman. He'd start lecturing me, and I'd tell him to take his father figure and stuff it. And that would end our night on a bad note.

He sliced a thick wedge of cheese and stuffed it into his mouth.

"So how come...and I hate to ask, but why can't you stay at Ondrea's place? Not that I'm complaining, it's just odd that the two of you would spend the whole weekend, uhm, and then not."

The tips of his ear lobes reddened. His right cheek puffed as he squirreled the cheese to the side and stuffed a cracker into his already full mouth. "She has mouse cakes," he said. Cracker dust blew from between his lips.

"What the hell are mouse cakes?" I laughed. "Is it contagious?"

"No. Housemates." He rolled his eyes. "Clean out your ears."

I scooted forward in my chair. "You mean like roommates?" He nodded and snagged another cracker.

I slid the crackers and cheese out of his reach. Roommates piqued my interest because Ondrea always made it sound like she lived alone in what used to be her mother and father's house. I would get to the bottom of this, but first I had to draft the perfect statement that wouldn't cause the lawyer in my brother to double answer me.

"Huh." I drummed my fingers on the table.

"Huh what?" Matt squinted at me.

"I thought she had moved out of her parents' house last year," I said.

"Oh nooooo. She wouldn't leave her parents alone."

Bingo! "Seriously, Matt?" I laughed. "At her age, who still lives with their parents these days? Isn't she too old, or maybe in this case, too young? For you?" I drummed my palms on the table, completely smitten with myself. "Sucker," I said.

"You, dear sister, suck! You played me." He shook his finger at me. "Just leave it alone, Kate, please."

"Oh, I won't deliberately pick on her for living with her parents, but the first time she tries to attack me, she's going to eat crow." I laughed.

Matt smothered his face in his hands and shook his head. "Just leave it alone, Kate. It's none of your business." He pushed his chair back and stood.

"Where are you going?"

"Shower and shut eye." He flung his backpack over his shoulder and headed up stairs.

"Hey, don't you want to hear about the silver sedan that followed me from the airport?"

"Really, Kate? I bet a dozen or more silver sedans were on that same route, and you decide to pick one to follow you?" His laughter bounced down the stairs.

"Oh sigh." I hated that sarcastic, logical lawyer lip. But he was right. Each time I lost sight of the car I thought was following me, I picked another.

CHAPTER 8

After I cleaned up our little picnic and changed into my bed shorts and tee, I plopped down on the couch in front of the TV. I stopped channel surfing on *Dancing with the Stars*. I liked reality shows, although I imagined some of the reality was clipped out. Too bad it wasn't that easy to adjust reality. Every now and then I could use a scene break or a change of costume.

Then again, maybe I should be careful what I wished for. My last reality adjustment caused me to make a major scene change. George had ended our fifteen years of marriage with two words, "I'm gay." We sold our house, and he took his bat and balls and moved in with Ethan. I bought a condo, and Emma and I condensed our lives into 1,200 square feet, minus a man, except for my brother on occasion, who was now mad at me.

I didn't expect Matt to join me, as the shower had shut off and the bedroom door had slammed. He was right about Ondrea's living arrangements being none of my business, but Ondrea never missed an opportunity to insult me or stick her nose in my business. Besides, I hated that the two of them were becoming a couple and worried that Matt was settling for a relationship because as he had said no woman his age wanted to start a family. It worried me that Ondrea could lose interest in Matt when he was sixty and she was forty.

I muted the TV when the commercial screamed at me to buy K-Y Intense Gel for her and him. The only things mating around here were the cats howling outside.

Matt's car alarm chirped, and I jumped from the couch to peer out the front window. A calico cat sat on the car hood, and the other ran across the street. "Well, we know who won that fight."

The alarm chirped again as the cat launched itself onto the roof. The dome light in Matt's car flickered on. Apparently, his anti-theft device wasn't as sensitive as mine. My alarm squealed if the wind blew too hard, but I didn't own a Lexus loaded with push button gadgets.

"Get off of there," I hollered. The cat pranced in a circle a couple of times before it curled into a ball.

I didn't care if the cat slept there all night, I just didn't want the car alarm to start echoing through the condominium complex. I left the window and opened the front door.

"Scoot," I hissed through the front screen door. The cat raised its head and looked at me before sprawling across the roof. The dome light flickered off and on repeatedly for a few seconds and then stayed lit. Another push button gadget, no doubt.

"Oh boy." Then I remembered Matt's rifle now in clear view in the backseat. I ran to the kitchen table and grabbed Matt's car keys.

"Okay, Calico. It's you or me."

I pressed the garage door opener, and the sensor lights pinged two-sixty watts of light off the white walls. The hinges whined, and the door staggered open. I made a mental note to spray the hinges with WD-40, and hoped the noise had scattered the cat, but Calico hadn't moved.

When I rushed toward the Lexus in my bare feet, waving my arms like a football coach to the end zone, Calico leapt to the trunk and ran off toward the bushes. I set the alarm again and waited for the dome light to fade out, but after what seemed like an hour's worth of minutes, it stayed lit.

"Dammit, Matt." I looked up toward Emma's window to see if by chance he was laughing at me. The window shade was at half-mast like an eyelid, and the blackened window glared down at me.

I unlocked the car, turned the interior light switch on-and-off, grabbed the rifle off the back seat, and stuffed it in the Red Rider sleeve. The interior light faded, leaving me in total darkness when I shut the door. A shiver ran across my shoulders even though it was near eighty degrees. A car across the street started up. I flinched. It coasted away down the hill. I ran on tiptoes to the end of the driveway with the rifle hitched up under my arm. The car coasted to the stop sign, turned on its lights, and sped off toward town. Probably one of the neighbor's one-night-stands. But I still wondered if it was the car that I thought followed me.

The bushes behind me rustled, and I spun around, aiming the car remote at the bushes.

Calico was back, meowing at me and weaving back and forth across the driveway. It stopped and looked into the open garage.

"Oh no you don't."

Calico snapped its tail at me and skittered in under my Jeep.

"Oh no you're not!" I ran up the drive after the cat and stepped on a pebble I'd swear was the size of a golf ball. It flicked out from under my foot and my foot went out from under me.

The rifle flung from my hand, along with Matt's car keys. Both hit the garage floor at the back of my Jeep and slid under the car. I fell to my hands and knees and my teeth slammed together. After several hammer-slamming-thumb cuss words and knee cradling moans, I crawled far enough under the Jeep to retrieve the keys and rifle.

The cat hissed at me, but didn't move.

"Oh come on, cat, go, get out. I'm missing *Dancing with the Stars*."

I didn't mind cats. I liked cats, just not my neighbor's cats. And didn't figure they'd appreciate me locking their cat in my garage all night. I limped around to the driver's side and lay down on the cement floor.

With the rifle stock in hand, I swept the barrel back and forth as if it were a broom. "Go, go on, get out, cat!" I crawled further under the Jeep.

Calico cowered up against my right front tire. He hunched low, his ears swiveled sideways like a swing-wing fighter and his tail swished in wide arcs. Shit, he was ready to attack. He hissed and raked his front paws at the rifle sleeve like a boxer delivering a one-two punch. His right paw caught hold and he tugged. "No, no, kitty. Let go." He pulled back, flipped over sideways and inside out, I'd swear, before his claw released. I yanked the rifle back before he could attack again. And when I did, a click and a whoosh vibrated my hand. A bang like a rock bouncing across a cobblestone road echoed through the garage.

"Shit!" I screamed, and jerked my head back, but not in time to miss the rifle's recoil. The butt end slammed into my brow, and my head bounced against the undercarriage. My heart lobbed into my throat, and the gunshot rang in my ears. My vision blurred, my nose stung, and my right front tire hissed stale air in my face from the huge grin in the rubber. But Calico had screamed his way out of the garage unscarred. I lay there dazed and stared at my flat tire. All I could think about was the hole in Matt's Red Ryder sleeve. At least until a warm tickle ran down my nose to my lips and I tasted blood. Shit, I shot myself.

I began to wiggle my way out from the Jeep just as a pair of feet entered the garage. I froze.

Whoever was attached to the bare feet said nothing and stood still with his toes curled against the cement. Another click jolted me, and I was doused into darkness when the garage sensor light clicked off.

"Where are you?" a man's voice yelled.

I held my breath and clutched the rifle. The hum in my ears sounded like a train whistle, but I could hear the feet shuffle along the floor and stop.

The garage lit up with a snap and I flinched. Hell, I couldn't even stand up and run out if I wanted to.

"Kate?"

Matt? "Matt, is that you?" Tears mixed with my blood and I spit it from my lips.

"Where are you?"

"Un, un, der da Jeep."

Matt's hands hit the floor, then his knees and his face peered at me sideways.

"Whoa!" He swiped the gun barrel out of his aim. "Your head, it's bleeding. Did you shoot yourself? Oh my God, Kate."

His face, knees, and hands disappeared. I was frozen in place and couldn't understand how I shot myself.

"Kate, say something, for God's sake." Matt tugged me from under the Jeep.

I nodded and kept nodding while he flipped and turned every part of my body looking for the bullet hole. The nodding was soothing and in rhythm with the thumping in my ears.

After Matt carried me into the kitchen, he patched up the slice in my brow with several tiny band-aids while I held ice against the back of my head and alternated another ice pack on my knees.

"You need to go to the hospital," he said. "No bullet holes, but you could have a concussion."

"No. I'm fine." And I stood to prove it. But fell to my knees and hurled my cheese and wine.

"Oh jeez, Kate." Matt gagged. "That, I don't clean up." He grabbed the end of the paper towels and spread five yards on the floor, covering my mess.

CHAPTER 9

I got an early start the next morning after Matt changed my tire and lobbed the injured one into the back of my Jeep. He suggested I drop it off at the Tire Tread Shoppe to have a new tire put on the rim. Hell, not even Fix-A-Flat would fill the hole.

I thanked him and gave him a tip for changing my tire. "Don't leave a loaded rifle lying around," I said. And he warned me about living alone, using a rifle as a broom, traipsing outside in the dark barefoot, and chasing cats.

"And you need to go to the hospital for stitches," he said for the fifth time.

I waved him away. I was fine. I had slept well, but staggered out of bed on my stiff knees. And by the time I drove to the Tire Tread Shoppe, my knees were well worn in.

The guy at the tire shop laughed when I told him I shot my own tire, but I hadn't been driving when it happened. I didn't explain the details, but told him to toss the .22 bullet if he even found it. He kept staring at my black and blue, which spread overnight from the outer edge of my eyebrow down across my temple to my ear. Hell, I couldn't even explain how that happened. I obviously jerked my head sideways and tried to stand up under the Jeep when the gun fired. I didn't know; it was all a blur. And the rain that the weatherman had promised now blurred my windshield. I pulled off my sunglasses, but quickly put them back on. Rain or not, the daylight stung my eyes.

Instead of turning left out the tire shop, I turned right and headed up the hill to the Glenwood Cemetery in search for some strange smell. At the top of the hill, I turned left into Glenwood and passed under the granite arch. The opening was just wide enough for me to drive through without scraping my side mirrors against the granite.

Straight ahead, about one-hundred yards away, stood a garage with a pickup truck parked outside. I turned left down one of the gravel roads that weaved around grave plots. A path of green grass, perfectly trimmed, centered the gravel roads and muted the tires crunching over the dirt. I tried not to think about the phrase *wake the dead*, but it popped into my brain without a welcome.

Streams of rainwater collected in the tire grooves on the road, but the rain had stopped, leaving the leaves a shiny green. I sniffed the air. Fresh rain, and wet moss, which wasn't stinky air.

I stopped at the end of the road where rooftops about fifty yards away peeked through the trees. The backyards of everyone who lived on Sprinter Street and emailed me about the yuck smell faced the cemetery at this point. I turned right and quietly rolled parallel with Sprinter Street to the end. The garage was on my right but behind me. The road dead-ended, and my only choice was to either back up or turn right. After turning right, I stopped and pawed through my tote for the map I had ripped from the phone book. The other street I had highlighted was Old Glen Road. Only one resident from that neighborhood had emailed me, and I should be parallel with the road. But instead, a steep short hill led down to a pond. Across the pond, which was no more than thirty feet across, a cluster of dense fir trees lined the shore. The rain clouds hid the tops of the trees in a gray mist. If Old Glen was beyond those trees, I couldn't see it from here. Plus, I doubted that resident could smell anything from here to there. I rolled forward to the next crossroad, turned right, and pulled up beside the garage.

Maybe a maintenance man or gravedigger was holed up in the shed. I sniffed the air a few more times as I grabbed my rainbow umbrella and exited my Jeep. Drops of water dripping from the oak splattered like pebbles against my windshield and my head and startled me. What was I thinking snooping around the quietest neighborhood alone? And the only drumming sound was me knocking on the garage door.

"Hel-lo?" I tired the doorknob, but it was locked. I could smell apples when I walked around the pickup, and for good reason. Two bushel baskets full of reds sat in the truck bed. I tried to look in the shed window, but it was frosted. I sniffed the air, but only smelled pine trees mixed with wet moss. All the inhaling was beginning to give me a headache.

The desolate quiet seeped into my bones and I shivered. I could hear Matt in my head saying I could have told someone where I was going. I headed along the back of the garage back to my Jeep and stopped before turning the corner. Fear of coming face-to-face with a hockey-masked man swinging an axe made me want to pee my pants. The adrenaline hit my heart and it knocked against my ribs. I took a deep breath, held my umbrella ramrod straight out in front of me, and ran from behind the garage. I spun, wielding my weapon while looking for stalkers, and jumped in the Jeep. I whipped my head around in all directions, half-expecting a ghoul to pop up from my back seat. Nothing came at me except a dizzy spell, which concerned me for a minute, until I realized it was normal about this time of the month.

As I drove out of the cemetery faster than I had entered, I vowed to return over the weekend, but not alone. Mystic Luanne would be more than willing to traipse through the cemetery with me. But first, I wanted to know if any of the neighboring residents had called 911 to report yuck smells or loud drumming. Michael could tell me that, and I'd have a good excuse just to say hello.

CHAPTER 10

Safely parked in the garage at *City Scope*, I dialed the police station.

"Michael Earl, please," I said. My heart skittered as I rolled his name off my tongue.

"Is this an emergency?"

From the quick, jabbing words, I knew that I was talking to Officer Gleason, the young kid who manned the front desk. He was the last person I wanted to talk to as the last time we had a conversation, he almost pinned my mug to the most-wanted wall for harboring a missing person.

"No, this is not an emergency," I said as deliberate as I could. He had a habit of misunderstanding what I said.

"He's out on a case," he said.

"Oh, I thought he was the house mouse?"

"That was temporary. He's a detective. Who is this?"

"Kate Lambrose at *City Scope News*," I said.

After a minute of silence and some keyboard pounding, he said, "I'll tell him you called, ma'am."

Raspberries of relief buzzed my lips, but I was disappointed at the same time that Michael wasn't available.

The man excited me, and that wasn't safe. Oh, and the upcoming date with Michael kept flitting in and out of my thoughts. I wanted to go, but then I didn't want to go. I couldn't decide. I scooped up my tote, map, and cell and marched up the stairs to the newsroom on legs as rubbery as a deboned chicken. The stairs seesawed and I glanced down at my feet, making sure I'd worn a matching pair of shoes. The way the cement rolled under my feet felt like I had trekked with one flat sole and one three-inch pump. I grabbed the handrail for support and felt my stomach flip-flop. I had no time to be ill, but at this rate, date night would be history before it happened.

I had an idea about hunting down the portrait and need-ed to get busy. Terri Wolf had to know who picked up her junk. Even if she didn't know the person's name, the truck or van would have had an organization's name on the side pan-el. From that information, I could track down the driver to find out which thrift store they delivered to.

The scene in the newsroom was very déjà vu, except in-stead of Carlton Haywood the police chief standing in the re-ception area, it was Detective Michael Earl. I paused on the threshold and sighed. Seeing my hunky detective had my insides churning between a purr and a free fall.

My experiences with visits from Yardman's finest had meant bad news. But this déjà vu had no reason to repeat. I hadn't been near a hospital in weeks, and no one I had re-cently interviewed had died leaving me the prime suspect. At least, I didn't think so, unless someone saw me roaming around the cemetery. Many dead bodies there, but not my doing. It would be just my luck that something awful hap-pened at the cemetery just after I left. Like Abby dying just after I left the hospital. Ha. I blinked and the words of Mys Caller came back to me. "You haven't heard the last from me," he or she warned. Was Michael Earl here to demand my source?

Dan stood next to Michael and towered over him. Be-tween their chuckles, I caught the words baseball and Red Sox in their conversation.

Ondrea sat at Mia's desk with her notepad and pencil ready to write up her next *she-said-he-said* scoop. Her straight bob was pulled back in to a bun, making her neck even longer, and her usual French manicure still looked wet. I'd bet a week's worth of lattes she had spent the morning having the weekend's private ground grime removed.

Joyce warmed her hands around her teacup and hovered in the background like a wallflower. She wore tons of vintage costume jewelry. Her bangles and beads chimed and clunked with her every move. I admired her for being true to her hip-pie heritage.

Their heads whipped around toward me when I shut the door, and the ceiling tiles huffed.

"Ah, I just called you." I pointed at Michael.

"Oh my God, Kate, what happened to your face?" Ondrea raced to my side to inspect my black and blue—or gloat. I wasn't sure which, but I doubted her sincerity.

"It's your fault," I said to her. "Not that I mind seeing Matthew any day of the week, and he is always welcome in my home. Which is more than I can say for your home. And if his car alarm hadn't started blaring through the neighborhood..." I took a healthy gulp of air. "Oh never mind. Next time, maybe you can get parental approval for a sleep over."

Ondrea stepped back and frowned at me.

"Kate." Joyce shook her head no. I wasn't sure why, but she knew something I didn't know, and I didn't get a chance to ask.

"Jeez, Kate, are you alright?" Michael stepped between Ondrea and me. He reached to touch my face, but I flinched at the idea. His up-close scrutiny heated my cheeks and ears. "Who did this to you?"

"Wait a minute." Ondrea craned her gooseneck around Michael. "My fault?" She waggled her pencil at me like a fencing sword. "How is it my fault?" She stabbed her pencil into her bun.

I rolled my eyes at her, something I shouldn't have done. The barely formed scab needled my brow. And the panoramic view from ceiling to wall to floor released a swarm of butterflies that fluttered in my head. I reached back and gripped the door handle for steady support.

"Who stayed at your house?" Dan asked me, but then looked at Ondrea.

I leaned against the closed door, hoping to stop the nausea bubbling in my chest.

Ondrea answered Dan's question. "Matt stayed at her house," she said.

"When?"

"Last night?"

"Who's Matt?" Michael asked the room, but looked at me.

"Her brother," Joyce answered. She frowned at me, the best she could with her penciled-in brows, and kept shaking her head in short no's. Typically, that meant change the subject.

I stood still with my lips zipped and watched the vaudeville reenactment. Sooner or later, they would have the answers they wanted and have figured out who was on first without a word from me. At least until Michael turned to me and asked, "Do you know who shot out your tire?"

Damn, how did he know?

All eyes ricocheted off each other like a pinball scoring double points and landed on me.

"What? Someone shot at you, Kate?" Dan asked.

I shook my head slowly. "How do you know about that?" I asked Michael.

He handed me a piece of paper. "Report from Tire Treads. They found the bullet you told them to toss." The emphasis he put on the words *you* and *toss* tumbled my stomach. My face heated. I was guilty as charged. Living in a small town had its disadvantages.

"Oh, huh." I giggled as I looked from one questioning expression to another and down at the floor. The butterflies swarmed again, or maybe it was the carpet that made me dizzy. "Can we take this outside?" I asked Michael. I suspected that the tire guy had already told Michael that I shot my tire, but neither of them believed it. On the other hand, my co-workers would. And they would roll on the floor laughing at my foolishness.

Michael nodded and pulled open the door. Joyce and Dan sighed disappointment and headed to their desks, but not Ondrea.

"I want to hear this," she said, and followed Michael.

"No." He held up his hand, waving her aside for me to exit. I liked having a cop for back up. At least this time Ondrea couldn't write another verbatim *he-said-she-said* story. But guaranteed she would speed dial Matt as soon as the door shut in her face. And by the time I returned, she'd have it on page one of this week's edition: *Sassy Newspaper Columnist Targets Cat in Heat but Blows Out Tire with a .22 Meant for Calico.* For sure the Humane Society would arrest me. I glanced over my shoulder and smirked at Ondrea.

Michael and I walked out front to where he had parked. The morning drizzle had faded. The sun speared through the clouds, piercing my eyes. My hair frizzled centimeters shorter as it soaked up the humidity.

"This is really embarrassing," I said, gathering my hair, pulling it tight, and twisting it over my shoulder. Bad enough

I had to retell the story of I shot the car and the cat won, but I had to tell it looking like a freshly watered and beaten Chia pet. I pointed to his Crown Victoria. "Can we sit in your car? I'm suddenly really tired."

He opened the car door and I slid in. I sunk into the warm leather seat. My knee flipped the yellow deodorizer tree hanging from the glove compartment. Lemon scent swirled in the air.

"Did you go to the hospital? Do you have a concussion?" he asked.

I shook my head, answering both questions at once. Even though Matt had suggested it a couple of times, I honestly hadn't considered that possibility until now. Could a concussion make me dizzy?

Michael closed the passenger door for me and walked around in front of the car. Time had either slowed or he moved in slo-mo, I wasn't sure which. But he had cut his hair. It was still nearly down to his shoulders, but at least three inches shorter. His jeans hung low and hugged his hips. His black tee sported the YPD emblem on his chest.

"You cut your hair," I said to him when he closed the door.

The *thunk* of the door broke the stillness and I was tucked inside a bubble of warmth, suddenly very sleepy and breathing in lemon, leather, and man.

"Yeah, a couple of weeks ago." He ran his hand from his forehead through his thick, dark brown hair.

Gosh, I wanted to do that, but I was too tired and let my head fall back against the headrest. I may have sighed a little too, content in the near soundproof bubble of the Crown Vic. He turned the engine on, and the a/c vent stirred the air around us.

"Mmm, spicy."

He turned toward me and gave me a crooked smile. "I'm sorry, what?"

"Huh?"

"Wait. Do you think you could have a concussion?" he asked again.

"From the percussion?" I laughed. "I don't think so."

"Percussion?"

"Never mind." I waved my hand in a half circle until it flopped on the seat. "So this is what happened," I said.

My eyes drifted to the empty seat space between us. I could just lie down awhile, rest my head on his thigh, but I closed my eyes instead and explained about the cat, the car alarm, and the rifle.

Michael asked me something about calling 911. I smiled and may have chuckled. His voice echoed hollow, and I had a sudden urge to pick up a tin can and play telephone with him.

"I don't think the string is tight enough," I said.

"String? Kate? Are you okay?"

My head nodded to my chest.

"I'm calling nine-one-one."

Huh? He was 911 and I was the one who shot my tire. Who was he reporting? I didn't understand, and neither Matt nor I considered calling the police. Besides, the neighborhood would have been filled with sirens. I hadn't heard a siren after the gunshot last night, but I heard one now.

"Kate? Kate. Open your eyes. Can you hear me?"

I could feel Michael's hand rubbing my shoulder. "Yeah," I said. That felt nice. My head bobbled like a dashboard novelty, and my cheek rested on the back of his hand.

"Good, now can you look at me, please?"

I couldn't. As hard as I tried to lift my eyelids, the only sensations were my eyeballs rolling up and down, which nauseated me.

"I'm going to reach across and pull the seatbelt around you," Michael said. The siren revved up and Michael's words faded—en route, hospital, ER, forty-two-year-old female, head trauma, and semi-conscious.

CHAPTER 11

Back at my desk after my twenty-four hour stupor, I felt rejuvenated and ready to own the world. Once the ER nurses finished leading me around by the IV for a CT scan, which revealed nothing, a CBC, and an electrolyte panel, I was diagnosed as dehydrated, slightly anemic, and an uncooperative patient. At least that is what my discharge papers read.

I was discharged around midnight. Michael sat in the waiting room the whole time, which was sweet and embarrassing. He refused to drive me back to *City Scope* so I could pick up my Jeep and insisted on sleeping on my couch so he could drive me to work in the morning. He did a lot of nodding while I argued the point. At least he hadn't issued any warnings about guns, stray cats, and locking doors, which I appreciated. I gave up my battle for independence when he tucked me in and planted a kiss on my temple. If I had been in my right mind, I would have at least kissed him back. I think he understood my embarrassment, which was more than I could say for my co-workers, who were gathered around my desk for the scoop.

Ondrea had already filled them in on the cat fiasco, as she had heard the story from my dear, dear brother.

"And the doctor said you didn't have a concussion?" Joyce asked.

"Right, nothing wrong with my head. I didn't hit it hard enough to cause any damage."

Ondrea snickered and I stood from my chair with my hands fisted on my hips. "Ondrea," I snapped. "I'm glad you are so entertained, but the truth is, if you weren't still living with your mother and father then Matt would not have ended up at my house with his rifle." I ticked off the events on my fingers. "Then his car alarm wouldn't have gone off. I wouldn't have had to deal with the cat, and none of this would have happened."

"Kate, don't go there." Joyce squeezed my shoulder.

Ondrea's face paled and, for a second, regret kicked me in the butt.

"And didn't you tell us last year that you bought your parents' house?" I asked her.

"It's not important." Joyce pulled on my arm. "Let's go get a cup of coffee," she said.

"It is important that she's lied to us. Don't you think so, Dan?"

He shrugged and turned back to his desk.

"I think it is important." I looked from Joyce back to Ondrea. "See, I care about my brother, and don't want you using him to take you on crow-hunting trips or anything else if you can't be honest about your life."

"And what makes you think I'm not honest with Matt? It's you that I don't have to explain myself to," Ondrea said.

"Oh but you do! He is my family. By extension, you owe me the truth."

"Oh gosh, Kate, please stop," Joyce said.

"No. Never mind, Joyce," Ondrea said. "Yes, Kate, I do live with my folks because they are both blind." She turned and walked away, which pleased me. At least she didn't stick around to watch me eat crow. I squinted my eyes shut as if that would help erase the moment and Matt's words to leave it alone bounced around in my mind like a pinball, scoring no points.

"I didn't know that," Dan rolled from behind his desk and whispered.

Joyce shook her head at me. "I tried to stop you."

I flopped into my chair and stared at the ceiling. The pin-holes in the acoustic tiles were plenty big enough for my small self to squeeze into.

At some point, I would apologize to Ondrea, but for now, I was off the hook. She had left the building, and regretfully, I wished I had listened to my split second of regret kicking me in the butt.

By mid-morning, I had excused myself from feeling bad about Ondrea, but vowed I'd listen more and talk less.

I wrote up the new requests I had received the other

day. A knitting Nana had run out of yarn and couldn't find dye lot #508 to finish the afghan for her daughter's baby shower. She'd have to drive fifty miles, but I found it for her.

The second one was from *undisclosed,* who continued to wear her oven mitt to hide her missing wedding band. She was sure she served it up in the meatloaf she had made the week before and wanted me to recommend a jeweler. My third response was to my biggest fan, Sadie Arnold, who never missed a week emailing me or leaving me voicemail messages.

Dear Sadie, Don't go jumping on any comet tail just yet. Those lights in the sky that you saw aren't predicting the arrival of aliens among us. I have it on good authority from NASA that what you saw last Tuesday were the strobe lights announcing the opening of the new K-Mart on Pitchel Street.

Sadie was a bit eccentric and entertaining, but most of the time, I simply replied to her emails rather than write a post for the paper. This particular request met one of the goals Helen Beck had outlined for me.

"When you can mention a prominent person, place, or thing in your column," she had told me, "it has the potential of bringing in sales for valuable ad space."

Next I would leave a note for Simon that read, *K-Mart on Pitchel, The Yarn Yard in Worcester, and Spicemann's Jewelers on Main.* He in turn would hit them up to buy ad space.

Huh. I sat back in my chair and stared at my thought-spot, one of the cacti flowers. In a roundabout way, I was also advertising persons, places, or things, which brought me full circle back to the stench in Yardman. I opened my copy about the reports of dreadful odor and deleted, "near, in, or around the Glenwood cemetery." Advertising a stale smell around the cemetery certainly wouldn't guarantee plot sales.

I called Luanne at the real estate office to tell her about my trip to the ER and ask if she wanted to camp out at the cemetery with me on Saturday night, but she was out doing a showing. Next, I called Terri Wolf. I hadn't heard back from her about my mystery caller claiming the portrait of Grandmother. Also, I wanted to find out if she knew who picked up her donations items.

After five rings, Terri hollered hello and sucked in a long out-of-breath gasp.

"Sorry to make you run to the phone, Terri. This is Kate Lambrose."

"Oh, hi, Kate."

"Are you free to talk?" I hoped Albert wasn't home.

"Oh yes, of course. Why not? What can I do for you?"

What an odd question. Had she forgotten about the secret she had sworn me to and her precious frame she wanted back? "Did you get my message about the caller claiming to be the grandchild of your husband's grandmother?"

"Yes, yes, I did. Odd. I don't know who or how that could be. And you know I can't ask Albert if he has any hidden siblings because then he'd know I'd lost the portrait."

"Yes, I understand that, but I'm wondering if he—Albert—was the one who called me. Would he do that?" I asked.

"Uhm..." she said, then nothing else.

While I waited for her answer, the door to the newsroom clicked shut and a man's voice hollered, "Hello?"

I stood and looked over the cubicles. Joyce did the same with her phone pressed to her ear. She turned and looked at me, shook her head no, and sat down, which meant it was my turn to greet our guest.

"Hold on a minute, Terri." I put the phone down and dashed up to the front.

"Can I help you?" I asked the man wearing a green jump suit.

"Yeah, I have this for..." He waved an envelope at me and looked down at his clipboard. "For Helen Beck," he said.

"She's up one flight, or you can leave it here." I pointed to Mia's desk.

"Okay." He shrugged, dropped it on the desk, and left.

I went back to Terri. "Terri, sorry about that." The line was silent. "Are you there?"

"Yes, but I really have to run, Kate."

"Okay, just one question. Do you recall anything about who picked up your boxes or anything about the driver or the vehicle they drove? And did they give you a donation receipt?"

"Uhm, it was a woman, I think, in an orange van. Hideous color. No receipt, and like I told you last week, no one I contacted had seen the frame or portrait. That's why I wrote to you. I really have to go now." Without a goodbye, she hung up.

I growled at the dial tone and strangled the handset. Perhaps her hasty hang up meant Albert had arrived. But last week, Terri had a panic attack over her loss, and this week, she couldn't even return my call. I had to reach out to her, which translated to, why should I continue this hunt if she wasn't willing to help?

The truth, I loved the mystery. I needed to chase down the what, where, when, why, and who. It fulfilled the investigative reporter blood bubbling in my veins. My column was small scale compared to Jack White, but my small town column kept me safe and at home for Emma's sake. Gosh, I was missing Emma, and hoped, no prayed, she was safe on her cruise and parasailing. In all her fourteen years, we had never been apart for more than a weekend. Loneliness stabbed my heart and my breath hiccuped. I had lots of things to look forward to, but loneliness had a way of reminding me of my distant family. My mother, Emma, George, my sister, and Matt, who was becoming more distant every day, and that was my fault.

I shook my head before I went into a full-blown pity party. At least I could reunite a family with their heirloom easier than I could pull myself out of my tizzy.

The next item on my list was to find out which organization used a driver with an orange van to pick up goodies. None of the other eight emails about the portrait were of any help. Mostly those emails were good luck wishes. Even the one this morning from Sadie simply stated that she thought she might know where the frame was, but she would get back to me. I wouldn't hold my breath.

I pulled out my list of thrift stores in the area and prepared to call each one of them.

"Hey, Kate, are you on the phone?" Joyce asked.

"Not yet." I replaced the handset. "What's up?" I walked up to Mia's desk where Joyce was spinning the envelope around the top of the desk with her hot-red glued-on nails.

"Wonder what's in this," she said.

"What's to wonder about?"

"Well, why was it hand delivered and not mailed?" She spun it one more time and it flung to the floor. Her dozen or so bangles chimed around her wrist. "Oops," she said, "now we have to pick it up and feel for paperclips or staples."

Joyce was a mystic kind of gal who studied her tea leaves, so maybe she was having a psychic moment. But what paperclips and staples would tell us was a mystery to me.

She spun around and smiled at me. Not one strand of her white blonde hair fluttered, and the fumes from her Aqua Net tickled my nose. We both looked down at the envelope, but neither of us made a move to pick it up.

"Not me," I said.

"And I'm not adding my fingerprints to it," Joyce said.

"At least it didn't blow up."

"Oh no!" Joyce kicked the envelope closer to the door. "I didn't even consider that."

"I'm kidding, Joyce. It's just mail."

The newsroom door clicked open, and we both jumped and hooted rather than screaming out loud.

Ondrea stood staring at us, and we both laughed. "What are you two up to now?" she asked.

"Can you pick that up?" Joyce pointed to the envelope. "And feel for paperclips or staples."

Ondrea scooped it off the floor. "It's for Beck," she said.

"Yeah, we know, but it was hand delivered."

"So what?"

"Just feel it," Joyce said.

Ondrea sighed and rolled her eyes, but ran her fingers along the top, down the sides, across the bottom, and up the other side.

"Well?" Joyce asked.

"Yes, three staples across the top here, and no paper clips."

"See I knew it. It's a legal doc. Those are always stapled three times."

I couldn't argue with that theory, but so what? Ondrea laid it back on the desk.

"Well, so much for that mystery," I said. "I have an orange van to find."

"For what?" Joyce asked.

"According to Terri Wolf, the person who picked up her donations drove an orange van. So, if I can find out which thrift store uses an orange van, maybe I'll find the portrait."

"It's too bad we didn't know the grandmother's name," Joyce said.

"Why? What would that matter? That's not going to help find anything," Ondrea said.

"I know that, but it's interesting just the same."

"I know some part of it, I think. But I agree with Ondrea. It's not going to help find anything," I said. "Besides that, it was my Mys Caller that claimed it was his or her grandmother Petra something-or-other. And who knows if that is true."

Joyce walked back to her desk. "I'll see what I can find." She giggled liked a kid and rubbed her hands together. "Petra...something," she mumbled.

"Kate," Ondrea said. "About the orange van. That belongs to the Down Stage Shop."

"How do you know?"

"We donated some of my parents' things that they couldn't...didn't need any more, and the Stage van picked them up."

If silence was truly golden, we'd all be dripping in gold at that moment. Things Ondrea's parents couldn't use anymore because they were blind, was the message ringing in my ears.

I walked over to Ondrea. There wouldn't be a more perfect time for me to eat more crow, humble myself, and close the gap between my brother and I. "Ondrea, I'm sorry for everything I said earlier and hope you can forgive me."

I stepped forward and gave her a quick hug. She didn't return the hug, but that didn't matter. The hug was for Matt.

CHAPTER 12

After calling the Down Stage Shop for the name of the van driver, I gathered my belongings and left the *City Scope* office.

Finding a portrait in the two square mile radius of Yardman shouldn't be difficult. After all, I had a finite number of thrift stores to visit. It should be simple enough to double check incoming donations.

According to Down Stage, the van driver volunteered twice a week for their shop. Usually, he picked up at three regular donation sites, one in the Market Rite shopping center, one at Yardman's public library, and one at Memorial Faith Church. Last week's log had him doing an extra run to neighborhoods, and Terri's house was on his route. I was on to a good lead for sure.

Being a volunteer driver could be profitable, especially if they dabbled on eBay. They would have the first pick of hoarding one or two items that appealed to them. It might not be morally correct to pilfer from the donation box, but I could see it as justified barter. Discarded treasures for community service, but certainly no reason to call out the National Guard.

I glanced down at my notepad and verified I had stopped at the correct address for Bobby Rumfield. I had considered calling first instead of barging in on him, but most often asking for an invite resulted in a "don't bother me." Crashing in gave me a chance to flash my toothy smile, and I was the least threatening-looking person I knew. Hell, I couldn't even threaten a cat. The yellow sleeveless rayon blouse I chose to wear this morning matched my shiner. I was just one ray of sunshine waiting to illuminate the day.

As I sat looking at the name Bobby and a front yard cluttered with hoarder's debris, my stomach rolled and a cold sweat stuck my blouse to my pits. When would I escape the trauma of the name Bobby, as in Bobby Maleck, aka Mack? Good and dead, Mack.

I sucked the last drops of my latte from the cup and smacked my lips. Chocolate and coffee—my battery was charged for at least four more hours. After a cleansing breath, I exited my Jeep and skillfully followed the round stepping-stones through the debris to the porch. I had entered another dimension, as the well-kept porch stretched across the front of the house.

Shiny ivy twined around the baluster. Just past the front window, a two-seated glider rocked to the rhythm of the breeze. On each side of the front door, red and white geraniums poked their heads over rust covered clay pots, and hanging from the porch light, purple flowers cascaded from a basket. Huh, Rumfield had a green thumb.

I rang the bell and fingered the leaves on the hanging basket. They were real. Keeping plants alive and thriving in captivity amazed me. My thumb only knew the color green when I slid the cap off my highlighter pen. Heck, I was fortunate my condo association cared for my lawn and not me.

The front door snapped open. I snatched my hand from the basket, accidentally taking a leaf, which I hastily tried to drop. I ran my fingers through my hair, hoping to cover up my faux pas, but the damn leaf stuck between my hair and ear.

"Hi." I smiled.

A woman in her mid-sixties dressed in a mismatched red sleeveless blouse and peach-colored Capris stepped up to the threshold. Her pixie cut gray hair stuck out at odd angles. She outweighed me by maybe thirty pounds and stood eight inches taller. The wrinkles around her mouth deepened as she frowned.

"Can I help you? Or do you normally go around beating up plants."

She crossed her arms over her chest, and I took note there was more muscle than turkey flab. "Sorry, sorry," I said. "I was just admiring." I pulled the leaf free and offered it to her. When she didn't take it, I stuffed it in my pocket. "I'm looking for Bobby Rumfield."

"Oh?"

"I'm K—"

"Kate Lambrose, *In Sight* columnist," she finished for me.

"Yes." I smiled. "That's right. Is Mr. Rumfield home?"

"There is no Mr. Rumfield," she said. "I'm Bobbie. Bobbie with an 'ie,' that is."

"Of course." I blinked.

When would I learn to stop assigning a gender to a name? First, there was Emma's friend. I was dumbfounded when Emma informed me she and Sam were having a sleepover. At least until I learned that Sam was short for Samantha. Then there was a nurse who abbreviated his name to "B," but was a muscle-bound Barney. And now, Bobbie with an "ie"...driving a van, carting load after load of discarded items.

"It's short for Roberta," she said.

Okay, I could visualize it. Throw her in some jeans and a pair of work boots. Her thick calves seemed well adapted for heavy lifting once or twice a week. I offered a handshake and clenched my teeth when she took my hand and squeezed.

"What brings you to my doorstep, Ms. Lambrose?"

"Call me Kate, and I was wondering if you have a minute to help me with a story I'm working on?"

"Oh? A lost story or a found story?"

"Lost," I said. She really did read my column. I wasn't just a pretty face in the paper. "I think you might be able to help."

"I doubt that." She took a step backward to close her door.

"Wait." I jammed my sneaker against the door. "It'll only take a moment. I think you may have picked up the lost item I'm searching for."

"I doubt that," she said again. The door bounced between us as she tried to shut me out, but I wedged my way in. "Persistent, aren't you? Looks to me you have already had one door slammed in your face."

"No, not a door, and yes, I'm persistent. I'm looking for a framed portrait. If I could show you a picture, I'm sure you'll recognize it."

"I already saw it. In your column. And haven't seen it since."

I wanted to say I doubted her, because only a guilty person would run away, but I didn't. "Maybe you didn't notice. I mean, after all, you do so much." I smiled and hoped flattery would motivate her. "And this would have been picked up almost two weeks back. I'm sure you have done more important things since then."

"I do and have." She smiled and squared her shoulders. "I picked up at least two dozen boxes and crates that week." She rubbed her biceps.

She stepped back from the door and I stumbled into her. She caught me around the chest and hefted me upright.

Reclaiming my dignity, I hoisted my tote back up onto my shoulder and pulled my shirt down. "Sorry. It's just...Ms. Rumfield...Roberta...Bobbie, it's important to my reader that she be able to reclaim the framed portrait of her grandmother."

She sighed. "Fine. But don't expect tea and cookies after that kind of entrance. Have a seat." She pointed to the Queen Anne chair and sat across from me on a fainting couch—or was it a divan?

I perched on the edge of the seat so I wouldn't wrinkle the tatted doilies. "Do you remember picking up a private donation on Pleasant Street?"

"Yep, of course. I'm not senile. They wouldn't let me drive, would they? I had two private donation pickups that day. Both were laid out at the curb. The first house was a foreclosure clean up. Had a bunch of odds and ends a family had no room to cart along on a swift move. " She rambled on about how people needed to save money for a rainy day and not over spend. I nodded in agreement as I looked around her living room.

Her décor reminded me of my nana's house, crammed with glittery, gaudy dust catchers that fascinated me as a child. When Nana died, my mother refused to part with the trinkets and she had labeled many items, literally with a sticker and black sharpie, with either "Matthew," "Allison," or "Kate." Family baggage I wasn't ready to inherit anytime soon.

If only I had a chance to roam Bobbie's house and poke around, I might see that portrait or frame. "Your home has so much character," I said. "I love big, old houses."

She nodded, but didn't offer the tour I had hoped for. The living room alone looked like the Antique Show had set up camp. All she needed to open her own storefront was a *wel-*

come sign. Terri's frame could be right in sight and I couldn't tell it apart from the sheer volume of stuff.

"So, the piece I'm looking for was donated from an occupied house," I said.

"Oh, that one. The couple that was screaming bloody murder at each other. I didn't stick around there long. Just grabbed the boxes and skedallied."

Uh oh, Terri and her husband screaming at each other wasn't a good sign and meant Albert probably knew about the missing portrait. And I doubted Bobbie skedallied. She probably heard the color of every piece of Terri and Albert's dirty laundry.

"Huh, what were they screaming about?" I asked.

"Something about who had rights to the car. I don't recall exactly. Why is that important?"

"Just curious. Do you recall where you delivered the boxes?"

Bobbie shrugged. "Depends on what was labeled on the box."

"What labels are you talking about?"

"Goodwill, Rags to Riches, Faith Rummage, Down Stage, or nothing."

Terri had said Goodwill, but she could have just used that as a generic reference. And I didn't know if she had labeled the boxes. But what interested me more were boxes with no labels.

"Nothing? What happens to those boxes?" I asked.

She shrugged and her eyes shifted around her room. "Sometimes they go to the dump," she said.

Great, the dump. I hurled at the smell of raw onions, garlic, or yeast. I wouldn't survive a trip to the dump and wasn't sure I would go that far for Terri's search. I made a mental note to ask Terri if she had tagged her donation boxes to a specific charity.

I settled back against the seat trying to get comfortable. Whoever Queen Anne was, I was no fan. She sat too ramrod straight for my liking.

"So did you take any unlabeled boxes to the dump?"

"No." She shook her head.

"But some didn't have labels?"

She nodded.

Again, I looked around the living room. The size of Terri's framed portrait, as well as the gaudiness of it, would be easily spotted. It wasn't here, at least not in the living room. But Bobbie Rumfield had more than just the average amount of family baggage. "I imagine sometimes people forget to label their donations altogether, don't they?"

"It happens."

I stood up and headed over to the fireplace mantel where a myriad of small knick-knacks and music boxes clamored for space. Two of the music boxes looked freshly polished.

"Don't touch those," she warned.

"You keep the items not labeled, don't you?" I said.

"We're done, Ms. Lambrose." She rose from the couch and herded me toward the door.

"I'm not saying it's wrong." I sidestepped around the end table.

"You de-leaf my plants." She pursed her lips. "You barge into my house, and then you call me a thief? How do you steal something nobody wants?" Her face flamed red.

If she was about to stroke. I hoped it was before she tore me apart so I could at least help her.

"Why, you are just like all the rest of your baby boomer generation. Golden-spoon-fed ungrateful...get out of my house."

Whoa, I was far from the baby boomer generation, but I hit some nerve she'd been hoarding awhile. "Please, calm down. I can't say I wouldn't keep some of these wonderful treasures." I waved my arms around her living room. "And you've done such a nice job displaying them all," I lied. "Can you at least tell me if you saw the portrait I'm looking for? I can't imagine you would hoard it...I mean display it. After all, it is pretty gaudy and wouldn't match your decor. And if you still have it, you could be the hero mentioned in this week's article about rescuing a family's grandmother!"

"Yeah, I saw that gaud-awful frame, and it either went to Faith Rummage or Down Stage. Now get out." She pointed at the door.

I stared at her. First, she had said she hadn't seen it since seeing it in the paper, and now she claimed it got dropped off at one of two places. I was about to point that fact out to her when she growled to get out again.

"Okay, okay." I grabbed the door handle and stammered an apology.

"Wait." She jerked my shoulder back, holding me in place with her thick vise-like fingers. "You might be taking a piece of my plant, but you won't be taking this." Her fingers grazed down my back, snatching a few strands from my head.

"Ouch!" I clutched at the back of my head, probing for a bald spot. "What are you doing?" I asked, and turned toward her.

In her grip was the doily from the Queen Anne chair.

CHAPTER 13

My scalp still tingled a bit from the hair plucking, and my pride had taken a symbolic kick in the butt. Nevertheless, Bobbie Rumfield sure had acted guilty. She hadn't wanted to invite me in at first, which was suspicious. I would have expected her to be more than willing to help locate the portrait she had picked up, especially since she was a *rah rah* community service volunteer. She hadn't even offered the proud homeowner tour when I said I loved old houses. Bobbie Rumfield was definitely hiding something, and it darn well could be Terri's missing portrait.

But she hadn't stolen it, as I had stupidly implied. After all, Terri had accidentally discarded it. It could have been picked up by anyone, and that didn't tag them as a thief.

I needed someone to explain the whole nine-tenths of the law was possession rule before I could decide my next move. My dear brother would be more than willing to quote it for me, but not without his parental finger shake in my face.

Michael Earl, on the other hand, didn't know me well enough to question my motives. Besides, I hadn't seen him since he whisked me off to the hospital. And I had promised him that I would stop by to fill out the police report about the death of my tire.

I sped up to make the light and turned on Brown Avenue toward the police station. I had a civic duty to follow through on my promise. I owed him a thank you, and certainly wouldn't mind filling my eyes with his sexy body.

The smile on my face lasted up to the moment I opened the door and saw Officer Gleason riding desk jockey.

He cradled the phone on his shoulder as he stuffed a cleaning brush down a gun barrel. Gun pieces lay scattered across a chamois on his desk. Somehow, that seemed wrong and un-lawful, or at least unsafe. He looked up long enough to frown at me. I flashed my toothy grin, which was more of a sneer.

The last time I was in the police station and Gleason was on the phone, he had signaled me, like a traffic cop, to park my rump on the bench. Then he had brought me front and center for an identity check.

This time I turned away from his line of sight and busied myself, looking over the community bulletin board and waited, eyeing him every few seconds. He turned a half circle away from me and dropped his megaphone voice into a whisper. But his whisper was just as loud as his inside voice.

I had no trouble eavesdropping. I caught the word Sabbath, which brought the song "Heaven and Hell" to the surface of my cerebrum. Then he said something about the three-quarter moon and that reminded me that I had a date with Michael about that time of the month. The last thing I heard Gleason say was, "last chance for holy water." That puzzled me. Did he intend to pump it, bathe in it, or drink it? I filed the information away for later and hoped my rendition of "Heaven and Hell" would escape my brain by the end of the day.

I planted my butt on the bench and stared at the near dead ficus tree. The poor tree dripped leaves like raindrops from the rooftop. It needed a healthy watering, or feeding, or whatever it took to spring new sprigs. Although the poor little tree hadn't succumbed yet, some of its branches were definitely naked.

Naked, hmm. I hoped Michael Earl was in the building. I pulled my notepad out of my tote and used it as a fan. Naked had me thinking about sex, and the only sex I had recently was in my dreams. And my imagination debuted Michael as the all-star in my dreams. I wanted him very much. But after George announced he was gay after fifteen years of marriage, I had to wonder if I was the cause and effect. Not to mention, I had kept Jonathan at arm's distance forever. I squeezed my eyes shut and knocked my head against the wall, partly to ditch my rampant thoughts and knock "Heaven and Hell" back into the depths of my memory. The ficus teetered from my movement.

Gleason dropped the phone on the cradle and peered at

me. "Here to file another missing person report?" he asked. "Or report a beating?" He pointed to my face.

"Neither," I said, jumping off my seat and bellying up to the counter. "At least you know who I am."

He frowned. "Pretty hard to forget. You had the entire PD tied up looking for a seventy-six-year-old man—"

"Who was an opportunistic murderer, and you're forgetting he tried to kill me too."

"And his wife, a pet shop owner."

"Who harbored a fugitive." I slapped down my notepad.

Gleason shrugged. "No reason to be defensive. It is what it is."

Okay, I didn't like him the first time I met him, and I liked him even less now. He may have just stated facts, but it sure sounded like a challenge.

I blew out a steadying breath then pasted a smile on my lips. "Should you be doing that here at the front desk?" I pointed to his dismantled gun.

"I can do what I want during my shift." He wrote my name, the date, and time in his logbook. "So, no missing person?" His eyes widened and the corners of his mouth turned up like the Cheshire cat.

"I would think having a gun visible to anyone walking in here would be a safety hazard."

"It's dismantled. To hurt anyone with it, I'd have to throw the pieces at you."

"At me?" I asked.

"You, as in anyone walking in here. Like you said."

"Well, I wasn't thinking of you hurting anyone with it as much as I was thinking of someone having open access to walking off with it."

"What do you want, Lambrose?" He tossed another chamois across the gun, hiding it from view.

"Oh, that helps." I smiled.

Gleason was Ondrea's personality only in reverse drag. He even seemed to be the same age. Huh. "Do you know Ondrea Franklin? She's our town government column writer."

"No, why?"

"You should make a point to meet her. She's about your age, smart, and gorgeous." My smile grew wider. "Is Detective Michael Earl in?"

"Is he expecting you?" Gleason tapped away at his keyboard.

"Yes, no. Well, uh, yes, I suppose so, but maybe no, not today."

He stared at me like I had just recited an algorithm that explained the universe. "I can wait while you decide."

"Yes," I said. "He's expecting me."

"Okay then." He pressed something along the lip of his desk.

A loud buzz echoed off the cement block walls. My fingertips tingled from the vibration rattling through the countertop, and the door next to me clicked open. For a moment, I thought he had stun-gunned me.

He pointed me down a corridor and toward a room he called the bullpen.

Before I closed the door behind me, I turned back to Gleason. "Let me ask you something, Gleason." What I wanted to know was if any of the residents around Glenwood had called the police about the weekend stench and drumming.

"What now?" He planted his fists on his hips.

"Aren't nine-one-one calls public record?" I asked.

"Sometimes, why?"

Sometimes? Was he kidding? And I knew better. "Well, let me ask it this way. If a resident called to complain about their neighbor having a loud party, would you have to do something about it?"

"Of course, why?"

I shrugged. "Just curious. Thanks." Rather than ask him to check if there had been any such calls logged, I'd ask Michael.

As soon as I peered around the corner into the bullpen, Michael Earl spotted me and waved.

I swiped my hands through my hair, unhooking the strands from behind my heated ears. I sighed and my vision blurred with fields of windswept flowers as we met halfway across the room. The YPD emblem on his black Polo rippled over his muscles.

"Everything okay?" he asked. His paddle-sized hand rested briefly at the small of my back as he turned me in the direction of his desk. I had pings that had my Wonder Bra wondering.

"Fine." I sat in the chair across from him. My eyes traced

the gold desk plate that read *Detective M Earl*. I wasn't sure if it was his quick smile, the warmth in his whiskey brown eyes, his light touch, or just that damn nameplate that had me purring, but I was. "I wanted to thank you for getting me to the hospital. I don't normally faint, but then I don't normally shoot my tire or try to stand up under my Jeep. And I really do know how to use a gun. My father taught me. He taught all of us. Well, not you, I mean, Jeez, I know it's not a broom, right?"

"Kate—"

"And just so it's all on record, I like cats. It might have looked like I was trying to shoot the cat—"

"Kate."

"But I just didn't want it stuck in my garage. I'm really a good neighbor, but—"

"Kate." Michael reached across his desk and squeezed my hand.

"Oye. Sorry, sorry," I said.

"It's okay." He smiled. "Just let me finish this report, then we'll finish yours."

Oh gosh, how on earth would I make it through a date with this man? I couldn't shut up. I couldn't sit still. I was a nervous, bumbling idiot. That's it. I wasn't going. End of story.

I sighed, relieved with my decision. I watched him mark up the reports, flipping back and forth between pages. I had seen him three times now, and each time I noticed something more interesting.

Of course, this time, I actually had time to gawk at him. The first time, I had been sidetracked by his heavily made up dinner date clinging to his arm and overcome by his Dennis the Menace orange striped jersey. Besides, I had been with Jonathan at the time. The second time, I had no time to pant out his name because I was too busy coughing up smoke. Then the third time, I had stared at him through the haze of semi-consciousness. This time, I studied him.

Smoke-grey rings outlined the warm brown irises of his eyes. A faint jagged white scar trickled under his chin, and one of his top teeth had a small chip along the edge. On his left arm, barely peeking out from under his Polo sleeve, I spotted the edge of a tattoo. There were stories buried beneath each marking. Stories that I wanted to hear.

Oh my God, I was leering. I swiped my lips, checking for drool, and looked to his nameplate then the wall on his left and back to his desktop where he carefully closed a manila folder. "Oh, I wasn't trying to sneak a look." I pointed at his folder. At least not at that.

"I didn't think you were," he said.

"I can come back if you're busy."

"But you're here now."

"Yes," I tucked my hair behind my ears. "Yes, I am. Huh, in the bullpen…" I hadn't meant to say bullpen aloud. It just tripped off my tongue with visions of red capes whipped around my hips. *Gore me now—olé!*

"Are you okay?" Michael asked. "Do you need a glass of water?"

"Oh, no. Just a little, uh…" I scoped out the room, looking everywhere except at his face. It surprised me that the office space didn't have one cubicle in the place. The random glances coming my way by the other officers had me even more uncomfortable, especially the one from one of the female detectives seated toward the back of the room. I'd seen her before, but couldn't place her. "Huh. Wow. I thought you'd have an office."

"Do we need privacy? Would you rather go into one of the interview rooms?"

"No. Yes. I mean, God no." I fanned myself with my hand. I'd never make it as a criminal. I was in the hot seat with my only crime being illicit thoughts, and I was sweating bullets. "Well, I've always wanted to see the inside of a police station. I just haven't been in this deep," I said. "Wait. That didn't sound right." I rubbed my palms down my face, hoping that he'd assume the friction was the cause of the heat rising to my cheeks. "I mean, I don't want, need…um…I don't. I just want to fill out the report about the bullet in my tire, okay?"

Michael's smile curved up the right side of his face. He pulled a file folder from his desk drawer and stood up. "Why don't we do it over coffee at Rubys? I could use the company and the caffeine."

Oh yes, please get me out of here before I'm arrested for idiocy. "Sounds perfect," I said.

CHAPTER 14

Rubys had plenty of open seating. With the breakfast crowd gone and the lunch hour just minutes away, Michael and I were two of six patrons. The welcome sign read, "If you see a seat, take it," rather than, "Please wait to be seated." The menus were double-sided, laminated pink sheets of paper that doubled as the table placemats.

Michael led me to the booth just inside the door along the windows. He took the seat facing the entrance, but then scanned the empty tables at the back by the kitchen door. Most likely on the lookout for Paulie or Rudy, the top two Yardman Sicily Boy's Club members.

I had the same habit anytime I came in here. The Sicily boys were a blight on Yardman, and although it hadn't been proven, it was rumored that they had their hands in everything from town politics to fencing stolen jewelry to laundering dirty money. Rudy Santora actually owned Rubys. Word on the street was his sign maker was dyslexic, making the name of the place Rubys instead of Rudys, period.

"Huh, I do the same thing every time I come in here," I said, and nodded toward the empty captain chairs along the back wall.

"Do what?" Michael asked.

"Look for Rudy and his fans."

"What do you know about them?" Michael's eye lit up.

"Oh, I don't. Sorry, no scoop here." At least not yet, I thought.

"Don't believe all the rumors you hear, Kate. Sometimes it's just crap."

Huh. Was Michael defending them? That piqued my interest. I wanted to know what he knew and why. But at the same time, I worried Michael might be buddies with Rudy.

"So, are you saying that Rudy isn't up to his elbows in...illegal matters?" I asked.

"Some might say he's given a lot to this town." He flipped the menu over and eyed the desserts.

"Would you say that?"

He shrugged. I sighed. I didn't push the subject further, but waited for Michael to sum it up. He didn't.

He had an annoying habit of dropping a subject off a cliff never to be seen or heard from again. And he never left the door open long enough to push in for more information. But at least we had something in common. We both were scoping out the scene waiting for guns a-blazin', maybe.

Silence settled between us and I took a deep breath. Now was not the time for an attack of Kate Lambrose Syndrome when I'd forget to censor my thoughts before they dribbled out my mouth. I shook the anxiety from my shoulders. It wasn't the fact that Michael had a detective badge that rattled me. It was the heavy attraction film that floated in the air between us. We had a professional relationship, but neither of us had clawed our way through the film yet. However, I was determined to let go of my junior high crush syndrome.

Dee, the waitress who never seemed to go home, hollered across to us. "You two want coffee?"

"Iced coffee," I said.

"Make that two," Michael said.

"You want your usual croissant with jam, Kate?" Dee asked when she brought our drinks. "Or are we trying something new?" She nodded her head toward Michael and winked.

Oh Jeez! Had he seen that? I took a sip of the cold coffee before answering to flush my embarrassment down the hatch. "Yes, the usual. Thanks, Dee."

"That sounds good. I'll have the same," Michael said.

Rubys had been the place that Jonathan and I had frequented. We never became the item everyone believed, and I certainly didn't want Michael to get the wrong impression. I came here all the time, and not necessarily with Jonathan, but with Emma too.

"About that usual thing she said, I can explain."

"You don't need to explain."

"I don't?" I cocked my head sideways and looked back and forth from his left eye to his right eye, searching for his thoughts. Jonathan would have needed an explanation. He had such a hard time understanding the figurative from the literal. He would have needed to know what my interpretation was just to be certain we were on the same page. And during my relationship with George, he had been so insecure in who he was, I always had to redefine who I was and self-explain. Not needing to explain myself was a new world.

"Why would you need to explain someone else?"

Huh. Why exactly? Even so, old habits die hard. "Just so you know, Jonathan and I were regulars here."

"I know." Michael smiled.

"You do?"

He nodded. "You're done with him, right? Or are you still doing the long-distance thing?"

"You know he moved?" My jaw dropped. "Oh. You're a detective. I imagine you know a lot."

He chuckled, and it tickled me that he laughed at my sarcasm. "Well?" he asked.

"Oh. Done. We never got more serious than an All-American special. I never got a taste of Rubys Wild Rose Omelet."

A slow, lazy smile hiked up his right cheek. I remembered the very first time I saw his crooked grin. I was at dinner with Jonathan, and Michael introduced himself with Ms. Cling wrapped on his arm. Aw! Ms. Cling was the female officer that threw the sour looks my way earlier in the bullpen.

"Are you still seeing her?" I asked.

"Who?"

"I don't know, but the woman you were with when we met at Red Dragon."

"No." He shook his head.

And that was it. No why, because, if, then, or but about it. Another subject he heaved over the cliff.

I started thinking I should put on my rock climbing gear if I was daring to date this man.

Before I had the chance to broach that subject, he had shuffled the folder open and pulled out a blank incident report. "Let's get your statement down about the night you wounded your Jeep and you."

I touched my forehead at the corner of my eye. "Doesn't hurt anymore at least," I said.

Somewhere between our second or third iced coffee refill, we ended up off topic while I explained Matt's expertise was in law and not first aid. Michael confessed that he had the same lack of doctoring skills and had I not conveniently passed out in the passenger seat of his Crown Vic, he would have called for the EMTs.

"I'm glad it didn't come to that. Ambulances draw the lookie-loos. And I don't think I was wearing my good bra that day."

His eyebrow raised, and I shook my head. So much for censoring my thoughts before the words drooled from my lips. "You know," I explained. "They cut off your clothes...oh...never mind. Erase that." I waved at the air between us.

"No, no, no. I like how you just say what comes to mind." He laughed.

"That's a good thing, because it happens more times than not."

"That's probably what makes you a good writer."

"Thanks." I smiled. I hadn't thought of that and logged that in my memory to use as a defense the next time I was up against my brother, mother, sister, or Ondrea.

Michael scribbled some additional notes on the report and flipped it around toward me. "Review that and then sign it there." He pointed.

I scanned through it, adding a few periods and commas before adding my signature.

"Okay, good, that business is out of the way," he said. "So where and what is planned for our Friday night date?"

Wow! At least he could have tied a bungee cord to that before he flung it out there. "I, uhm, I don't know."

"You don't?"

"No. It was all Luanne's idea, and Izzy too, I think. Or yours?"

"No, not mine. Izzy came to me, so I thought you went to Luanne and she went to Izzy with the idea," Michael said.

"Oh boy. I think we've both been set up. I'm sorry," I said.

"Don't be. I wanted to ask you out, but didn't know how or if you would." He looked down into his iced coffee.

I did the same. Did he think I'd say no? "Are you sure it's a good idea?" I asked before I even knew where that thought came from. "I mean, you being a detective and me being a reporter. Isn't that a conflict of interest?"

"Maybe," he said.

And over the cliff that went, but not so fast. I wiped the disappointment from my face with my napkin.

"Wait." Was he giving me an out? "I'm not just going to let you toss this over your proverbial cliff. Out of sight, out of mind," I said.

Michael smiled.

"I'm not sure I want to go on a double date."

"You don't?" He set his glass down with a thud.

I met his eyes and shook my head, "No. Did you?"

"I'm not sure how to answer that. No—I don't want to double, but yes, I want to see you on Friday night. How's that?"

"Perfect. I'll tell Luanne," I said.

"I'll let Izzy know they are on their own."

I glanced at my watch. "I have to get going, but can I ask you a question?"

"You can ask me anything, Kate."

And a few dozen questions raced through my mind, but I'd save those for later. "Can you check if there have been any complaint calls from residents near Glenwood?"

"What kind of complaint calls and about when?"

"Noise, and say, like, within the last two weeks."

"I can, but can I ask why?"

"Can I tell you later?" I smiled.

"So this is that line of conflict of interest, I guess. But if it's a big deal, you'll let me know?"

It wasn't a big deal, and I didn't have any information to make it important. "I promise," I said. "Oh, and let me ask you one more question?"

He laughed. "Go for it."

"If you thought someone had something that really wasn't stolen, but lost, how would you get it back from them without accusing them of taking it?"

"I'm not sure I understand." He frowned.

"You know, like you have something of mine." *Like my heart*, but I didn't say that. "And I know you have it, but I'm the one that lost it, so you didn't steal it from me, meaning you accidentally found it. I didn't give it to you, but now I want it back. How do I get it back?"

"Is this about the portrait?" he asked.

"Yes."

"Aw, so you think you know who has it?"

"Maybe, and I'm not sure how to get them to admit to it or give it back."

Michael took a long time digesting that. I worried he wasn't going to answer, but then he finally said, "Possession is nine-tenths of the law in this case."

"I was afraid of that." That meant if Bobbie Rumfield had the portrait, it was hers for the keeping. "Finders keepers."

"Pretty much, yes."

"Well, I'm not giving up just yet. I'm headed to the church to rummage through their rummage." I pointed across the street. "It could be there."

"So about Friday..." Michael said. "How about we skip to a second date? Rubys being our first." He winked. I smiled.

"I like to cook," he said. "Would you be okay with me making dinner at your place?"

"I think I'd like that." I pitched all my anxiety over the cliff.

CHAPTER 15

Bobbie Rumfield was guilty of keeping Terri's portrait for sure. I could feel it in my bones, but hadn't a clue how I'd prove it. I just hoped she would agonize over it and return it. In case I was wrong about it being in her possession, I crossed Main Street from Rubys, and walked past the burnt out shell of *City Scope* to Memorial Faith. After climbing the half dozen cement steps to the arch doors, I peered in the cross-shaped windows.

The last time I had set foot in a church with any purpose was when my sister Allison married Jackson. Matthew was preoccupied with surrogate father duties that day, and while Allison primped, Jackson begged me to distract my mother. "Just ten minutes," he had said, "until the ceremony begins."

My mother had good intentions and ideas, but despite her five-foot-three stature, delivered them with overbearing menace. Like a backlit fire firefighters use to clear debris, Mom had to be watched and raked into place.

In my rush to rescue the videographer's camera away from my mother, my shoe strap broke, sending me sprawling at their feet in a cloud of peach taffeta.

"You can't go barefoot in church, Kate," she had said.

"You have a better idea? God told Moses to take his shoes off on holy ground, so why can't I?"

Thanks to Mom's antics and my face plant, Allison and Jackson had a DVD of wedding bloopers.

At least I had both shoes on today. If Mom could forgive me for walking barefoot in church then God could forgive my absence from His house. It wasn't like I didn't pray or talk to him. We had conversations daily, well mostly one-sided—my side—but I did genuinely invite Him to comment even if I didn't leave Him room to answer. I certainly didn't blame Him

for His silence over trivial matters. He was there when I needed Him. Nevertheless, Luanne threatened to break me of my
"Oh my God" outbursts. So far, she'd done a pretty good job.

I swung the hefty door open, stepped inside, and paused,
blinking my eyes like a stuttering candle, adjusting to the
dim light.

Through the clear panes along the west side of the
church, the sun streamed a shaft of light and spotlighted the
pastor's pulpit. Dust motes floated in the air, and made me
think of a trail of tiny angels. I tiptoed down the center aisle,
following the light. Overhead, three ceiling fans stirred the air
with the scent of lemon and beeswax. It was months until
Christmas, but I wondered what frankincense and myrrh
smelled like.

"Hello?" I yelled in a soft whisper. My voice echoed back
and I stopped at the front pew. On a small step up stage to
my left, the church organ sat silent. The Devil tempted me to
climb the two steps and rock out a wicked rendition of "Mary
had a Little Lamb," a tune I could finger over the phone during terminal hold. I had taken two steps toward the instru-
ment when my mother's voice echoed in my head. *Mind your
manners, Kate. You are visiting.* I did an about face and
headed toward a door tucked inside a small alcove to the
right of the pulpit.

"Hello?" I called again, and knocked. Huh. I should have
called ahead instead of traipsing around on my own. I was
the only soul in the place with a physical body.

I jiggled the handle and raised myself on tiptoes to peer
through the window.

Smashing my right cheek against the glass, I could only
see the hallway white walls. I swiveled my head to look in
the opposite direction and came face to face with a shaggy
brown-haired, mustachioed man.

"Oh my God!" I jumped back from the door and slapped
my hand over my outburst.

"Can I help you?" the man asked as he opened the door.

"Hi. Oh boy, you scared me," I said. "I'm, uhm, looking
for the person in charge." I blew out a long breath.

His lips turned upwards, the corners of his mustache
poked into his chipmunk cheeks. "The Big Guy or the middle
man?"

He motioned with his hand for me to take a step back.

"Oh, sorry," I said. "Sorry." He swung the door and propped it open with a kickstand. "The middle man, I suppose. Umm, Pastor Lawrence?"

"You found him." He stuck out his hand for me to shake.

He was maybe in between his late twenties and early thirties. Dressed in a light blue jersey shirt, dark blue gym shorts, and black Vans tennis shoes, he didn't appear pastorish at all. I tried not to notice the sweaty patches under his armpits, but he caught me staring.

"Not my normal garb," he said. "I referee the teen basketball camp. We just finished about ten minutes ago. Haven't had a chance to clean up yet." He swiped his fingers through his wayward hair and snagged a sweatband that he tucked in his pocket. I was glad that he removed it after I shook his hand. "You're the Insight lady, right?" he asked.

I smiled wide. "That's me." I bit my tongue to keep from making a dumb joke about him being the Insight man. "I was hoping you could help me with a lost portrait."

"That's a request I haven't heard before." He chuckled. "Come, follow me to my office. I desperately need water."

His Vans squeaked on the tiled floor as he took one step to my two. He pushed his office door open wide. A manmade breeze from a box fan in the window fluttered papers weighted down by Psalms books and Bibles. Effigies of Jesus from birth to crucifixion decorated the walls and shelves.

Pastor Lawrence rounded his desk and plucked a towel off the back of his chair. "Please, have a seat." He mopped his face with the towel.

"Oh, that's all right, I'll only be a moment." I should've called for sure, as I was having a hard time trying not to look at his naked knees. They stuck out below the hem of his gym shorts. It seemed inappropriate, especially with the portrait of the Virgin Mary peering over his shoulder. Shouldn't preachers be fully clothed from head to toe?

"Are you in crisis?" he asked, and took a bottle of water from the small refrigerator in the corner.

"Crisis? No, yes, no... Wait. What do you mean?" I sat down on the edge of the chair. Thankfully, he seated himself behind his desk.

Crisis seemed to be my middle name. I conjured it even

when life was boring just to keep extra busy. Crisis? Well, Emma was somewhere out at sea dodging the ghost of Rosalyn Kohler. I had a date with Michael. I nearly shot a cat, practically killed myself, and had to file a police report about how I killed my tire. I survived a plane ride to and fro, and by God's grace—*thanks, by the way*—I nodded slightly at a crucifix—I survived a fire that destroyed the historical building that once housed *City Scope*. Beck avoided me, Ondrea hated me, and my brother was disappointed in me. Oh, and my mother was coming to visit, not to mention I felt that someone was watching me besides the Big Guy upstairs. I had crisis stamped on my forehead and my backside. When I walked in dirt, the tread of my shoes stamped the word in my wake. Hey, crisis was my brand name. I snickered at my thoughts. My life sounded like a sitcom. At the very least, a soap opera if I threw in my gay ex-husband.

My snicker turned into a snort.

Pastor Lawrence's eyes widened. His brows raised his hairline. "Is there someone you'd like me to call? Forgive me, but you look, uh…" He waved his hand, gesturing toward my head. "Beaten."

"Oh." I cupped my cheek. "Thank you for not saying what I thought you were going to say, which is crazy. But this isn't what it seems. I, uh, walked into a Jeep. The Jeep came out worse for wear. And thank you again, but no, I'm not in any crisis." I paused a second, waiting for God to strike me with lightning. Pastor Lawrence didn't seem convinced, but God did. "I'm here to ask you a favor. Bobbie Rumfield said she dropped off a few cartons of items for your rummage sale."

"Yes. We were excited for the donation. The general population doesn't give much during the off holiday months. Nothing like a blizzard during Christmas to up the ante. During the summer, the donation treasures supplement our rummage sale with items that we sell and use to support our youth camps."

"Like the basketball camp?" I asked.

"Yes, exactly."

I swallowed a hairball of guilt and made myself a note to make a donation. Maybe a scavenger hunt in my closet would give him means to buy a uniform for next year, or at least a pair of longer shorts. "Well, see, one of my readers accidentally discarded a framed portrait of her grandmother, and I think it may have ended up here." I looked around for another lightning bolt, because I was sure Rumfield had it hanging on some wall in her house. "Would you mind if I rummaged through you rummage items?"

"Oh is that all?" he asked. "Sure, no problem." He rounded his desk, naked knees and all, and invited me to follow him to the basement.

He hit the light switch and a hundred-and-fifty watt bare bulb elongated every shadow into creatures scrambling to climb the walls. A hoarder's paradise I didn't relish wading through, especially when I knew where the frame was hiding.

"The newest arrivals will be on the right, the older items on the left. I don't think you'll have to trouble yourself with the bags and cartons in the back. Those are mostly items that didn't sell last rummage sale."

I shuffled down a few steps, keeping my hand on the block wall for balance. Thankfully, it was five degrees cooler in the cellar than it was upstairs. Although, with all this junk occupying space, I wasn't sure how much air that left me to breathe. On my descent, I scanned the tops of piles, praying I'd see a gaudy gold frame.

"You need any help?" Pastor Lawrence asked.

"No, but I think I'll need a miracle."

"All right then." He laughed. "You've come to the right place."

As soon as he stepped away from the door, it swung shut, rattling the bulb in the ceiling and sending the shadows into jitters. Wonderful.

CHAPTER 16

I spent an hour treasure hunting in the basement of the church, shuffling and pulling boxes of books that were so heavy pall bearers would need to lug them out to the lawn on the day of the rummage sale. I prodded bags of clothes, searching for the four corners of Terri's missing portrait. I unearthed china place settings that I fell in love with, and promised myself to attend the rummage sale early in order to buy them. I found baby dolls and board games, and over-sized costume jewelry that would make my mother drool. I even stopped my digging to ponder over a carton of behead-ed Barbie and Ken dolls with their arms duct taped behind their backs. What exactly went on behind the closed doors in the two square mile town of Yardman?

My last unearthing was a one-eyed, slack-jawed mounted deer head. I hauled ass up the basement stairs and ran out of church like a Boston marathoner on a final sprint. I wasn't out of ideas just yet, and continued my sprint across the street to Abbott's pharmacy. They had perky African violet plants that I was sure Bobbie Rumfield would love to have.

If I couldn't get her to admit she had the portrait, I could at least give her a gift for her help and hope she would feel guilty enough to hand it over.

I stood outside Bobbie Rumfield's front door with my small peace offering in hand and rang the bell.

She wasn't the type of woman who gave second chances, but I at least owed her an apology. After all, I had sort of called her a thief, assaulted her plant, barged into her house, and had nearly stolen her antique-lace tatted doily.

Plus, an apology might grant me access for another stealthy look around her living room.

I rang the bell again and waited while absently stroking

the velvet leaves until I had snapped the green leaf clean off the stem. I tossed it into the bushes before I was caught red-handed brutalizing another plant. If Bobbie didn't answer her door soon, I'd kill it for sure.

"Mrs. Rumfield?" I called. "It's Kate. Kate Lambrose." I peered through the front window, but the gauzy curtains distorted any movement. "Bobbie?" I knocked on the glass, but the curtains never parted.

I walked the stretch of porch around the side of the house and spied through windows along the way. Nothing and no one moved inside.

A wheelchair ramp led down to the driveway and the porch narrowed to the right and wrapped around the house out of sight. Gravel extended the concrete driveway and followed the narrow porch.

Whatever type vehicle Bobbie drove, it was huge. The stones smashed deep into the dirt, leaving parallel rivets. Huh, a tank would fit her personality.

"Hello, Mrs. Rumfield," I called before rounding the back corner.

A small back porch with matching Adirondack chairs greeted me, but no Bobbie.

Her back door was wide open. Only the screen door barred my entrance. I called out again and listened for her answer, not really expecting one. Yardman didn't exactly have a high crime rate. Probably a lot of people left their doors unlocked. I just didn't go around trying them.

But I could now. I hugged the violet a little tighter.

It wasn't breaking and entering. I just wanted to leave the violet and take a quick look around. I didn't plan on touching, moving, breaking, or taking anything even if I found the portrait. I just needed to know without a doubt that Bobbie Rumfield didn't have it in her possession. And if she did, I'd tell Terri to go fetch it. Bobbie couldn't possibly deny a poor old lady her family heirloom. Besides, Bobbie had a ton of antiques and Terri was an antique dealer. A perfect match.

I opened the screen door, stepped up and over the threshold, and stepped right back out, letting the door slam.

Trespassing, it echoed in my mind, was a real crime that carried jail time. Was I ready for that? Would I be out for good behavior by the time Emma got home? Jail would severely hamper future dates with Michael Earl. Or would it?

Huh. Jack White would use every opportunity to get his story, and I had a chance to hone my sleuthing chops. What was I going to do, chicken out?

Oh hell no.

With one hand on the screen door handle, I looked over my shoulder. The well-kept garden was my only witness, except for the crows that *caw-cawed* from atop the power pole wires. I swallowed hard, pulled the handle, and stepped across the threshold into Bobbie Rumfield's kitchen.

My eyes flitted from sink, to the magnet-covered refrigerator, to kitchen table and back. Dishes cluttered the drying rack. The countertops were crowded with flour and sugar canisters. A red and white checkered tablecloth decked the kitchen table. A fresh baked pie perched on a cooling rack, center stage. I sniffed. Apple—and my stomach gurgled. I set the violet on the table and hitched my tote strap over my head, crossing my heart. The last thing I needed to do was swipe trinkets off tables with a swing of my tote.

"Bobbie, you here?" I asked in a breath above a whisper.

I crept into the dining room from the kitchen and into the living room. If she was napping somewhere, I didn't want my bellow to scare her into a coronary. I did a cursory glance about, looking behind the couch and opening a coat closet. Trinkets and knick-knacks crowded every corner, but no framed grandmother portrait.

I stepped carefully up the stairs, wincing at every creak, certain but not certain that I was alone. On the second floor, four open doorways lined the hallway. Two on each side.

I scanned the bathroom walls first and peeked in the linen closet. Next, I ran from bedroom to bedroom. The first two didn't even have beds, just a mattress on the floor and the closets were empty. No portrait to be found. In the last bedroom, I bent on hands and knees and lifted the bed skirt. My nose met with a line of shoes as long as the bed frame. Pulling a pair out of the way, I peered deeper into the darkness. Still no portrait.

I dusted my hands on my knees and knocked dust off my pants. The smacking sound echoed from downstairs at the same time. My heart leapt to my throat when the sound continued after I stopped. For several long seconds, I couldn't breathe or move. The doorbell rang at the same time some-one banged again on the front door. I hit the floor hard and tried to wedge myself under the bed. My tote bunched up under my stomach, preventing my backside from clearing the bed frame.

With my ear pressed against the wood floor, I heard a muted ringing. And a vibration like butterflies swarming in my gut that tickled my stomach. Someone was calling my cell phone.

By the time I squeezed free from under the bed, the door banging and phone ringing had stopped.

I raced downstairs into the kitchen and grabbed the violet off the table.

"Hey. What are you doing in there?" A silhouette standing outside the screen door spoke to me and snickered.

The plant slipped from my fingers, spraying potting soil across my white sneakers.

Fear and adrenaline collided just under my kneecaps, and I folded to the linoleum with the African violet.

"Whoa." Luanne laughed from outside, still in silhouette form.

"I think I just wet myself," I said.

Luanne let herself in. "Jeez, Kate, you're whiter than Elmer's glue."

"Am I breathing?" I huffed. "Check my pulse." I held out my arm and Luanne pulled me off the floor.

She pointed to my face. "Jesus. What happened to your face, Kate?"

"What are you talking about? Oh..." She hadn't seen me since I nearly shot the cat out from under my Jeep. "It's not as bad as it looks."

"That's some pretty black and blue. When you told me about the cat under the car, I expected a quarter-sized bruise, not the Pacific Ocean. Does it still hurt?"

"No, but it was Ondrea's fault," I said.

"How do you figure that? Was she there too?"

"No, no, no, it's not like that." I explained how Matt end-ed up at my house and how I armed myself with his shotgun and rammed my head into the underbelly of my Jeep.

"I see why you think it is Ondrea's fault." She rolled her eyes.

"Are you saying it isn't?"

"Well, in the Kate Lambrose school of thinking, I suppose so, as convoluted as it is."

"One would not have happened without the other. Einstein's Law of Cause and Effect."

"True. But it's Newton's Law. Don't get me wrong, she's not on my fave list either. I'm just curious why you put so much energy into tying everything back to her."

"I don't." Did I?

Luanne's eyebrow arched.

I didn't spend a lot of energy reasoning it was Ondrea's fault. It was. Yet, I did spend much of my day trying to outwit Ondrea. For heaven's sake, I was fifteen years older than her. I had life experience she didn't have. Why did I care?

"You do," Luanne said.

"No. What are you doing here anyway?" I asked.

"I knocked. Didn't you hear me?"

"That was you?"

She nodded. "When you didn't answer, I called your cell."

"Why?" I asked.

"'Cause I thought you needed help. What are you doing in here anyway?"

"Wait." I held up my hand. My fingers shook like I had overdosed on one too many Hot Joe's lattes. "How did you know I was even here?"

Luanne squeezed my shaking fingers. "I followed you."

I shook my head, spreading my arms until my entire upper body did a shrug all at once. "Why?"

She rolled her eyes, and blew out a breath. "Well, I was stopping by to ask you to dinner when I saw you at Abbott's, but you blew right past me, so I figured I'd just follow you. And let me tell you, for someone who is constantly harping about driving the speed limit, you sure as heck raced through town. And then I lost you."

I stared at her, waiting for the rest of the story.

"Anyway, I spotted your Jeep and pulled up just when you made your way around back. I thought I'd just wait for you to come out, but then you didn't. So I knocked, and then I called. When no one answered the door and you didn't answer your cell, I got worried."

"But why?" I asked. For some reason, her concern bothered me. I appreciated her friendship, and I loved her for being my best friend and all that jazz. But this motherly concern was a bit more than I liked.

She squinted at me and jabbed her long forefinger in my shoulder. "Because, Kate. I know stupidly fearless when I see it."

My jaw muscles slacked and I rolled my eyes. She was right about that, and this wasn't the time or place to discuss friendship boundaries. I let it go.

"I'm looking for Terri's portrait. Now help me clean this up."

"You broke into this house? Whose house is it anyway?"

I explained about Bobbie Rumfield's alleged part in the alleged taking of Terri's heirloom. "But I didn't break in. The door was open," I said. "Now help me clean this up."

"Oh, well, as long as you're not a destructive criminal, and thank God I set you up with a cop. You'll have to sleep with him to secure a get out of jail free pass." Luanne smiled.

"Wait." I handed her the broom like I was handing out marching orders. "How do you figure you set me up with Michael? Besides that, you're in here with me now too. So, who's your get out of jail free pass, huh? Certainly not Michael Earl. I knew him before I knew you."

"Seriously?" Luanne said. "Did you just say that?"

I frowned at her. "I did. And why are you irritating me?"

"I didn't know I was." Luanne swept the plant debris into a neat pile without another word.

I held the dustpan while she gently pushed every last speck of dirt onto the pan.

Then we debated over putting the dirt into the kitchen trash. We argued if a person inspected their current trash before adding more.

"What difference does it make? Is she going to call the cops and tell them someone's filling up her trashcan?"

She had a point, but I was still too irritated with her to give in.

"What is your problem?" I stood, holding the dustpan over the trashcan.

"I, uhm, I don't have one, but I'm guessing you do."

I did, but hell if I understood what and why.

"I'm sorry." I said, "I guess I..."

I didn't get to finish what I was saying. Gravel crunched alongside the house. I dropped the dustpan, dirt and all, in the trash. We bounced off each other like billiard balls looking for an open pocket. A car door slammed and the two of us squeezed through the cellar door at the same time. The door clicked closed and we crouched low on the dark stairway.

"What if she comes in here?" Luanne whispered against the back of my neck. Her breath was hot and heavy. I turned to answer her and we bumped noses. I slapped my hand over her mouth to stop her laugh from escaping.

"Scoot down to the bottom."

"I can't see where I'm going," she said.

"Butt-walk it," I said.

By the time we were at the bottom of the stairs, my eyes had adjusted to the dim light. Ceiling-high windows let in just enough light to see the dust motes as they floated free from the shadows. The corners of the room were darker, but I could make out shapes, shelves with mason jars, a washer and dryer, an old stainless steel sink, and an old coal-burning furnace.

Luanne stood on a wood crate and tugged at the window. "It's painted shut. Do you see a hammer anywhere?" She dance-stepped her way to another crate and pulled at the next window.

I found a box labeled "trains," a basket full of hats, a trashcan stuffed with Ken dolls, and a shelf lined with at least ten microwave ovens. But no hammer. "Nope."

"Seriously? Who doesn't have a hammer?" She hopped off her two-foot perch. "How the hell are we gonna get out of here?"

"Well, it's not like we can break the glass and slip away unseen," I said.

"Shhh!"

The ceiling above us creaked. We both looked up and followed the footsteps. I walked over to the old coal eater, bent my head to the fire plate, opened the grate, and listened. Bobbie's humming trilled through the vents. I grabbed Luanne by the arm and pulled her to the furthest place in the room away from it.

"If we can hear her through the vents, then she can hear us," I whispered.

Luanne nodded at me, wide-eyed.

"She'll have to leave sometime," I said.

"Right. Or go to bed. Eventually, right?" Luanne agreed and hunkered down on a three-legged stool. "And we'll go out the way we came in."

"Yup." I took out my cell and used the display as a flashlight, highlighting the corners of the room and boxes of junk.

"What are you doing now?"

"I figured I'd look for the portrait while we're stuck down here."

"I have to pee," Luanne said.

"There's probably a bucket somewhere."

"It's one thing being caught red-handed." Luanne sniffed. "But I won't be caught with my pants down too."

"Suit yourself."

After a few moments, Luanne called me again, "Kate?"

I turned back toward her, shining my weak light on her. "Yeah?"

"What is it with you and me and basements?"

"Huh." I hadn't noticed the parallel until she pointed it out. I looked at the furnace one more time, just to be certain that was as far as the similarity went. "No worries," I said, pointing to the coal eater. "No fire."

"No dumbwaiter either."

"True—" The basement door opened. Luanne covered her gasp with her hand, and I dodged for the nearest shadow, stuffing my phone under my shirt. From my vantage point, I could see Bobbie from feet to knees. She stood on the top step and dropkicked a duffle bag down the stairs then slammed the door shut again.

I scrambled over to Luanne, who scurried under the stairs. We clung together like grapes. "Oh my God, oh my God," she said. "It's a body. It's a body."

I grabbed her hand and squeezed. "No. It's not a body," I said. "You really need to stop taking Izzy's stories so seriously."

Peering through the open slats of the steps, I studied the large duffle bag. I recognized the black logo with white lettering. Yin-yang laundry. "Uh oh."

"What?" Luanne's nails dug into my hand.

"I think she's going to do a load of wash."

The door ticked open and Bobbie clomped down the

steps. We ducked low. In the barest of whispers, Luanne said. "Great. I don't have to pee anymore."

After Bobbie whistled her way through loading the washer and stomping back up the stairs, Luanne and I sighed heavily. At least she left the light on.

"Kate, I don't think she's going to leave anytime soon," Luanne whispered.

"I think you're right. We need a diversion so we can get out of here."

"If we just knew where in the house she was right now, we could make a run for it."

"Yeah, and run right into her."

We both looked up at the painted shut windows again and shook our heads.

"I got an idea." I pulled my cell from my pocket.

The main phone line in the *City Scope* office rang at least ten times before Ondrea answered.

"Ondrea," I whispered. "It's Kate. Is Joyce there?"

"Why are you whispering?" she asked.

"Never mind that. Is Joyce there?" I asked again.

"No."

"Dan?" I asked.

"No."

I looked at Luanne and strangled my phone. Ondrea was the last person I trusted to do anything for me without making matters worse.

"Kate? Are you all right?" Ondrea asked.

I sighed. She was our only option at this point. "No." I begged her to listen carefully. After I explained the situation and after she finished laughing, I asked her to come keep Bobbie Rumfield busy at the front door.

"And, Ondrea, ring the doorbell a couple of times, please."

"Sure thing, Kate. I'll send help." She laughed and hung up.

CHAPTER 17

Thirty minutes after Ondrea hung up promising to send help, she still hadn't shown up. Luanne and I set up camp in the far corner under the stairs, in the shadows. The hum from the washer and dryer soothed our nerves and we huddled over an abandoned Scrabble board. As the moments ticked away, our words became gloomier. Dung became dungeon, ark became dark, and earth became dearth.

"Stop that!" I knocked Luanne's hand aside when she added a D in front of my Anger. "You aren't helping. Where's that positive side?"

"I left it out in my car. Tell me again why we are here? You saw the portrait here?" She looked around the basement.

"No, not *here* here." I pointed to the floor. "This is my first visit to her basement."

"Shh." Luanne pointed to the creaking ceiling. Rumfield was on the move again. We held our breath.

I was just about to dial the office number again when we heard a car door shut. We both crossed our fingers that it was Ondrea and not the police. I feared she was sending help via Yardman's finest. It would be just like her to do that.

We tiptoed out from under the stairs, ready to make a dash up and out the back door. I didn't know who would be on the other side of the doorbell.

It rang. Footfalls scuffed along the hallway above us. The doorbell rang again. That was our cue, and we both charged the first step at the same time, wedging ourselves between the railings. I pushed my way through and up and out the door. Luanne flew up behind me and we both stopped.

The back inside door was now shut and the security chain was draped in place. We looked at each other for a split second, both mouthing, "what do we do now?"

Bobbie Rumfield was saying, "No. No, thank you. I said no. No thank you." And the front door slammed shut.

Luanne and I moved together like choreographed swimmers. I slid the chain off. She turned the doorknob. I squeezed out first and she followed, closing the door gently behind her. We jumped from the porch and rustled through the hedge into the neighbor's backyard. I didn't want Bobbie to see us walking down her driveway and across the street to our cars. We ran across the neighbor's backyard, down their driveway, and across the street, laughing—at least until we spotted Ondrea.

"I can't wait to hear this one, Kate," she said with her arms crossed as if she were the scolding parent.

"You're not hearing it tonight," I said.

"I gotta pee," Luanne said. "Kate, I'll stop and get food." She jumped in her car and sped off.

"Thanks for the rescue, Ondrea." I waved. "Talk to you tomorrow."

Now I owed her one, and I hated that. And worse than that, I was no closer to finding the portrait.

***

I stared at my kitchen wall phone, expecting it to ring any minute. Ondrea would have called Matthew by now, and he'd be calling to spit orders and preach the law of trespassing. However, it was my cell that rang instead.

"Hola, buenos noches," Luanne said.

"Spain?" I asked.

"Mexico." She laughed.

"How'd we get to Mexico?" Somewhere over the last few days, she traded continents and I had missed it.

"I've got take out for two. Nacho chips, tacos, carne asada burritos, and Spanish rice. Open your front door and bring a broom. There's something dead on your welcome mat. Hasta." She hung up.

"What—" I grabbed the broom, raced to the front door, and flung it open.

"What's dead on my door step?"

"Mmmm, something that once had feathers, I think."

Luanne stepped closer, and I turned the porch light on to get a better look at the dead animal in the growing dusk.

"Ohhhh, it's a pigeon," Luanne said. "Or what's left of a pigeon." She tiptoed over the battered bird, her take-out bag held high. "Someone tagging you as a stool pigeon?"

"Damn cat," I said, but stool pigeon rolled around in my mind. With one big swish, I swept the bird out into the yard and shivered.

"Have you heard from Emma? Get a post card or any-thing?" Luanne asked.

I shrugged, desperate to downplay how much I missed her. "She called. George took her on a cruise."

"Wow. Lucky girl." Luanne munched down on a loaded tortilla chip, pinching a thread of cheese that threatened to stick to her chin. "And you're okay with that?"

I sat down and passed her a full glass of wine. "Do I have a choice?"

Luanne shook her head.

Determined to put our self-inflicted Rumfield imprison-ment behind us, I led our conversation to greener pastures. "So, what did you find out about the land deed? What part of Macy's rests on your plot?" I asked.

"I looked up the real estate records and land parcel num-bers, and the nearest I can figure with the help of Google maps, I own the dirt under the fine jewelry department."

"Get out of here!" I laughed. "So it's kind of like owning a jewelry store without the merchandise or the liability."

"Exactly. That plot of land is my jewel in Manhattan and can't be stolen."

We toasted her millions with the opening of a new bottle of Shiraz wine. "So are you going to quit your job?"

"Hell no," Luanne said. "I just won't have to work as hard. Hey, I was thinking, maybe you could help me figure out what that rabbit's foot and turtle shell meant to my grandmother."

"Are you kidding me? How am I supposed to do that?"

"You're the finder of lost things. The mighty Insight woman."

I scooped up the last nacho. "Who keeps those things anyway? Okay, a rabbit's foot I can see. But a turtle shell...ewww. That's just crazy. That's as sick as the one-eyed buck in the church basement. I'm telling you, someone in Yardman is a bad taxidermist."

Luanne spit out her wine. "Wait. What's in the basement of what church?"

I explained the gruesome find, omitting the details of my hasty retreat.

"And you were there why?"

"Looking for Terri Wolf's grandmother's portrait. Rumfield dropped off a donation for the church rummage sale."

"Rumfield rummage and Terri the dramatist?" Luanne laughed.

"Not so much drama now. I think she is avoiding me, but I don't know why. Last week, she was hounding me about finding it, and this week, she has hardly enough time to take my phone call. It seems the more questions I ask, the more aloof she gets."

"Why didn't you tell me all this when we were locked in that woman's basement? I thought she wanted the portrait back. Isn't that why you were at that woman's house to begin with?"

"It is, and I thought Terri wanted it back too."

Luanne's eyebrow arched.

I shrugged and finished the last bit of my burrito.

"So, I have to ask about your meltdown in the kitchen at Rumfull's house," Luanne said.

"It's Rumfield."

Luanne shrugged. "Why were you so pissed off at me?" Her brow frowned in that worrisome way.

"Oh boy." I slapped my hand to my forehead. In the silence of the basement, I had figured that out, but was hoping to avoid explaining it.

"That bad?" she asked.

"No. Not bad, just hard to explain. And I don't want to say something I don't mean, you know?"

"That sounds bad."

"And it doesn't make a whole lot of sense. Because if I had asked you to come with me, you would have," I said.

"To Rumfield's?"

"Yes."

"Of course, but...?"

I sighed. I was so much better at writing what I meant

than verbalizing it. With no backspace button to wipe out the words I spoke aloud, I feared changing the course of our friendship.

"You know how it is with George and my brother Matthew, my mother, even Jonathan, and of course Ondrea and probably a few other people in my life, I'm always on the defensive side of what I say, do, or want. And it's always their way. I'm always feeling like I have to validate myself to them."

Luanne stared at me.

"And they're always intruding into my life with unasked for opinions, suggestions, and corrections. As if I need their guidance. I never quite feel like a grown woman with my own family when I'm around them." I paused, took a sip of my wine, and bit the tip off a nacho chip.

"And I made you feel like I was intruding?"

"No. Well, yes. That's how it felt when you—"

"Showed up uninvited."

"See, I knew I couldn't explain this correctly because it's not how I feel about you. It's how I felt at that one moment."

"No, I get it, and I'm sorry. The next time I show up un-invited—and I will..." She laughed. "I'll leave my suggestions and opinions in the car. Just don't ever, ever, ever leave me out of your life plans again. You're all I got."

Oh dammit. "Did you just flip this all around to make me feel bad or better?" I hung my head.

Luanne laughed. "A little of both. I hope." She wadded up the empty wrappers and tossed them into the trash.

"A whole lot of both," I said.

In silence, we trashed the rest of our leftovers and I wiped down the table.

"I have an idea." She dug into her purse. "Let's tell our fortunes." She slapped a deck of Tarot cards on the table.

"Get out of here." I flung the dishcloth into the sink. "You are not a fortune teller. The seal isn't even cracked on this deck."

"So? It comes with an instruction book."

I rolled my eyes.

"Besides, Izzy said I have healer's hands." Luanne examined her hands.

I laughed out loud and snorted. Ever since she met Isaac, the EMT, a lot of her conversations were Izzy said, Izzy thinks this and that. Come to think of it, I was surprised she hadn't mentioned Izzy up until now.

"So what? You think you have inherited divine powers?"

"Oh come on. We just need some candles," she said.

"I don't like open flames." I reminded her.

"It'll be fun." She searched the cabinets and drawers for candles. "And you won't need to worry about anything. I brought protection," Luanne said.

"What? A fire extinguisher?"

That moody brow of hers rose up to a new regal height. "Don't be silly." She tugged a silver necklace out from beneath her shirt, stretched the chain over her head and dangled the medallion in front of my face.

I stared at the outline of a palm, fingers pointing downward. In the center, surrounded by a filigree of silver in the shape of an eye, a single diamond winked back at me.

"Are you planning on slapping the spirits back or telling me to talk to the hand?"

"Neither," she said. "Izzy gave it to me. It's a Hamsa. It will protect me against the devil's eye."

CHAPTER 18

I sat at my desk the next morning, seesawing my pencil between my fingers and staring at Sadie Arnold's newest email. My concentration stretched in five other directions. We were all present and accounted for at our desks, even Simon Rutter who worked out of the front seat of his car most days. Ondrea was pecking very loudly on her keyboard, and Dan, Joyce, and Simon were all blabbering on the phone. Their voices increased in volume, fighting against each other to be heard.

I had already read Sadie's email four times, and each time the words floating through the room got caught up in her email. It wasn't making any sense. She claimed she knew exactly where the portrait was hanging, and she also had a lead on the stars and stripes missing from the flag outside the Governor's mansion.

I hadn't heard any other commotion about the flag except from Sadie. To her, it was a matter of national security. "Stealing from the government and all."

"Does anyone know anything about stars and stripes missing from the flag at the Governor's mansion?" I hollered out to the room.

Ondrea's pecking stopped. Joyce giggled. Dan, Simon, and Ondrea said no.

"But that flag costs a fortune," Ondrea added.

Fortune?

She meant dollars, but my mind thought Tarot cards.

After Luanne left last night with her Tarots, I searched the world-wide-web for a master fortuneteller. Or at least someone who hadn't just peeled the cellophane off a fresh deck.

Thousands of websites appeared and all wanted a credit card before allowing me to browse. Heck, all I wanted was a crisp picture of each card in some other setting than blazing candle light. After all, Luanne had said the cards were open to my own interpretation, and my reading lacked clarity. Psychic Revelation was the best site I found, and not only did it display the Tower card, but it detailed its meaning in seven different categories including love and work.

I had scrutinized the Tower card with bodies flung from windows set afire. Escaping a burning building had a way of putting life in perspective. I could attest to that. My finger traced the jagged lightning strike across the top of the tower. Change wasn't necessarily a bad sign, and I was good with that. I was even okay with the Five of Wands, men fighting and Death riding noble on a white horse—competition. My life was one constant competition, at least in love and work. And then Luanne turned over the High Priestess card and oo'ed.

"This is a good card for you, Kate! The High Priestess represents your inner self."

I studied the card and failed to see the connection. The woman on the card wore a long, flowing blue robe and a crown shaped like Viking horns. I was certain my inner self would rather wear silk or nothing at all. And even though Luanne explained the Viking horn was the crown of Isis, I doubted I would ever trade my super hero cape for a diamond studded tiara, let alone bullish horns.

Luanne pointed out that the moon rested at the feet of the High Priestess, which was the only good thing I saw. I liked the idea of someone giving me the moon. And the crescent moon represented intuition.

"Aha! I don't know how many times I need to tell you this, Kate. You need to trust your hunches. Even the Tarot is telling you the same thing. There is someone insisting things are true when they aren't and you know it."

Without a doubt, my hunches and intuition worked over time. They often screamed at me, but sometimes, they needed to repeat themselves because the riddles in my life were queerer than fiction. Like George. I knew from the first *I do*, that he was different, but ignored the truth for 15 years. I vowed never to be that dense again.

What was the Tarot telling me now? Someone had followed me even though Matt said it wasn't so? Was my curse-flinging mystery caller really Albert Wolf? Or was it true what Sadie had said. Was it possible Terri hadn't accidentally donated the portrait at all, and it was some elaborate ruse so

Albert would never get his hands on it?

I read Sadie's email one more time and cautiously replied. Sadie was a wannabe private eye who read too many supermarket tabloids. Still, she was my biggest fan.

"Dear Sadie," I wrote to her. "I'm on a trip right now, but as soon as I return, I'll give you a call. Thanks, Kate."

I hated lying to her, but I was about to call Terri to have her meet me at the library.

The librarian had emailed me saying that a framed portrait had been donated to the library. They intended to use the frame to display their 1920 map of Yardman. It was the perfect odd size they needed. But she'd return it if it was the lost treasure.

No sooner had I hit send when my inbox pinged with new mail. From Ondrea and to all of us, which wasn't anything new. She was always sending us trivial tidbits.

The subject line read, "Rumfield's backdoor." It sounded like a song title.

But the body of the email read, "You're welcome, Kate, for the rescue from the spider-infested basement. I would have hated to see you serve time for B&E."

I shot straight out of my chair. There she was, kitty corner to me through the cactus podium, grinning from ear to ear. I didn't care who knew about Rumfield's basement. After all, I had called that day for Joyce to rescue us and then Dan, but we got stuck with Ondrea. And of course, she had donned her superman cape. When the story didn't make front page news, she had to at least shine in her small *City Scope* world. I should have known.

I shook my head at her. "You are such a diva," I said. If I had something to throw at her, I would have. Everything was her business, but nothing about her was anyone's business. It didn't seem like a fair trade.

She shrugged, grinned, and batted her lashes.

Dan rolled around into my square. Simon squeaked back against the window and peered at me. Most days he kept his nose pointed to his laptop and didn't interact or comment about any of our conversations.

I plopped back into my chair, folded my arms, and waited for Joyce.

"Well," Dan said.

I rolled my eyes. "Might as well wait for Joyce. No sense in telling the story twice."

"So the black eye?" Simon said.

I frowned at him, as I did most of the time. He was one of those people that started talking out loud in the middle or the end of his unheard thought.

"So when did this happen?" Dan asked.

"Yesterday." I sighed.

"What happened?" Joyce sidled up next to Simon.

"Ondrea," I called. "Are you joining us?"

She might as well tell her side of the story first. It wasn't very interesting anyway. Come to think of it, none of her stories were very exciting. Neither were Dan's sports reports and around town fillers. Joyce wrote interesting obituaries, and Simon's advertisements had spiced up a bit.

Huh, no wonder they were all attentive to my column and up in my space. Nothing they reported was mysterious with dangling modifiers. I smiled at my epiphany.

Ondrea, in her own peculiar way, was interested in what was going on with my stories, but her competitive edge wouldn't allow her to care without malice. She just wanted to be included instead of excluded. I could do that.

"So, Rumfield," I said. "Bobbie with an IE, short for Roberta, was my first person of interest. She picked up the portrait from Terri's house."

I looked from Joyce to Simon to Dan and Ondrea. All eyes glared at me, waiting for the rest of the story.

"How did you get cornered in her basement?" Ondrea asked.

I sighed and ticked off the events of my day, starting at the church and ending with the mishaps of my second visit to Bobbie Rumfield's.

"And of course you weren't invited. You just helped yourself." Ondrea smirked.

"She had the portrait!" Simon pointed at Ondrea.

I nodded.

"Wait, back up." Joyce waved her hands in the air, wiping the facts off the imaginary white board. "How did Ondrea rescue you?"

"I was her only option." Ondrea squared her shoulders and bragged how she answered the phone when I called for help.

"I would have rescued you, Kate," Simon said.

I smiled. "Thanks, Simon. I'll remember that for next time."

"And I'm sure there will be a next time." Ondrea snickered.

We all sighed. Her snide remarks were tiring, and I think we all felt that.

I ignored her tsks and tats as I told them about how Luanne had followed me, the smashed African violet, playing Scrabble under the stairs, and Rumfield doing laundry. We laughed except for Ondrea.

"And that's where I came in," Ondrea said.

The room sighed again.

"Really, Ondrea, if ever I heard a reason for an award—that's it," Simon said and rolled back to his square.

"That sounded sarcastic," Ondrea said.

"Yup. Great story, Kate," he added.

Huh, maybe Ondrea was the reason Simon worked out of his car.

"Will you be going back to Rumfield's again?" Joyce asked.

"Why? Do you want to go?" Ondrea asked.

"I'll go with you, Kate," Dan jumped in.

"Not today," I said. "I have a lead to follow up on at the library."

"Another dead end, no doubt," Ondrea said.

Simon stood from his desk with his laptop under his arm. He shook his head, flipped his backpack over his shoulder, and walked out.

"Ondrea, give it a rest, please," Joyce said.

That was good advice, but I doubted she would heed the message.

"The only dead end I anticipate in my future, Ondrea, is your relationship with my brother."

Whether she heard me or not, I didn't know, and she didn't reply.

I called Terri and told her to meet me at the library. On my way out, Joyce handed me an envelope to deliver to the librarian.

"Secrets?" I asked.

"Genealogy," she answered.

CHAPTER 19

Terri beat me to the library. I spotted her standing in front of the portrait when I walked in, as still as a statue. The librarian was busy checking out books for a woman huddled by four small children. I laid the envelope on the desk. "From Joyce Hendrix," I said. She winked at me.

"Hi, Terri. Is it?" I asked her.

She shook her head. "No." She sighed.

"Are you sure?"

"Yes. It's similar, but not it." She sat down at the table.

I sat across from her, preparing to tell her that I believed it was a lost cause at this point.

"What am I going to do now, Kate? You promised to help find it."

"I don't know, Terri. If someone has it, they obviously have no guilt about keeping it. The best I can do is run the story one more time and plead for them to give it up. Make that person feel guilty for keeping it."

"A little guilt can't hurt," she said. "What about the driver that picked it up? Did you talk to them?"

I nodded.

"They didn't know anything?"

"Not really," I said.

"What do we do now, Kate?"

Across the quiet library, a newspaper snapped and rustled. I turned and looked down the history aisle toward the sound and could only see a white-haired head over the edge of a newspaper.

"Hold that thought, Terri," I said.

I stood and walked past the history row and through the self-help. If white-top was Scowl, I was going to be damn mad about it. But before I made a complete fool of myself, I stopped and tried to peer around and through the newspaper he had held up in front of him.

"Oh, the hell with it," I said aloud, and walked right up to who I expected to see. Mr. Scowl.

His gaze fixed on the printed page in his hands. His black-rimmed glasses sloped down his nose and his mouth was drawn in a grumpy frown as though he greatly disapproved of today's news. But that edition of *City Scope* wasn't even this week's. It was the same edition I had carried with me on the plane.

"Are you following me?" I slammed my fists into my hips. "You know, I do have friends on the police force here in town, and they would be more than happy to arrest you for stalking me. This is the third time you have been in my space in the same location and I want to know why."

He slowly eased the paper into his lap. Smart that he hadn't made it obvious that he was trying to hide from me.

I stood my ground even though his slow, deliberate movement intimidated me. After all, I was in a public library. What could he do to me here? Hush me to death?

He looked up at me over his black-rimmed glasses. The same damn black-rimmed glasses that he dropped on the seat next to me on the plane. The same glasses he perched on his forehead while he stared at me in the airport.

"I'm sorry," he said. "Do I know you?"

I rolled my eyes. "Why are you following me?" I said again.

He cackled. "Do I look like I'm following you, or anyone for that matter? I'm sitting here reading the newspaper, minding my own business, which is more than I can say for you."

"Oh please...don't even pretend you don't know me. You tried to steal my reader requests off my lap on the plane just days ago. And last week, you were at Hot Joe's having coffee or tea or whatever. And now you're here...here while I'm meeting—" I stopped, suddenly aware that I was babbling.

He folded the newspaper, tucked it under his arm, and slowly stood. I forced myself not to step back as he stepped into my bubble zone. Stand and confront. My heartbeat drummed in my ears.

"Oh. Oh! Now I know who you are." He pointed at me. "You're that newspaper columnist who thinks she writes funny stuff, right?"

"Yes, Kate Lambrose, and who are you? And why are you here?"

"Jeez, girl. What's your problem? I got a right to be here just like you. What reason do I have to follow you?"

He spaced his words with a pregnant pause that left my insides quaking. And I really didn't know of any reason he would follow me, except that I felt like a rabbit caught in a wolf's gaze.

"You seem a bit too self-important in your own mind." He took the paper out from under his arm and slapped it against his thigh.

I flinched. I didn't mean to, but I couldn't help it.

"Have a nice day, Ms. Lambrose."

He turned and walked past me. I squeezed my hands into fists. He was right, but I also knew what I knew. He was following me.

"Wait," I said, "Do you live in Yardman?"

"Do you want to see my library card?"

"Yes." I held out my hand, expecting him to drop it in my palm.

"Fat chance."

"Okay fine, at least tell me why you were in Phoenix when I was."

He stared at me as if he were trying to decide whether to tell me the truth or lie about it. "You first," he said.

I had nothing to hide, but I wasn't about to mention Luanne's inheritance. "I went there with a friend to comfort her. Her grandmother had died." Not a total lie, just old news.

"My daughter lives there. She had a baby girl." He looked down at the floor as if he had a sad story to convey. But I wasn't about to let him off the hook that easily.

"What is your name?"

"My friends call me Sly, but you can call me Mr. Fisher." He grinned and tilted his head.

Several responses ping-ponged around in my mind, but I kept them from bouncing out between my lips.

"Is that a nickname for Sylvester? Or your persona?" At least now I had his name. As fictitious as it probably was, I could still search records.

I turned and walked away. When I was back in Terri's

line of sight, I waved a come-along to her and stopped at the front desk to thank the librarian. When I looked back for Terri, Fisher had her cornered at Arts and Leisure. Her back was to me, and she kept stepping backwards. Fisher had his head down. His eyes glared at her over the rims of his glasses, and he spoke to her, but I wasn't a lip reader.

I took off toward them in a half sprint. "Hey!" I skidded to a stop, wedging myself between them. "Everything okay here?" I looked over my shoulder at Terri. She nodded and looked back at Fisher.

"You really are in every one's business, aren't you, Ms. Lambrose?" he said.

"Actually, I think it is you who has your nose where it doesn't belong, and I will find out why." I hooked my arm under Terri's and led her out of the library to her car.

"What was he saying to you, Terri?" I asked once she was settled in behind the wheel.

"Nothing of importance, Kate." Her face flushed and she looked back toward the library entrance.

"Come on, Terri. I saw how you were back-stepping away from him, and he was saying something. If that man was pestering you, you need to tell me. He's a bit odd and that bothers me."

Terri looked down at her lap and fiddled with her car keys. "He was charming to me, and I didn't think he was odd, uh, he just surprised me. It's been years since anyone has asked me on a date."

"A date?"

"Well...he asked me to lunch. Wouldn't that be considered a date?" She blushed.

I slapped my palm to my forehead. Terri was my mother's age and Terri was still married to Albert. And for some reason, I hadn't considered that her generation would date. Was my mother dating? Oh. I shook my head to rid the visuals from my mind.

"What did you say to him?"

"Nothing. I didn't have a chance." She looked up at me. She didn't have to say another word. I was in every one's business.

I sighed. Had I just ruined the next best romance since Romeo and Juliet, Matthew and Ondrea, and George and

Ethan? "What would you have said? And you're married."

"At the moment, yes, but I'm not dead yet, Kate."

I didn't know whether to apologize or laugh. "Don't you think it's a bit odd for a stranger to walk up to another stranger and just blurt out an invitation to lunch? Did he at least introduce himself?"

"How else do you meet people?" Terri frowned at me. "And yes, he did introduce himself. I don't understand, Kate. Do you know him or something about him? And wouldn't the library be a better place than a bar to meet?"

Oh no! My mother was dating. She went to the library every weekend and she was always thrilled to tell me. She was more than thrilled to preach to me about getting out of my hole and enjoying life. Damn, somewhere between thirty and forty, I became the old fuddy-duddy looking for everyone's ulterior motive. Is that what I had done with Mr. Fisher? Was it me and not him? Was he just in the library generation, meeting strangers, collecting new friends, straight up?

"Yes," I said to Terri. "I'm sorry I interrupted you and him." I nodded toward the library. Fisher had just exited. "I...I honestly don't know anything about him, Terri. I guess I just have trust issues." Issues I thought I had worked through, but I didn't say that.

"I'm not so sure any man can be trusted, Kate, but in the meantime, we can let them spend their money on us. And he looked expensive."

I had to agree with her there. He was well dressed and had just climbed behind the wheel of a silver Mercedes. And he was watching me watch him.

"I'm sorry," I said again to Terri. "I've got to run." I sprinted across the lot to my Jeep, leaving Romeo and Juliet alone without my daggers.

CHAPTER 20

I marched straight to my desk without a word to anyone. My mission was to find out who Sly Fisher was and why he kept turning up everywhere I went. He may have wanted to date Terri, but he was hounding me. Instead of being reactive, I would become proactive.

So many Fishers came to life on my computer screen, but only one named Sylvester. And he didn't live in Yardman like he claimed. He lived in the neighboring city, according to the newspaper article I found under the City Building department records. Close enough. After all, I wouldn't admit where I lived if Kate Lambrose accosted me about my whereabouts. The article talked about how Fisher ended up in a debate with the city because he wanted to build a new home on a plot of land he had inherited. It stated that he had survived his family's house fire and years later, he wished to rebuild it. Except, the required plot size for a new build had changed over the years. Nevertheless, he won the debate by paying for it. I wasn't exactly sure what that meant and scrolled down to read more details just as Eugene called my name.

"What's up?" I stood in the doorway to his office.

"Beck called. She wants to see you," he said.

"For what?"

It had been close to a month since I had any conversation with Beck. She took to her new office above us like a bear in hibernation. All her directives were delivered via Eugene, and even he huffed and puffed over it.

"I don't know. She didn't say, and I didn't ask." He shrugged and went back to work redlining copy.

I hovered in the doorway. The old-style clock hanging on Eugene's wall ticked louder than usual. Beck's summons upstairs brought Luanne's fortune telling fresh to mind. Spidery ghostlike fingers tickled the back of my neck just like they had last night when I pulled the Tower card from the Tarot deck. Was Beck's sanctuary my tower of doom?

Luanne and I had both closely inspected the Tarot card. A castle tower set aflame. Two bodies hurled toward the ground with clouds of gray smoke billowing in the background.

"Holy cow," Luanne said. "What the hell was your question?"

I didn't have just one. When Luanne told me to ask a specific question to the Tarot, several fought for first place. Would I find Terri's frame? Would I learn the name of Mys Caller? Would Matt and Ondrea's relationship work out? Would Emma go to college? Was I being followed or paranoid? Would I ever stay lucky in love? My brain traveled faster than the speed of light.

That was the trouble, Luanne said. My erratic thoughts had tuned into neurotic vibes and caused me to hand pick chaos. In the light of day, I doubted all her mumbo-jumbo. I did at least until now.

"Kate?" Eugene said.

"Huh. What?"

"Now would be a good time." He pointed a hitchhiker thumb to the ceiling.

"Right." I trudged down the hall to the stairwell. The Tarot booklet definition rang in my ears. Sudden change. Disruption. Conflict. Disturbance of well-worn routines. Be prepared, Luanne had cautioned, the situation could change rapidly. God, I hoped the next thing I wrote wasn't my résumé.

What could I have possibly done this time? The last time we butted heads, she had slapped my writing hand for being too apologetic to a reader whose dog had died.

The woman intimidated the hell out of me, but I had preached from my soapbox and defended my articles to her.

"You hand out apologies like a doctor hands out scripts for the common cold," she had said. "And you do it just to appease yourself. It doesn't cure anything. The animal is dead, move on."

I sputtered one too many responses at the same time. "Oh yeah, you think so?" I smashed my pointing finger repeatedly on her desk. "Well, you should try it some time.

Maybe it's not about appeasing yourself as much as it is about making the other person believe that you care. Even if it is just for one small moment in time. Even if you just are pretending to care or show an ounce of empathy toward another person." I could have stopped there, but I didn't. "Awh-ha I get it now—you might not be Helen Beck if you show respect toward others. You could have at least, I repeat, at least have told me you were sorry for me being almost fried to death in a fire started by *your* brother-in-law, but *no. You* just ignore me and the whole situation as if it never ever happened."

She bowed her head for one brief moment, and before pointing me out her door, she said, "I'm your boss, not your mother, Kate. You want to hear I'm sorry, call her. Don't cry to me. I have many things to be sorry for, Kate, but you being here is not one of them."

I stood outside her closed door that day, surprised she had only pointed me out of her office and had not thrown me from her kingdom's tower. Somewhere in her words, I did hear an "I'm sorry," even if it was backwards.

With no hint as to what today's conversation concerned, I took a huge cleansing breath before tapping on her nameplate. Helen Beck—Editor in Chief. Hell-n-back—sister-in-law to *City Scope* owner, I thought the nameplate could read. Beck was as old as my mother. She had a wardrobe of outdated tweed suits that Lois Lane would have shunned. However, I admired her for wearing Pretty in Pink lipstick.

The door swung open as soon as I knocked. Frank Walker, better known as Legal, invited me in. I looked from him to Helen, who sat behind her desk and peered at me over her rimless glasses. I was in big trouble this time, but not one clear thought or mangled thought popped in my head as to why. I couldn't even conjure up a command to breathe, walk forward, sit down, say hello, good morning, or was it afternoon already? My skin tingled as if I had just stepped out of a hot shower after using a whole-body salt scrub. I hated how fear left me senseless.

"I'll talk to you later Helen," Legal said, and closed the door on his way out.

I shook my head to clear out the muck. With Legal now gone, things didn't seem so bleak. He could have been here for some other matter, not me, and I felt foolish thinking it was all about me.

"How are you?" I asked Beck, and sat in the bucket chair across from her.

"I should be asking you that. I heard about your trip to the hospital. Hope all is well."

"Yes, all is good." I knew Helen Beck well enough not to offer the details. If there weren't any ramifications caused by the incident, she didn't need or want to know.

"So, uhm...what...?" I let my half question hang. I didn't want to ask what I had or hadn't done wrong or right this time.

"This is about your treasure chase portrait story." She handed me the envelope that had been delivered the other day. The one Joyce spun off the desk to the floor. The one Ondrea picked up and molested. The one I had no interest in at the time.

I pinched the envelope between my thumb and index finger. This wasn't good news. I pulled the stapled papers out of the envelope and studied them as if I knew what I was reading. A whole lot of legal mumbo jumbo, pretty much like Luanne's land lease agreement, sprawled across the page.

The adrenaline surged from my chest to my feet and singed my veins on its way to my brain. The last few hours of my life instantly became a forgotten memory.

"Do I need a lawyer?" My voice quivered. "My brother is a lawyer."

"No. Frank Walker will handle it."

"What is *it*?" I asked, still searching the document for one word I might recognize. I feared losing my house, my car, and all my possessions. Oh God, I'd have to live on the streets. Emma would move in with George and Ethan. My heart pounded double time, vibrating the buttons on my blouse.

"It is a cease and desist order," Beck said.

"Against me!" My voice squealed. "Look, my name, Kate Lambrose." I stabbed the document. "Oh hell. Bobbie Rumfield," I said.

"Who?" Helen asked.

"Is this from her?"

"Maybe. I don't know. Who is Rumfield, and what does he have to do with the portrait?"

"She. And she was the person who picked up the portrait from Terri Wolf."

"Then no, unless you mentioned her in the article," Beck said.

"No." I shook my head and fanned my face with the envelope.

"Don't worry, Kate. Legal assures me that all you need to do is stop printing anything more about it, the portrait that is. However..." She paused.

"However what? And I don't have much to put in my column this week about it anyway. Oh, and I already gave my copy to Eugene."

"I already pulled it, but do you have a short piece you can fill with?"

I nodded. "What the hell is a Copland Hangdlewag? I don't even know how to say that." I turned the papers toward her and pointed at the name.

"That is the plaintiff's lawyer, apparently. The plaintiff wishes to remain anonymous, according to Legal, but obviously has more than a few dollars in his pockets and knows someone well enough to be able to convince a court in *ex parte* to issue an immediate cease and desist order."

"Can they do that? I mean, not name themselves?"

She nodded. "Apparently."

"Oh my God! There's a court date on here." I stabbed at the papers. "Monday!"

"Frank Walker will be there in your stead, Kate. You work for *City Scope*. You're not a freelance writer. We represent you just as Attorney Hangdlewegner represents the plaintiff."

"But, I could go?" I whispered. "I'd like to see who this *ex parte* person is. Wouldn't you?"

"I would, yes, and I will be going, but you're *not*." She jabbed her index finger in the air at me. "Promise me, Kate, you will not set foot in that courtroom. We don't need you volunteering any information."

I had no information to volunteer except Terri Wolf's name, my dramatist. "Oh! I wonder." I scanned the document for the word dramatist. Of course, I didn't expect to find it, but it kept me in study mode long enough to stall for an answer.

"Kate?" Helen Beck said. My name sounded like a red flag

warning.

I sighed. "Okay, I promise," I said. Her glare had me wanting to promise that I would sit quietly in the back of the courtroom with duct tape over my mouth. "Really." I held up my hands as proof I hadn't crossed any fingers nixing my oath. I didn't promise I wouldn't sit outside in my car.

I stuffed the papers into the envelope and handed them back to Beck.

"Hold up." She pointed me back to the chair. "We're not done."

Reluctantly, I sat back down. I needed to pee badly now that the adrenaline had settled in my bladder. I just wanted to go home and bury myself in bed. Oh gosh, I couldn't even do that. I had a date.

"I want you to continue to track down this frame and portrait. Find out anything and everything you can."

"But don't print anything?"

She nodded. "There has to be more to this story than a simple misplaced heirloom. If we have an anonymous person filing a cease and desist order, I want to know why." Helen Beck smiled.

"Don't you think it's odd that anonymous didn't demand the name of the source of the story?" I asked.

"They will," she said. "This isn't over yet."

"We can't do that," I said.

"We might have to, but we will be given a time allotment to hand it over. In the meantime, you will find out why."

After sitting in the ladies room stall with my face buried in my hands, adding up all my pressures, I returned to the office.

I traded my bladder pressure for my co-workers' pressure-cooked questioning of what Helen Beck wanted from me. I summed it up in one long paragraph, leaving them all speechless.

"At least I have my cemetery piece for this week's edition," I said. That was a mistake, because next they wanted to know all about that. When I finished that story, I emailed my cemetery piece to Eugene and went and told him it was in his inbox.

"I'm leaving, Eugene. Just fix whatever you need to in that copy." I was too tired and stressed to wait for his rewrite suggestions. Besides, it was more of an exposé at the moment. At least until I dragged Luanne along with me to the cemetery tomorrow night for a bit of recon. Even then, we might not turn up anything useful.

He nodded.

"Kate, before you leave," Joyce said. "I never did research anything about the grandmother in the portrait. But now I've forgotten what name your mystery caller gave her."

"Petra something," I said. "And the portrait was painted in 1907, according to Terri."

Joyce wrote it down. "Thanks, and get some rest, Kate."

"I wish. But now I have to get ready for a date that I committed to."

"Oh? Who's the lucky guy?" she asked.

"Michael Earl."

"The cop?" three voices asked at the same time.

I nodded and left the three musketeers discussing it without me. It was time to prepare.

CHAPTER 21

All the way home from *City Scope*, I struggled with the decision to cancel my date with Michael or not. Not won.

My starved libido craved action, but just being around him made me shy and stupid. And anything that required an explanation had me rattling off run-on sentences faster than Superman could circle the world.

Luanne's advice was sound. "Kick up your heels, find a man, have sex."

It seemed like a good idea, even though Michael would have to see me at my worst first. Frazzled. Although the phantom George in my head said that wasn't the best idea I've had.

But George's opinions didn't influence me anymore. What bothered me were the three musketeers chiming in unison, "the cop?" when they heard I had a date with Michael Earl. Were they surprised that I had a date, or surprised "the cop" actually found me interesting? I chewed on that tidbit all afternoon and couldn't spit out an answer. At least Ondrea hadn't burned me with any snide remarks. But by now, Miss Diva, queen of he-said-she-said, had quoted everything I had said to Matt. And Matt would have an opinion, whether I wanted one or not. Just like he always had since I was sixteen. I expected he would deliver it in a face-to-face interrogation, a tactic we both had learned from our mother.

My mother, oh God. I rubbed my eyes until starbursts erased her face. Then I kicked every one of their questioning faces out of my head and straight to the curb. Behind their clutter, a smiling thumbnail picture of Jonathan remained. He would have told me to deal with the present moment and prepare. "You can't control the universe, Kate. At some point, you have to let go. Explore unknown territory." That I could do, and I jumped in the shower with a new blade in my razor.

I had no control over the cease and desist order. I had no control over Matt and Ondrea, and I had no control over Emma's vacation with her father. Heck, I didn't even have control over finding anything that my readers lost. The only thing in my life I had control over was my date with Michael. I was a willing participant and felt good about my choice. How could I say no when he offered to cook dinner at my house?

Although I had no idea what food was on the menu, the kitchen and I were clean and prepared.

I turned on some soft jazz and then shut it off. I fluffed and re-fluffed the couch cushions. I put candles on the dining room table and then stuffed them back in the drawer. With nervous energy left to burn, I changed out of my shorts into a skirt and then to a pair of Capris.

By the time I heard Michael pull into the driveway on his motorcycle, I had had one, two, three too many epiphanies. One—I was going to be me and to hell with good behavior. Two—I intended to throw the truth out there and not hide behind a wait-and-see verdict. I wanted to tell him how I felt about him, but I had relationshipitis because of George. And three—I wasn't going to cook and serve, as mother had taught.

Before he rang the bell or knocked, I'd flung open the door. To hell with playing hard to get. When I saw him all primped in yet another wide-striped jersey, but smelling like a Macy's cologne counter, my brain backfired as if I had forgotten how to speak a word of English.

I'd swear a herd of spiders circled my neck.

Michael held two plastic grocery bags, one in each hand, and a bottle of wine under his arm. "You've got great timing, Kate." He smiled.

I nodded and smiled.

His stonewashed jeans cinched at his waist with a shiny black belt. A flash of silver teased my eye, and I dared a quick glance at the buckle hovering right above his fly zipper. The top bar had the word "Just" imprinted with black letters, and the bottom bar read "Ducky." I giggled. Did I read that right? No way was I about to drop on my knees and inspect it.

"I'm not even going to ask how you carried all that on the bike," I said.

"Saddle bags," he answered. "You look nice." He leaned in and kissed my cheek.

I kissed the air back. "Thanks, so do you." As I stepped aside to let him in, I snuck a peek outside at his bike. Two well-worn, sandy brown saddlebags straddled the fender, and one black helmet balanced on the seat. Where was mine?

"Kitchen?"

"Oh." I pulled my head back inside and nearly knocked my noggin. "Straight ahead that way through the arch. Help yourself."

Oh gosh, even the backside of him was sexy, but those Dennis the Menace jerseys had to go. I couldn't move. It was more than his cologne that had me hungry. My hormones couldn't come together to utter a single word except to purr. Sprigs of soft brown hair lofted over his shirt collar. His pants hugged his hips and tapered down to a straight boot cut cuff. And why I would wonder if his feet were sweaty in his Harley boots at a time like this, I didn't know, but I did.

He sauntered through my living room into the kitchen. I felt like I was fourteen again, built like a two-by-four, trying too hard to be casual while begging for the attention of my brother's best friend. But I wasn't fourteen now. The two-by-four had expanded in all the right dimensions so my toes weren't visible with a simple duck of my head, and I wasn't begging. Oh dear. My next thought was R-rated, and I slapped my palms to my face.

The heat radiated to my fingers. Dammit, I was blushing. I raced across the room to the thermostat. After I punched the down arrow to sixty-five degrees, I raced to the refrigerator and grabbed two cans of soda. Michael had gone out the slider to the back deck. I wasn't sure why, but I let him go. I raced back to the front door with the soda can bottoms pressed to my cheeks, and swung the door shut with my foot. My black pump slid off my foot and sailed across the room. The slider door clicked shut and I spun in a circle, looking for my exit hole.

"Hey, Kate, I didn't see a grill..." Michael stopped in the archway.

I smiled at him and shrugged. Caught red-handed with the soda cans pressed against my face and one shoe on, I did the first thing that occurred to me. I kicked off my other shoe and shuffled it behind me.

"Are you alright?" he asked.

"Hot in here," I said. "Do you want a root beer?" I held the can out to him.

He smiled and his eyes twinkled into slits. He took the soda and set it on the table beside the couch. "You have perfect red circles." He touched my cheek. "Cold circles." He laughed. "Kate, you are so cute."

Oh no. He didn't just say that to me, did he? Who needs cute?

My face must have revealed a whole lot of disappointment because the next thing I knew, my soda can was placed on the table beside his. He had scooped up my little self in his big Popeye arms, and we were sweating against each other. I was suffocating under his long, soft, yummy kiss, at least until I got in opposite rhythm with his inhales.

"I...I...I...don't own a grill," I said when we came up for air.

Michael shrugged and led me to the kitchen without a backwards glance or comment about the kiss.

"I brought steaks. Is that okay?" he asked, and pulled two huge T-bones from the plastic bag along with a few other items.

I nodded and shook my head. God help me, I didn't know the answer. I was still in shock over the down and dirty kiss without an after hug. And I missed being prepared for it. The next one would be all mine.

"Why don't you have a grill, Kate?" he asked.

"I don't cook on open flames. Fire scares me. And before you ask—I don't know why."

"Because of the *City Scope* fire?"

I shook my head. "No, just always."

"Hmm. It's water that does it for me." He pulled the cellophane off the steak. "Platter?"

I pointed to the cupboard and watched his biceps flex as he freed the platter from underneath a stack of plates.

"I'm not talking bath water or swimming holes, I'm talking about open oceans, flood torrents, white water." He seasoned the meat using my black and white cow-shaped salt and pepper shakers.

"Why? Did you nearly drown once?"

"Nope. Not that I know of. Kind of like you. No reason. Just is."

Huh. He had control issues too.

"Do you eat salad?" He handed me a huge tomato and a bag of baby spinach.

I looked at what I had in my hand, which to me didn't make a salad. "What?"

"Salad. The rest of it is in that bag." He pointed. "And where is the on button for your oven?"

I giggled, only because Emma had to teach me how to work the oven. "You have to set the temperature first, then press start."

"What if I just want to use the broiler?"

"It will beep when it reaches the temp you set it at, then you press broil. There." I pointed.

"I'll buy you a hibachi, so I can grill next time." He laughed.

Next time? Huh. I liked that.

"Oh, and I found this in your driveway." He fished in his jeans pocket and handed me a perfectly round glass disc, about the size of a silver dollar.

"What is it?" I asked.

"An eyeglass lens." He shrugged.

I yanked my hand out from under it and it fell to the floor. "Oh my God!" I jumped back. As he bent to retrieve it, I backed into the counter. "It can't be. And you found this in my driveway?" My voice hit the same octave that Michael Jackson be-bopped to in Thriller.

"Why, what's wrong?"

"He's been here!" I shouted.

"Who has been here?"

"That man. Fisher. I know it's his. It's the same lens that fell in my lap on the plane."

"What?" Michael left the lens where it landed.

It glared up at me, and one thought lead to another. Like a nuclear reaction, I entered meltdown mode.

CHAPTER 22

Every emotion, every stress inducer, ache, and pain surfaced. Words and tears spilled out of me in one continuous stream. I listed a week's worth of woes, even the ones he already knew about.

Michael frowned at me. "Wait, what? Your ex is at a party?" The muscle in his jaw twitched. "And someone is stalking you?"

"No, yes." I wobbled my head like an unbalanced tire. "I thought so, but it wasn't who I thought it was." My sinuses clogged and I sounded like I had cotton balls stuffed in my mouth.

"Okay..." Michael nodded slowly. "Who was it?"

"Sadie. Sadie Arnold." I held out my hands like a magician announcing *tad-ah*. "I thought it was a silver sedan that had tailed me from the airport. But Sadie showed up in a gray Cadillac. What difference does it make now? Matthew was right. I traded cars like a kid trades baseball cards. Besides, when you are on the interstate, heading in one direction, aren't all cars following you?"

"I suppose they are." He scratched the back of his head. His bicep flexed. His tattoo peeked out from beneath his shirt cuff.

I walked in circles, swinging the bag of spinach and strangling the tomato. I wasn't done yet and sucked in a long breath. "Emma has been gone way too long—I can't stand it, but after that." I pointed at the offending lens lying on the floor. "I guess she's safer with her father. My brother is involved with Ondrea—my worst nightmare. Which is like if I were Donald Trump and Rosie O'Donnell was dating my brother. If Trump even has a brother. I dunno. But dammit she will not, I repeat, not let the incident at Bobbie Rumfield's house drop. Ondrea, that is. Not Rosie O'Donnell."

The more I rallied all my troubles together, the faster I paced. The faster I paced, the more I cried. Somewhere in the cluttered ramblings, it occurred to me that George would have laughed and asked if Rosie O'Donnell and Matt were now an item. Michael, on the other hand, let me run my course and rescued the tomato and bag of spinach from my hands as I circled around again. I stopped in my tracks and faced him head-on.

"And what about this?" I swung my arms wide around the kitchen.

"About what? Dinner?" Michael asked.

"Yes, about dinner. About us. What are we doing? Maybe I don't need to know right now, maybe even you don't know, but I don't do the *don't know* thing very well. And don't you dare kiss me again like that"—I pointed toward the front door—"without hugging me afterward!"

"Okay, I won't." He reached out and cupped my cheeks, brushing away my tears with his thumbs.

"Okay then. Fine." I squeezed my eyes tight. "You can go now." I sniffled and tried to step back, but his hands held me gently in place.

"I'm not the one backing away, Kate, and you can't make me."

"I'm not ready to have expectations again. Expectations lead to disappointments, which lead to heartbreak, and soon after that, I'm condensing my life into five rooms, left alone to wallow in grief. The only person I'm important to is—"

"Me," Michael whispered, and pulled me to his chest. The thud of his heart outraced mine.

Before I knew it, we were sitting on the couch. I was in his lap with my face buried in his shoulder. I tried to explain, but my sobbing choked my words.

"Shh. Kate, it's okay. Just cry. Talk later," Michael whispered, and wrapped me completely up in his arms. I had landed in a safe place. Even if I could talk, I didn't want to. I let my tears wash away the stress. When my hiccups subsided, Michael slipped away and brought a damp washcloth so I could wash my face. And he handed me a glass of wine.

As I stared into the liquid, I remembered the conversation I had with Luanne when she had turned over my last

Tarot card.

"Six of Swords," she had said. "A smooth passage from difficulties. See? It all turns out well."

I picked up the card and peered at it carefully. "Doesn't look all that smooth to me." Drawn on the card were a woman and child with heads bowed aboard a small boat. Six swords imprisoned their view as an oarsman carted them off to a destination unknown.

"Are you looking at the same card I am?" I asked. "Still looks gloomy."

"That's because your focus is too narrow. There's someone waiting to set you free. Who do you think is in the back steering the boat? Jeez, Kate. Your life isn't set in concrete. You have free will. Write your own caption," she said.

Huh, the man sitting beside me wanted to steer my boat.

"What do you see in there, Kate?" Michael leaned over and looked into my wine glass.

"Another kiss," I said.

My face superheated. What a waste of air conditioning. If I couldn't handle the heat from my emotions now, in another decade when menopause struck, I'd have to move to Siberia.

Michael sniffed the air. "Something's burning." He sniffed again.

"Ha ha."

"No, really, Kate. Something is burning." He raced into the kitchen.

Smoke vented from the stovetop. Through the oven door, I could see the cookie sheet Emma and I had used weeks ago and never washed.

"Oh my God! Fire." I didn't need to see flames to know what came next. I grabbed my fire extinguisher that I kept under the sink.

"It's okay. It's okay. We just need to get the pan out. Where's your pot holders? Or a kitchen towel?"

The two of us do-si-doed trying to get past each other. "In there." I used the nozzle of the extinguisher and pointed at the drawer beside the stove.

He grabbed the top one and slipped his hand into one. The matching mitt dangled by the plastic tether still attached from the store. He frowned and yanked them apart.

"They were a gift. I didn't want to ruin them." I danced in

place with the pin pulled free from the extinguisher's handle.

"Stand clear." He opened the oven door. The smoke rolled out in a tsunami wave and the smoke detector squealed to life.

The pan burst into flames with the new breath of oxygen and he ditched it into the sink.

I aimed the nozzle and fired a quick douse of retardant before it set my kitchen curtains aflame. White foam splattered across my countertop, onto the tile floor, baptizing my toes and Michael's jeans. We looked at each other and smiled, although I was sure I looked like a rabid mongoose the way my lips quivered.

The oven snapped and sparked.

"Oh shit."

A white-hot spot burned on the heating element. Smoldering lava burst into flames. My oven had turned into a Fourth of July fireworks show.

I aimed and pulled the trigger just as Michael swung the door shut with his boot tip. I doused the outside of the oven door and Michael's leg.

"Jeez, that's cold." He shook off the excess foam and coughed into the crook of his arm.

"Sorry, sorry. Oh my God. We have to call nine-one-one." I swung the door from the kitchen to the garage open and the smoked rolled past me.

"I am nine-one-one."

"No. I mean the other nine-one-one. Fire nine-one-one."

He pushed the oven *off* button and heaved the window over the sink open. Something clunked inside the oven and he stooped to investigate through the oven window door.

"Well, that shouldn't happen," he said.

"Shit. Shit." A foot-long piece of the heating element had broken off and burst into flames. I grabbed the cordless phone and rushed out the front door where I could breathe and hear the emergency dispatcher.

"There's a fire in my oven!" I rambled off my address and ran back into the house.

Michael had wrapped my kitchen towel around his nose and mouth while he doubled up on potholders around his hand. If I wasn't so terrified, I would have laughed at him looking like Dennis the Menace playing cops and robbers.

Between the grease fire and the flame retardant, an ozone smell singed the air.

"Do you have some pliers?" Michael asked.

I yanked open the junk drawer and handed him pliers like a scrub nurse hands a scalpel to a surgeon. The 911 dispatcher issued instructions to exit the house. "We have an engine en route, ma'am."

Why was everyone so crazy calm? My kitchen was on fire! "Come on, we gotta go."

Michael didn't budge. He had the pliers stuffed in his hand and tested opening and closing them while wearing the clunky mitt. I'd bet my life he could handle chopsticks like a pro.

"What are you doing?"

"Don't worry, Kate. I got this."

I was terrified to stay and too terrified to leave him battling alone. I skidded and slipped past him on the foamy tile and slammed my shoulder into the doorjamb.

Shit, that hurt. But I needed to give us an escape route and punched the button to open the garage door. It rolled up, and a fresh wave of air blew past me, wharfing the smoke in circles.

"Ma'am! Are you out of the house?" the dispatcher crackled in my ear.

"Yes. Sort of..."

Michael pulled the oven door open and clutched the flaming element between the pliers. He dropped it in the sink and ran water over the entire mess. A cloud of steam rolled out the kitchen window and up along the ceiling.

"Fire out?" I sounded like a vocabulary challenged cave woman. I panted and my chest heaved. My shirt twitched above my left breast with each extra beat of my heart.

"Yup. Is that the fire department still on the phone?" he asked.

I nodded, and he gently peeled my fingers off the phone and explained to the dispatcher what had happened. "Everything is fine," he assured her. He took my hand and towed me through the debris and out the front door. "You okay? You are shaking like a Chihuahua." We sat on the stoop and he wrapped his arms around me.

The smoke detectors staggered off one by one as the smoke cleared and my air conditioning blew out the front door. I closed my eyes against the dizzying stripes on Michael's shirt and concentrated on steadying my breath. His bear hug stilled my shivers and after a moment, our breaths fell into tandem. His lips brushed my forehead and I lifted my head. I put back on my superhero cape, took control, and kissed him hard.

The double honk and straining engine of a fire truck sounded around the corner. "I thought you told them it was all clear?"

"I did."

The fire engine pulled into the driveway and turned an abrupt right onto the lawn to avoid Michael's bike. Streaks of red and white reflected off the house and yard. Michael went around to the passenger side and greeted one of the firefighters that had hopped off the moving truck. "Pac Man," Michael said, "I told dispatch to call you off."

"Hey, Ducky, so ya say. But the chief wants us to make sure you don't have an electrical fire smoldering in the walls."

Pac Man? Ducky? I wondered if it was a nickname or if he belonged to the belt buckle label club.

Michael slapped him on the back and nodded for him to go ahead. Five men hustled past me as I stood at the entrance of my garage. Each dipped their head and sized me up with a "ma'am" before bullying their way into my house.

Michael and I took the short cut through the garage and met up with the fire crew in my kitchen. I stood in the doorway while Michael explained and listened to the fire captain say it wasn't the first electric stove he'd seen catch fire.

"Sometimes, the heating element develops a thin spot...." The captain explained all the technical blah-blah. "Nichrome wire...ceramic insulator...electrically grounded."

It was all a blur to me, at least until I heard, "something flammable—not wiped up," and all eyes swiveled toward me.

"Cookie dough?" I said.

They all nodded.

After pulling the oven away from the wall and checking my breakers and walls for hot spots, the five-man crew piled back on the truck with an all clear.

Michael and I had walked out with them. "Do they have water in that truck?" I asked.

"Not that one. It's not a tanker. Why?"

"Then why is the driveway wet? What are they leaking?"

The engine revved, the truck jerked backwards to the edge of the tar driveway, and rocked forward. The rigs wheels spun, digging a trench of mud in the lawn, and the driveway disintegrated under the wheels. A ten-foot geyser shot into the air from the lawn.

Within minutes, the lawn sprinkler water line drenched the truck. I had a pool in my front yard and a fire engine stuck in a muddy rut.

After the town DPW shut off the water, and after the tow truck arrived to heave the engine out of the rut, Michael said, "Fire and water. That about covers our fears, wouldn't you say?"

We laughed. "I suppose you're right." I slipped my hand in his.

"How do you feel about take-out?" he asked.

"How do you feel about a bowl of cereal, a glass of wine, and me?"

"In any particular order?"

We raced back in the house.

"Just ducky." I hit the garage door button and let the fire-fighters figure out their own rut, because I was certainly out of mine.

CHAPTER 23

The wide-ass grin on my face hurt my cheeks. Michael was still sleeping when I slipped out of bed to make coffee and mop the kitchen from ceiling to floor. Unfortunately, all I had to offer for breakfast was apple juice, milk, coffee, Milano cookies, and some leftover stale nacho chips. Except we had already agreed we'd head out to Rubys for an omelet after a cup of coffee.

Thank God it was only Saturday and not Sunday, as I'd have another whole day to catch up on my sleep and clear the stench out of my house. Michael and I talked for hours in between a few other activities. But our conversations where almost as orgasmic as the rest of the night. We laughed until we hurt, telling each other stories. And we almost saw the sun come up. I couldn't think of one thing that we weren't compatible over, except maybe family, which explained why he felt I was "out of his league," as he had put it. I had grown up with a mother, father, sister, and brother in a twelve-room secure home. Michael had grown up with six foster sisters in a six-room house with his foster parents. Even though I assured him that he was wrong about me having more opportunities than he had as a kid, it was going to take more times than one to convince him. The other thing I understood after learning he had six sisters was why and how he had such a receptive and appreciative respect toward me and my Venus culture.

"Kate?" Michael's voice echoed down the stairs.

"Yeah?"

"Everything okay?" he asked.

I smiled more—if that was possible. After all our conversations last night, his question really meant, "Are you still with me?"

"Every...thing is wonderful! Coffee is almost ready."

I could almost hear his smile bounce down the stairs and wrap around me.

It wasn't long after Michael and I cuddled up on the couch with our coffee that the doorbell rang. Luanne hollered and banged on the door. "Let us in. We heard you had a fire."

"Us" was Izzy and Luanne. Shortly after that, Matt and Ondrea showed up. I expected Luanne and Izzy, as we were all headed to Rubys for omelets. But what Matt and Ondrea stopped by for was a wide-eyed mystery.

I made another pot of coffee, introduced everyone, offered juice and cookies, and watched big brother Matt scrutinize the other two men at the table. And explained again the fire story.

"We are headed to Rubys for omelets if you want to go?" I asked Matt. I extended the invitation, expecting them to leave.

"Sure." He looked to Ondrea.

"Or we could all go to Bobby Rumfield's, sneak in, and ransack her house for an antique portrait, right, Kate?" Ondrea said.

Luanne did a slow turn and faced me. That twitchy brow of hers raised and posed the unspoken threat of "shut her up!" And here I thought Ondrea had used up all her adjectives describing her heroism for rescuing us from Rumfield's basement. I should have known Ondrea was waiting for the perfect time to spotlight the information—again.

Luanne and I had vowed secrecy about Rumfield's, at least to Izzy and Michael. Even though we admitted to each other that we didn't know how either of them would react, we weren't going to take the chance of being told we shouldn't, couldn't, or wouldn't do that or this. We both had struggled in the past with men who needed to control our every move. And as grown, independent women who only needed a man for one reason, we pinky swore not to let our independence disappear into a relationship.

However, I'd told Michael, and I was pleased that all he did was laugh.

"Who's Rumfield?" Izzy asked, and looked from Luanne to me and back.

Michael stopped mid pour of his second cup of coffee and

kneed me under the table. He knew all about it and even knew that Luanne wasn't talking about it to Izzy. God, what a blabbermouth I was.

I glanced past Luanne at Ondrea. She tried to hide her smirk behind her napkin as she blotted orange juice from her painted lips.

"Don't look at me," Matt said. "It's the first I've heard about it. What have you done wrong now, Kate?"

If my gaze could throw Ninja stars, Ondrea would have taken one to the heart.

"Rumfield is just an old lady with a lot of plants and she needed one more. So Kate and I delivered it to her," Luanne said, trying to cover for us.

I, on the other hand, didn't have a clue what to say.

"Oh, Kate," Ondrea said. "I'm sorry, I thought you would have told everyone about your cry for rescue." She grinned.

Luanne's head turned toward Ondrea like a possessed mechanical doll. Her brow nearly cleared her hairline.

"So this is it?" Luanne asked. She hooked a thumb and jabbed it in Ondrea's direction. Her head whipped back at me so fast I feared she'd be in a neck brace before noon. I nodded one time. She was experiencing Ondrea's deliberate shakedown for the first time. And now I was a bit scared. "Wow. You know what I would do?" Luanne said.

I knew exactly what Luanne would do, but Matt wasn't her brother who was smitten with Ondrea. I cut Luanne off before she told Ondrea where to stick her nosey nose.

"Ondrea, look...we just didn't want to cause the woman a heart attack by popping out of her basement when she already thought we had left. Nothing more."

"Really?" she said. The sarcasm in her voice was more than Luanne could handle.

"You sound like a twelve-year-old, giddy and ready to tattle on big sister," Luanne said.

Crap. And now I was deeper in crap than I wanted to be. Matt glared at me as if I'd made Luanne talk. I opted to continue to back pedal and answer all the questions that were still open.

"Nothing was done wrong to anyone," I said, answering Matt's last question. "Well, that's not exactly true. I mean, I suspect Rumfield has Terri Wolf's husband's grandmother's portrait and she won't give it back." I laughed and looked at Michael.

He already knew all this and he knew how I felt about Ondrea. I had told him several stories of her deliberate be-heading, and how it had gotten worse since she started da-ting Matt.

Michael had said that Ondrea was jealous of me. One, for having a big brother I could count on, and two, for being smarter than her. It had made sense last night when he said it, and he suggested I not let her suck me in to her little game. But it was easier said than done.

He squeezed my hand and winked at me. In my head, I heard, "I got your back." Damn, he was one fine detective and he didn't even have to try.

"So let me get this straight." Izzy tapped the air in front of him as if he were making check marks on some invisible whiteboard. "Rumfield has Wolf's portrait?" He laughed. "Am I the only one that thinks that is a bit weird? Why would a complete stranger want a portrait of someone else's grand-mother?"

Luanne and I nodded. "That's what we wanted to know," Luanne said.

Izzy turned Luanne's chin toward him and kissed her. She mewled like a stroked kitten. "You're so sweet."

"Okay, I'm hungry. Is anyone else ready for Rubys Wild Rose Omelet?" I said.

"Oh yeah, that was the plan, and I'm starving," Izzy said.

"Hold on. I know that change-up Kate does when she's up to no good," Matt said. "Something's up."

Up to no good stuck deep in my heart. And Matt had that father look on his face, the one he used when I was sixteen.

"You don't know anything, Matt." I grabbed the juice glasses off the table, taking myself out of the loop. I would have loved to dump the remnants over Ondrea's head, but there were too many witnesses, and I doubted Michael would appreciate having to cart me off for assault.

"Oh yes I do, Kate," Matt said. "I'll be bailing you out of jail, no doubt."

A huge gust of air escaped my lips. "Okay. Fine." I looked from Matt to Luanne to Izzy to Michael and back to Ondrea. And I talked directly at her. "Everyone at this table already knows the whole story. So if Ms. Ondrea wishes to reiterate it to you Matt, she's welcome to...on her own time. Not mine. That's it, and I don't need to discuss it because it is my business, my story, my mystery." I narrowed my gaze at Ondrea and said, "Understood?"

"Yup, up to no good again." Matt needed the last word, as usual. "And don't be getting in her face because of your mistakes." He thumbed at Ondrea.

My mouth hung open. Had he just defended her over me, his sister? Mistake? The only mistake I made was opening the door and welcoming them in to my home.

"Hold everything." Michael held up his hand toward Matt. His voice deepened to that authoritative cop drone. "Kate is *not* up to *no good*, as you put it, Matt, which I find offensive toward her. And secondly, this is her home and we are her guests, and that in itself gives her all rights to ask anyone to leave." He looked directly at Ondrea and back to Matt. "I don't hear Kate belittling your faults in front of your girlfriend or in front of your boyfriend." He looked back to Ondrea. "And what's Thumper's rule? Oh yeah, if you can't say something nice—shut up."

The room settled in total silence. Luanne had a grin a mile wide plastered on her face, and I half expected her to stick out her tongue at Ondrea. I didn't know which way to turn or who to look at.

Michael stood from the table, grabbed my hand, and said, "I'm ready for that omelet."

***

Rubys Wild Rose Omelets were as good as ever, if not better. The breakfast cook, Rose, made the omelets with a secret cream cheese sauce, egg whites, crumbled sausage, diced black olives, chopped rose petals, and topped with fried tomato slices.

After the six of us had filled our guts, we disbursed in six different directions. But not before Matt caught up to me outside.

"I like Michael, Kate," he said.

I was still feeling triumphant over Michael defending me and said, "It wouldn't matter if you did or didn't, Matt. After all, it doesn't matter to you that I don't like Ondrea. Right?"

That hit home with him, because he hung his head and agreed with me. I could have stopped with that, but I had his attention.

"Let me tell you something about your girlfriend," I said. "I wouldn't be surprised if someone at the office doesn't make a formal complaint against her."

"And that would be you?" he asked.

"No. I don't think I'll have to, because everyone is pretty annoyed with her insults. But the fact that she insults your sister..." I pointed at me as if he needed to know who I was talking about. "Right in front of you, and if you plan to introduce her to Mom, you better reel her in. Because Mom will chop her off at the knees. Blood is thicker than water."

"Yeah. I got that message from Michael."

I left him standing in the parking lot, looking after me as I drove away. I hoped he would either talk her down, if it was worth it to him, or find an adult to date. Although, I had to admit that they made a cute couple, when they were quietly smiling.

Chores at home were my next stop and then a nap before Luanne returned later for our trip to the cemetery.

CHAPTER 24

The sun had set by the time Luanne arrived. She had brought a pizza with her, and we devoured that before leaving the house.

"You just drove right past the entrance," Luanne said. The gothic stone arch entrance hugged the curbless road.

"I know. I can't turn in under the arch from this side of the road." On each side of the pillars, century-old maple trees stood guard. The cemetery existed long before Grant Street had two lanes.

"Why?"

"It's too narrow to swing the Jeep around straight."

"We should have brought Sporty. It turns on a dime." Luanne had bought herself an Audi S4 and hadn't stopped bragging about it since. I rolled my eyes and turned left down Dove Street. Dove Street was better known as Hearse Circle. It dead-ended at a circular cul-de-sac. Perfect for funeral processions coming from the same direction I was to turn around and squeeze though the arch.

Since we were only one car, I didn't bother to drive down to the circle. I flipped a U-turn and headed back to the cemetery.

"You better shut your lights off," she said.

"I will." I slowed to make the turn.

"You better shut them off now."

"I will as soon as I clear the arch," I said.

She *tsk'd* at me. "They will see you come..." Luanne didn't finish her sentence. The car jolted. My headlights blinked off with a smash and a clang.

"Well that takes care of that." Luanne laughed.

"What the hell just happened?" I said.

"I think there was a chain across the arch and you just

took it out along with your headlights."

"Great." I stopped and opened my door. Sure enough, a snapped chain lay on the ground. "Oh boy," I said.

"So, this is really called breaking and entering, I guess."

"Oh my God."

"Don't just sit here, go." She pointed toward the grassy mound. "Drive around there. We can hide from the street and the shed."

The moon spied through the tall evergreens, stretching the shadows across the lawn. I rolled down my window and drove with my head hanging out, watching for the edge of the road. The last thing I wanted to do was roll over a grave plaque. I clicked off my lights, not that I needed to, and shut the engine off.

"You know we will be walking home now," I said.

"Don't you have a flashlight?"

"Yeah, but..."

"And I have this." Luanne pulled a small, silver CSI like flashlight from her backpack.

"What are we supposed to do, hold them out the window while I drive down the street?" I was kidding of course, but she wasn't.

"No, I also have this." She held up a roll of duct tape. "We can tape the flashlights to the front bumper."

"Oh my God, are you kidding me?" I laughed. "And what else do you have in there?" I pulled the pack off her lap and dug through it.

Among a pair of socks and two black stocking hats, I pulled out a screwdriver, a hammer, mace, her camera—complete with telephoto lens—and a Billy club.

"What are you thinking?" I looked at her.

"Protection," she said. "And I didn't have time for a gun permit."

"Thank God." I stuffed everything back in the bag.

"But I think I will get one."

We stared at each other for a moment before laughing, and together, we said, "You'll shoot your eye out."

An hour later, all was still quiet at the cemetery. No stench to smell and no loud drummer noise to listen to. We had donned our black long-sleeve shirts to match our black jeans and tromped around from tree to tree and gravestone to gravestone, hiding in the shadows. We toured the area around the shed and back to the Jeep before deciding to head home.

"It would be easier to call a tow truck and a taxi," I said.

"True, but I bet the tow will call the police before they show up at the cemetery."

That did seem like a logical assumption, especially when the tow company was the same garage that had reported my murdered tire.

"Okay, well let's get to it. Nothing exciting happening around here anyway." I picked up the duct tape.

"Move over, MacGyver." Luanne laughed.

As it turned out, it was easier than I thought. We stuck the butt end of the flashlights in through the broken plastic.

We had just finished taping my flashlight to the driver's side when a horn tooted, and a voice yelled, "Dude!"

We plunged into each other's arms and hit the dirt at the front of my Jeep.

"What the hell was that?" Luanne said.

"I don't know, but maybe the party is about to start," I whispered.

A circle of light swept around both sides of the crypt, and I covered my head with my hands.

"Stay down," I said. Car engines whined in the dead quiet. Another arc of light split around the crypt, which meant two cars.

"Where's your backpack?" I asked. "I think we need the mace and Billy club."

"In the car. I'll get it."

"No." I pulled her back. "Shh, did you hear that? Someone just banged on the shed door. Come on." I crawled away from the Jeep and around the burial vault to the first large grave marker. From there, we had a clear view of four people milling around outside the shed. And I hoped that they didn't have a clear view of our white faces staring at them.

Just then, the music rocked the silence as the door swung open. The bass boomed so loud I couldn't even recognize the song.

If this music was the disturbance the neighbors had complained about, then why hadn't the police checked it out? That didn't make any sense to me. And shame on me for not following up with Michael to see if he located any police reports.

"I think we're going to need my backpack. Either that or we just get in the Jeep and get the hell out of here," Luanne said.

"I know, but we can't just open the door and grab the bag. The inside light will turn on."

"They won't see. The Jeep is behind that crypt." She pointed behind her.

I looked back and couldn't see the Jeep, but light traveled faster than I could grab a backpack.

"You stay here," I said. "I'll go get the backpack and our cell phones."

Luanne nodded with both her thumbs up. "Just hurry back."

I crawled back around the burial vault on my hands and knees like a dog. My heart knocked against my chest, and my breathing was shallow. None of this seemed as much fun as it had when we were planning our recon. We were outnumbered five to two. And those five people milling outside the shed each had a man's physique.

It upped the ante of our stealth operation, but only if we got caught. I didn't intend to confront them. I'd take notes, snap some pictures, gather enough recon to write my column, and uncover the stench in Yardman.

Move over, Jack White. Dressed in Ninja black and on the trail of a news story, I had joined the ranks of those that uncovered the underworld. I just hoped the world beneath my feet stayed buried.

I hoisted myself up over the open driver's side window, and clunked my head on the headliner. Half in and half out, I grabbed the steering wheel in one hand and the headrest with the other. After waddling my hips over the door edge, I flipped over and slid butt first into the driver's seat. Maneuvering my legs and feet over the steering wheel was harder than scaling Red Rocks in Gloucester.

Once I had gathered anything in the Jeep that we could use for defense, including our cell phones, I escaped and crawled back to Luanne.

I grabbed one of the black stocking caps from the backpack and pulled it down over my face. It was now darker than midnight. Turning the hat every which way, I felt around for the eyes and mouth openings. "I thought these had eyes, nose, and mouth holes," I whispered.

Luanne laughed and pulled it off my head. "Not yet." She dug in the front pocket of the pack. "Scissors." She held up a small silver pair.

"Now you tell me. We could have used those instead of my teeth to cut the duct tape."

She shrugged and went to work cutting holes in the hats.

After we had our sweltering black hats on, with holes that didn't quite line up correctly, Luanne attached her telephoto lens to the camera. She fiddled with the settings and balanced the camera on top of the gravestone.

"Wait." I grabbed her arm. "Is the flash off?"

"Yes," she whispered, and pushed the shutter button.

Fifteen seconds later, the shutter released and the aperture closed. She pressed the button four more times. In the dim shadows, we stared at the grainy digital display. I squinted until the picture focused.

"They look like a bunch of kids," Luanne said. "What do you suppose they're doing?"

"I don't know. Waking the dead?"

"Seriously? That's a little twisted."

"I know, right?"

"And if the neighbors are complaining, why aren't the cops here?"

"That's what I thought." I studied the picture. "Hey, that *kid* looks familiar." I tapped the image with my finger. "Quick. Take another pic."

The solid bass continued to boom. My body absorbed the percussions and stirred a memory that stayed just out of reach. It drove me insane that I couldn't determine what was so familiar about the song.

One by one, the men disappeared into the shed. The last man who had opened the door turned toward us. Luanne and I hit the ground and I tasted grass. The camera perched on the headstone took the final shot.

"Do you think he saw us?"

I pulled the stocking cap tight, lining my eyes up with the holes, and poked my head up just far enough to peer around the gravestone. "No," I said. "He went inside. And left the door open."

We settled back against the cool granite. She scrolled through the images.

"Wait." I grabbed her wrist. "I do know that guy, and he's not a kid. He's a cop."

"What? Who?"

"Jeez, that's it. 'Master of Insanity.'"

"What the hell are you talking about? Don't make me slap you," Luanne said.

"That song that's playing. That's Black Sabbath. 'Master of Insanity.'"

"*This* is insanity. I thought we were talking about a cop."

"Yeah, that's Gleason, or at least I think it's Gleason. Distance isn't doing his attitude any justice."

"Oh my God, Kate. We're staking out an undercover operation."

"Could be," I said. "But we'll have to get closer to be sure."

My brain hummed with the word Pulitzer. Although, if this was a police sting, I wasn't sure what information I could use even if I did uncover something big. I didn't want people thinking that I had pimped a relationship with Michael Earl for inside information.

"Come on." I tugged her in a sprint across the clearing. The three-quarter moon stunted our shadows into midgets that ran beside us. With every rise of our footsteps, it looked like a hand swiped out from a grave trying to trip us.

We skirted around the side of the shed, keeping our distance from the open door. I led the way. We ducked under the frosted window at the back. My heart pounded and I sucked in air to feed my adrenaline.

The music stopped. We smothered our labored breathing, Luanne cupped her hand over her mouth, and I pulled the fabric of my shirt over mine. I'd suffocate for sure or die of heat stroke. At least they wouldn't have to carry my body far.

From inside the shed, hinges whined and a door or person slammed against the wall.

"Hey, T-Bone! Get down there and get that pump primed." The megaphone voice from inside was Gleason.

"You got it, boss," a voice as thick as rocks replied. Heavy footfalls clomped across floorboards and disappeared. The willies tickled my neck. I turned a 360 looking for the five guys. For all I knew, they were standing behind us with guns pointed at our heads.

The shed was no bigger than a 20' x 20' square with the entrance door and a roll-up garage door side-by-side along the front.

Luanne tapped my shoulder and pointed at the window. I shook my head and pulled her head toward me. "We won't be able to see through—it's frosted," I whispered.

More footsteps thudded over the floorboards. I smashed my ear against the building. Were they walking in circles? One by one, the shed swallowed the footsteps, and the voices disappeared.

CHAPTER 25

A loud rumble roared to life and we clutched each other. 'Heaven and Hell' bellowed from inside the shed. We bumped into each other trying to flee and bounced hard to the ground. My hand landed on something slick and round that grew hard beneath my fingers. I scrambled to my knees and knocked Luanne back down. She let out a giant *oomph* that blasted me in the eye.

"Snake...snake..." I squeaked, and crab-walked backwards.

Thank God for the blaring music and the grumbling motor. It was louder than me.

"Kate. Kate. It's a garden hose," Luanne whispered.

"What the hell?" I yanked the stocking cap off my head and sucked in a giant lungful of air. *Inhale, exhale.* I willed my pulse out of the aerobic red zone.

She hauled me to my feet.

"Look. They must be pumping water inside," she whispered directly into my ear. The hose dead-ended into the baseboard at the corner of the shed. We followed it back across the road where it disappeared into the darkness down the hill and into the pond.

"That doesn't make sense. Why pump water up from the pond?"

Luanne shrugged.

"Give me your backpack," I said.

Luanne slipped it off her shoulders and I rummaged for the can of mace and Billy club. I kept the club and gave her the mace. She nodded and shook the mace can like a bartender shaking a dirty martini.

With the club resting over my shoulder ready to swing, I motioned Luanne to follow me. We tiptoed up to the front door, and like Heckle and Jeckle, stuck our heads around the doorjamb. It was nice of them to forget to shut the door tight.

But the shed was empty, at least of men and for as far as we could see.

We stepped away from the door and stared at each other wide-eyed. Luanne tugged on her necklace, freeing the chain from under her shirt. For a second, Izzy's Hamsa glinted in the moonlight before Luanne fisted the protective hand in her palm.

"Where did they go? They can't just disappear."

"They could if they were spirits," Luanne said. "Don't you remember the Death card from the other night?"

"Wait a minute. You were the one that said Death didn't mean death. Besides, Gleason is not a ghost."

"Seriously? We're in a cemetery, Kate. We're surrounded by death. It's got to be close to midnight. Do you see them? 'Cause I sure don't."

"I think you've overdosed on Tarot Cards and Izzisms. Come on." I pushed the door in with my palm, just wide enough to poke my entire head through and look around. The creak vibrated in my fingertips as the door hinges protested. Luanne had a death grip on the waistband at the back of my jeans. If she got any closer to me, she'd be in front of me.

A naked light bulb hung from the rafters. It wasn't lit, and yet, a sliver of light cast shadows around the room. Maintenance equipment, weed eaters, and push brooms leaned against the wall in front of me. Unmarked containers of varying sizes and large, empty flower baskets lined shelves to my right. A wheelbarrow partly filled with apples stood under the shelves. But no boom box or stereo system was in sight to explain the screaming music.

I pushed on the door again and stepped inside. The door butted against something and banged back against my head. I froze like a statue in a game of freeze-tag, and Luanne rear-ended me. My heart bubbled in my chest, stealing my inhale.

The wooden floor rumbled beneath my feet. The music, thankfully louder than my knocking knees, blanketed my footsteps. Fright had stolen my flight, and even though I knew five big guys couldn't fit behind the door, I expected them to jump out at me.

But when no booted foot stepped from behind the door, I whirled around it and swung the Billy club, sweeping a protective bubble in front of me.

My wild swinging motion carried me forward, and I tee-tered on toes inches away from a large, yawning hole in the floor.

Luanne steadied me with her fierce grip on my waistband and kept me from flopping over the floor door and tumbling down into the ground. She pulled me backwards right out the door and around to side of the shed just as Black Sabbath shouted the last strains of "Heaven and Hell."

"Ah jeez, Kate, I don't know about you, but this is foolish. The only answers we're gonna find is death. I think we should get out of here," Luanne said.

Officially, my clamoring heart and adrenaline-spent knees wanted to agree with her. But the wanna-be underground investigative reporter inside me kept me planted in place. "Not until we find out what they are doing in there."

Luanne rolled her eyes. "They're doing the same thing we are. Trespassing, breaking and entering..."

"Wait. What's that smell?" I scrunched up my nose. A turpentine stench drifted through the air. "Did something break in your backpack?"

Luanne glanced over at the pack where we had left it sit-ting along the side of the shed. "I don't own anything that smells that bad."

"I smell apples too."

"There were apples inside and there are apple trees planted around here," Luanne said.

"No. This is more...uh...saucy."

Luanne sniffed. "It smells like applefied benzene."

"Or turpentine. Huh." I slid down the shed wall and sat cross-legged. Luanne followed.

I had tripped over exactly what my readers had com-plained about. I now knew who caused the complaints, but I still didn't have the what or the why. My fright battled with my curiosity to flee the scene.

Gleason was a part of it, and Gleason was a cop. Cops carried guns. I recalled the gun and ammo magazines at Gleason's desk and how he almost drew his weapon on me the first time I had met him. I hadn't even been threatening then, just asking about a missing person. And recently, how he had practically spit-polished his weapon to a gleam at the police station's front desk. He'd have no problem drawing his gun on me if he caught me spying on him.

I lifted my head in the air and wiggled my nose like a cartoon character following a scent. The moon had reached its apex, and without the shroud of trees, I saw all three quarters of it. Another Black Sabbath song screamed from down under. The hose next to us gurgled.

"Sabbath, three quarter moon, last chance for holy water." Those were the words I overheard Gleason say the other day at the Police station. "Holy cow! It all makes sense now." I grabbed Luanne's wrist and squeezed.

"What?"

"Moonshine." I dug my cell out of my pocket. "I know that smell. It's hootch."

"Who are you calling?"

"Michael Earl," I said.

"Just what exactly are you going to tell him, Kate?" Luanne grabbed for my phone, and I shrugged out of reach. "We're breaking the law too."

Luanne had a point. But the phone had rung three times already before I snapped it closed. "What do you suggest?"

"I say we get the hell out of here, and make the call to regular nine-one-one and not involve your boyfriend at all."

"They might get away."

"So? We have pictures."

"Pictures showing they were outside this shed. Whoopee," I said. "This is bigger than trespassing. Bigger than B & E. They're bootlegging. This is a *big story*."

"I agree. Which is why we don't want to be anywhere near here when we do call the cops."

"No, it's not going to work. All these people in the neighborhood have made calls in the past and no one arrives. I think I know why too."

"All right, I'll bite. Tell me why?"

"Gleason. Think about it. He would know what to say or do to keep the cops from rolling on a call. Being a cop is the perfect cover if you wanted to do something illegal. Who's going to question him? He could even say he responded to the call and cleared the scene. And besides that, we can't say we weren't here if we have pictures to share."

"Well hell, that's true."

My phone rang in my hand and I jumped. Michael's number displayed. "Oh boy, it's Michael." I sat on my phone to muffle the sound. "Now what?" I asked Luanne. "If I don't answer, he'll worry."

"Oh hell, I don't know."

I didn't have to make a decision about answering it as it stopped ringing. I waited for the vibration and chime telling me that I had a voicemail, but none came. That hurt.

After a few moments, my other pocket trilled. I pulled Luanne's cell phone out and tossed it to her like a hot potato. She promptly sat on it too. "Izzy," she said.

"Is he what?"

"Izzy's calling. Michael must have called Izzy. And Izzy's calling me."

"Great. Now we're both not answering."

"They'll GPS us for sure," Luanne said. We debated our next move before I dialed Michael back. He answered on the first ring.

"Where are you Kate? Are you at a party?"

"Huh, sort of. I'm at the cemetery."

"Why is there music?"

Oh that explained the party question. I didn't answer his question, but plunged into what Luanne and I had uncovered. Michael asked direct questions that stopped my Lucy Ricardo explanation of what I discovered.

"Kate. Listen to me. Go back to your Jeep and stay put. Okay?"

"But I won't be able to see if they leave."

"You don't need to see. Just go back to your Jeep. I'll be there soon." Michael hung up and I stared at the phone in my hands. He hadn't made me promise to leave.

"What did he say?" Luanne asked.

"He said he's coming. Let's go see if we can get some pictures in case they close up shop before the cavalry arrives."

Luanne unzipped the side pocket of her backpack and pulled out a small pouch that she tossed at me. "What is it?"

"My makeup bag," she said.

"Really? You think a touch up of mascara is going to hide my sweaty hat hair from Michael?"

"I'm sure Michael has already seen your sweaty hair, but you can use the mirror compact to look down the hole."

I couldn't stop the grin that spread across my face—for a moment anyway.

We snuck back into the shed. Laughter bubbled up from the cellar below. I recognized two voices, Gleason and the man he called T-Bone. T-Bone couldn't carry a tune, and Gleason didn't miss a chance to poke fun at him. I slid on my belly over the floorboards and inched the mirror over the edge. Once I located the direction where the men had gathered, Luanne handed me her camera, minus the telephoto lens. Holding my breath I lowered the camera over the side and snapped pics. I had four of them taken when the music stopped. The final snick of the camera sounded loud in the deafening silence.

"Hey. What the hell was that?" Gleason asked.

I jerked the camera up and rolled over on my back. Chairs shuffled and heavy boots clomped on the floor beneath me. One set of boots had hit the stairs when I motioned for Luanne to flip the trapdoor down.

She was already on the move, lifting and shoving the door over its balance point. The top of Gleason's head had just appeared over the threshold. His eyes met mine.

"You!" he shouted.

Flat on my back, I stared back wide-eyed, unable to move, but snapped one last picture. The door slammed shut. The heavy slam blew my bangs out of my face, and I rolled on top of the door. The slice of light now gone, we were plunged into total darkness.

"Oh shit, oh shit!" I yelled. The door shuddered beneath me, lifting inches then falling back and bouncing in place. My teeth rattled in my head. "Hurry, hurry. Find something to lock it shut," I yelled to Luanne. Death may have pulled my name card, but I wasn't about to roll over for the Dark Angel.

Luanne cleared shelves, moving storage containers and the lawnmower next to me on to the door. Apples rolled around my head.

Gleason pounded the door beneath me. I could hear the men swearing below and thanked God that only one of them could fit on the stairs at a time. Despite my lack of dieting, my weight wouldn't hold them back for long. At least I didn't think so.

Gleason called to T-Bone to switch places. The next shove

of the trap door lifted me three inches off the ground. Luanne screamed and stomped down on the door. My head bounced hard against the floorboard as it dropped back in place. I reached out for anything that could help leverage me in place. My fingers fell against a loop, like a padlock loop, and I slapped the floor, feeling for the other side of it. The hasp.

I shouted to Luanne to feel around for the lock or anything that could be fished through the eye to hold the hasp in place.

The thumping below stopped.

"Here." Luanne dropped a strap in my hands.

"What is it?"

"It's the leather strap off my camera. It's all I could find."

I stuffed the strap through the loop twice and tied it in a knot. It wouldn't hold them back for long, but long enough for us to run like hell out of here.

"Listen up, nosey bitch," Gleason bellowed. "You have five seconds to move or I'll shoot you dead."

Luanne grabbed my feet and pulled me off the trapdoor. In less than those five seconds Gleason promised, a shot rang out. We screamed our way out of the shed and right into the arms of Michael and Izzy. Surrounding us were four patrol cars and eight officers with guns drawn.

CHAPTER 26

Let the puns begin, I thought after typing my eight-word copy title. My fingers tapped the keyboard while I waited for the words to paint my screen:

Hard Rock Churns the Still in the Night
The graveyard rallied alive to the riff of Black Sabbath's lead guitarist blaring from boom box speakers. Propane burners torched copper drums filled with fermenting apple mash. The stench in Yardman wafted around the neighborhood near Glenwood Cemetery—all the byproduct of an illegal still undertaking.

Aha, I was on a roll now and snuggled up to my desk.

As you recall, many concerned residents reported loud drumming and sour air in the neighborhood. This past Sunday, law enforcement uncovered the cause of the disturbance.
Five seedy individuals operating a still were hauled out of the root cellar beneath the maintenance shed at Glenwood Cemetery.
Anthony "T-Bone" Scapula, Chuck Upling, Bart "BB gun" Barrett, Ollie Randall, and Yardman's rookie officer Jake Gleason were taken into custody and charged with trespassing, operating a still without a license, trafficking and producing mass quantities of moonshine, and Federal and State tax evasion.
Two of the five men, Barrett and Randall, were also charged with public intoxication. Currently, the five men are detained in the Yardman Jail awaiting arraignment, which is set to take place Monday morning.

Two cars carrying four of the suspects veered into Glen-wood Cemetery just before midnight Saturday. There they met up with Chuck Upling, caretaker of the sacred grounds. In his off duty hours, Mr. Upling allegedly took charge of maintaining and concealing the still.

Ollie Randall, a recent graduate of Worcester Polytechnic Institute [WPI], admitted on scene that he manufactured the still. His blood alcohol content at the time registered 1.8, which is 100% proof positive that alcohol does loosen the tongue.

Luanne and I had laughed at the shaggy red-headed kid as he boasted his construction skills. Too drunk to know he had copped to a felony, but full of pride over his creation. Sympathy needled at my heart for the kid. He was book smart, not street smart, and apparently manipulated into joining Gleason's ragtag group. Luanne had shouted from the sidelines that she wanted all her tax dollars back that had gone to the kid's financial aid package. "What a waste of a degree," she had said.

Detective Michael Earl, responding to the scene, suspect-ed the still had been in operation for the past six weeks. "It's an elaborate copper drum mechanism, capable of producing large quantities," he said on record. "They used a clean burn-ing propane apparatus, not the traditional wood burning or charcoal operation, which would have sent suspicious smoke rising from the area. They had quite the set-up, cooling the still with lake water." When asked for a statement about Of-ficer Jake Gleason's involvement, Detective Earl declined comment. A source on scene suggested that Gleason was involved in covering up potential 911 calls that allowed the operation to go undetected.

I flipped my hair behind my ears, drummed my fingers on my desk, and re-read what I had typed. My relationship with Michael would be a tight-wire walk at times, and I wanted to stay unbiased and true, but not cause either of us grief. I back arrowed to my last sentence and changed it to read, *An eye-witness on scene*, and added that, *Officer Gleason was said to have threatened to shoot, and did shoot at the eyewitness.*

That will teach him to mess with me. Oh wow! Was that considered attempted murder? Yikes. A shiver rattled me. If Luanne hadn't yanked me off that door in time, Joyce would be writing this story instead of me.

I added one last line to my copy before putting it aside until after I attended the arraignment.

Remember, dear reader, an apple a day may keep the doctor away, but a bushel in the shed brings a raid.

Huh. Not too bad. A little rough and choppy, but Eugene could smooth the edges. It was, after all, first draft, and after the arraignment, I'd have more details to add. Maybe I'd even have to admit that I was the eyewitness. Luanne too. Even though we led the police to the crime, we had committed a crime too. Breaking and entering and trespassing. The police chief, Carlton Haywood, delivered that news to us instead of Michael. He wasn't charging us with anything, but he did say we may have to pay a fine and damages.

"Yeah, well, what about the damage to Kate's Jeep?" Luanne had asked.

I tried to shush her, but she went on to point out that there was no warning sign hanging from the chain across the opening. And had there been one, we would have stopped. I doubted that, but didn't say a word.

I dialed my dear brother after that. He wasn't too happy that I woke him up after midnight to ask a hypothetical question.

"Say someone drove into a cemetery at midnight, and in doing so, they broke the un-posted chain across the entrance," I had said. "Would that be considered trespassing or breaking and entering and should someone contest paying a fine and damages?"

"Oh boy, Kate. Just pay the fine," he said, and hung up.

I worried about it all day on Sunday, which pumped my adrenaline into overdrive. In less than five hours yesterday, I cleaned my house inside and out, did two loads of laundry, and grocery shopped while Walmart replaced the headlamps in my Jeep. The tow truck guy, who had not only towed my Jeep home, but gave Luanne, Izzy, and me ride, said they couldn't fix my head lamps until Monday.

My Jeep was all fixed pretty, and I was pleased and proud. I propped my feet on my desk and lounged back in my chair. I had blown the roof off a real crime story. I revealed real criminals operating in Yardman. I was on my way to becoming the next Erin Brockovich. Maybe for my next piece, I'd find out if Rudy laundered money through Rubys. Yes. I pumped my fist. I'd take on the Sicily boys. Huh. Maybe I'd aim a little smaller at first and find out how to make the secret cream cheese sauce in those Wild Rose Omelets.

The ceiling acoustic panel above me sighed and I poked my head over my cubicle. The tile settled back in place and Joyce whisked into the office calling my name. The bangles circling her wrists chimed like the Disney fairies dancing in Peter Pan.

"Kate, Kate! Oh my stars, I got here as quick as I could." She rushed toward me. The layers of her green gauzy skirt bounced, but not a hair on her snow-white head moved. She slid to a stop. Her silver-beaded sandals had picked up friction on the carpet, and when she grabbed my arm, we both said "Owee." Tinker Bell had bit me.

"Oh my gosh, you have to tell me everything." She dropped her purse to the floor and sat me down while she plopped into Dan's chair. Her grip never left my arm. "Holy Moly. I don't think I ever heard as much traffic on my cop scanner in my entire life. Are you okay?"

Her painted on brows couldn't climb higher up her forehead, and if her eyes got any wider, she'd be a Japanese anime.

"I'm fine," I said.

"Nearly every cop on duty showed up at Glenwood. And I heard they called for the hazmat crew."

"I'm safe. No worries, Joyce." I patted her hand and twisted my arm free from her grip.

"So, it's true? Were there shots fired?"

"Morning," Dan said. Joyce had me so preoccupied I hadn't heard the tiles sigh.

"How's our bootlegger butt-kicker this morning?" Dan asked.

"You heard too?"

"Yeah, of course."

"How?"

"On my Find a Crime."

"He means his scanner," Joyce said.

"Does everyone have a scanner but me?" Maybe I didn't even need to write my article.

"Don't you worry, we'll get you one for Christmas," Joyce said.

Dan shrugged. "You might not even need one. If the cop and you get serious, you'll have inside information. Undercover intel." His eyebrows shimmied.

Joyce and I both shouted, "Dan!"

"Not appropriate..." Joyce scolded.

"Like I'd ever..." I rolled my eyes, not sure of how I intended to respond.

Dan shrugged, and I flipped my hair over my heated ears.

"I heard your cop was there," Dan said.

"Yes—"

"And most of the Yardman PD," Joyce said.

"I heard that too...they called for backup," Dan said.

"Did you catch the part about Internal Affairs being called in?" Joyce said.

"I did. Must be someone on the force is a bad apple."

"Oh that's funny." Joyce laughed. "Bad apple. And with them making apple hootch."

"So who's the bad apple, Kate?" Dan asked.

"Jake Gleason," I said.

I sat back in my chair and watched the two of them tell my story. Their excitement was contagious. If my little underground undercover story created this much hoopla in the office, I couldn't wait to see what it would bring once it hit the newsstands. I grinned from ear to ear at—least until Ondrea appeared behind Dan.

"Good morning, everyone," she said.

"Oh, Ondrea. Did you hear what happened to Kate?" Joyce asked.

"I did indeed. Heard you got yourself into a little trouble, Kate. More B&E," Ondrea said. "You're making it a habit." The central air kicked on and swirled a cloud of Light Blue in the air. I didn't mind the fragrance. I still had the stench of fermenting apples locked in my sinuses. What I did mind was the saccharine smile pasted on Ondrea's face.

"Well, as a matter of record, I didn't get into trouble," I said.

"That's not what I heard," Ondrea said.

"What are you talking about?" Dan sidled up to me and bear-hugged my shoulders. "Kate took down a bootleg operation."

Ondrea raised her chin. "She"—Ondrea pointed at me—"did not take down a bootleg operation. The police force did. Honestly, Dan, that's as bad as saying, 'we won the game' when your Patriots play. You aren't part of the team, you just watched. It isn't your win."

Dan's face paled like a kid who just discovered the tooth fairy was a myth. How did my brother put up with her? She'd ruin Christmas morning and Santa, the Easter Bunny, and green beer. I narrowed my eyes, crossed my arms, and dug each of my ten fingers into my arm one by one. My temper was about to lift off.

"Spoken like someone who never gets involved," I said through clenched teeth.

"Don't forget just how involved I am, Kate."

"Even if you blinded me, I couldn't forget." The minute the words came out, I was reaching after them. I hadn't forgotten that her parents were blind, I just misplaced the information for a moment.

Spots of red darkened the rouge on Ondrea's cheeks.

Oh crap, Matt was going to kill me if I made her cry. "It was a rotten choice of words," I said.

Dan shook his head ever so slightly before making a grand show of studying the floor.

Joyce squeezed my arm so hard one of her press-on nails fell off. "Oh my goodness, I'm falling apart today." She laughed and picked up her fingernail, holding it in front of her face. But that didn't lessen the tension.

"I think there's glue in my desk drawer." My eyes never left Ondrea's face. In truth, I was waiting for her to deliver a hard left uppercut to my jaw.

"Maybe you could glue your tongue down," Ondrea said.

"I could," I said. "But the tongue is the strongest muscle in the body, and I salivate a lot. It would just come loose."

She chuckled just a little, enough to give me an opening.

"I am sorry."

"No doubt," she sniffed. "Did you tell them the rest of the story?"

Dan and Joyce looked back and forth from Ondrea and me like they were watching a tennis match. Right now we were at a stalemate, zero—love.

"Oh? There's more?" Joyce asked.

"Do you have a scanner too?" Dan asked Ondrea.

"No, I don't have a scanner." Ondrea wrinkled her nose. "I have Matthew."

I took a deep breath and squared my shoulders. Either Matt hadn't reeled her in yet or she didn't care.

I knew exactly where she was going with this and where I intended to go next. My hypothetical call to Matt had made it back around to her like a poorly played game of telephone. And I'd be reminding him of client-lawyer confidentiality.

"Well?" Dan asked, rubbing his hands together. I'm sure he expected an adventure. "Is there more you're holding out on us?"

"Uh, yes, no." I toed my sneaker into the carpet. "Well, not anything pertinent to the take down."

"Kate got arrested last night too," Ondrea said.

Both Dan and Joyce gasped.

"I wasn't arrested. Nor was I charged. I was detained. D-E-T-A-I-N-E-D." I spelled it out for Ondrea's benefit.

"Arrested," Ondrea corrected. "For trespassing and damaging private property."

"Look who has the rotten choice of words now," I grumbled.

Dan hooted. "Who'd have thought Kate, of all people, would end up in a cell."

"I would," Ondrea said.

"Oh my stars, Kate. Why didn't you call? I would have bailed you out."

"Did your cop date get you off?"

Oh my God, for a bunch of journalists, we all had issues with poor word choices.

"No." I laughed out loud. "Look, it's not how she is making it sound."

I explained to them after Gleason's wannabe moonshine gang was rounded up, Luanne and I had to make our statements. We both had to admit that we were there, had pictures, and flushed them out. But our intentions were solid. With the plastic headlamp casing lying next to the snapped chain, I couldn't deny it was my Jeep that broke through the entrance.

I left the three musketeers mulling over my criminal status while I rushed off to the courthouse. I didn't need to be at the Gleason and pals arraignment, but I chose to. Besides that, I had an excuse now to bump into Beck and get the scoop on the cease and desist order.

CHAPTER 27

The courthouse was a solid red brick and mortar building that stood three stories tall and dated back to the late 1800s. Two years back, after a homeless couple held the building hostage, automatic glass doors and a metal detector were installed. The Historical Society had been hysterical over the modifications, but security came first.

I shuffled through the front doors and smiled for the right in sight security camera. Yardman's founding father's portrait hung on the mahogany wall as a permanent greeter.

As I waited for my turn to walk through the metal detector, I reviewed potential items in my tote that could set off an alarm. My keys or my cell phone. I had traveled this road before when I covered town council and school board meetings.

My tote passed the screen test with no problem. The security officer called, "Next," and waved me through the metal detector. Just two steps in and the machine dinged. The overhead light flashed red.

The guard held out a plastic tray. "Empty your pockets and step back through."

"I don't have any pockets," I said.

He thumbed me out of line, where I got up front and personal with a handheld security wand.

I held out my arms like wings, and separated my feet a modest distance. He swiped in between, up, and down both legs and around my waist. When he passed it across my chest, it buzzed.

Oh God. I was going to be frisked. "I don't have anything in there," I said. My hands clutched the girls before I even realized I had. "Well, that's not true. I mean, I'm wearing a bra, but it's not a deadly weapon," I rambled. "Unless you believe the Victoria's Secret ad."

His eyebrows rose and he grinned. My ears heated and I swept my hair free. Damn those underwires that propped up my girls. What was I thinking this morning when I had gotten dressed? But I knew what I had been thinking, and it hadn't been about security wands.

"Not my first rodeo, lady." He pointed for me to gather my tote and move on. "Next," he called.

My navy Keds squeaked across the tile floor as I walked to the courtroom directory. I cringed and considered going barefoot, but tiptoed instead. Striving to appear nonchalant, by the time I got to the directory, my calves ached from the awkward stretch of keeping my heel off the ground and my presence under the radar.

The third floor courtrooms were reserved for civil matters. That would be where Beck and Legal were dealing with the cease and desist order. Criminal cases and arraignments took place on the second floor. I trotted up the middle of the stairwell, passing a line of people carrying jury summons. They hauled themselves up using the handrail as if they were mounting Everest.

Like a good citizen, I silenced my cell phone as I entered the courtroom. In the first row of seats, I spotted the five men scheduled for arraignment. Each of them were dressed in Tic Tac orange jumpsuits and sat in every other chair. Huh, in my Tarot card reading, I'd drawn the Five of Wands. Five men fighting, deception, litigation—that's what Luanne had said the card meant. Gleason's rag tag gang certainly fit the picture. Their lawyers unloaded briefcases on the defendant's table. Three bailiffs hovered nearby with their hands cupped around their handguns. The creases in their khaki pants were pressed to precision, and their chests puffed with bulletproof vests. It made the arrestees look like a fashion week reject pile.

I took a seat in the back and scanned the room.

Behind the first row, the chief of police took up two seats with his girth. Chocolate glazed doughnuts popped to mind. His size and profile mimicked Santa to a tee. How a man his size ever landed the nickname Bonzie had stumped me for years. The Assistant D.A. sat at the prosecution table. He scribbled wildly across a yellow legal pad. Oh how I wanted to get my hands on his notes.

I searched the room for Michael, and came up disappointed.

Other than me, court employees, defendants, and attorneys, half a dozen other spectators scattered the courtroom. Four women and two men sat on the defendant side. No one I recognized. I assumed they were somehow related.

"All rise for the Honorable Judge Hopp," a fourth bailiff demanded as he entered from behind the bench. A woman as compact as Judge Judy followed him and hoisted herself into the big, black leather chair.

The United States flag stood to the left of the bench, and on the right, the Massachusetts state flag furled. The Judge's clerk took her seat, and *thunked* the microphone twice with her index finger.

I was set to say the Pledge of Allegiance, hand on heart, ready to go when the bailiff said, "Be seated."

The door to my right opened and Michael crept in. My insides purred as I watched him stride down the aisle and take a seat next to Bonzie. They whispered to each other and they both glanced back at me, which worried me. And although Michael didn't smile, he winked. I felt warmed all over, nearly melting in my chair.

"Court is now in session," someone up front announced.

Behind me, the door creaked open and I turned. Rudy Santora towered in the aisle until the door shut behind him. Once he had everyone's attention, he zigzagged through the rows before he settled in a seat. Of all the seats he had to choose from, he sat next to me.

I squirmed, sitting a little taller and stiffer in my chair. I stared straight ahead at Michael. His gaze narrowed at the hulky man next to me.

"What's gone down so far?" Rudy asked, leaning into me.

The leftover aroma of salami and coffee wafted in my face and I rubbed my index finger under my nose. The subtle maneuver barely covered what the man ate for breakfast.

"Nothing yet," I said.

Rudy shrugged.

Judge Hopp banged her gavel.

The bailiff handed her a document. "Your Honor, Court docket seven-ten, State of Massachusetts vs. Bart Barrett, Ollie Randall, Chuck Upling, and Anthony Scapula," the bailiff said.

As the men were called, their attorneys urged them to rise. Only Gleason remained seated.

I wasn't the only one who thought that odd, because Judge Hopp rose from her chair, leaned across the bench, and stared down at him.

"Which one are you?" she asked.

"Your Honor." Gleason's attorney stood and hoisted his client out of the seat by his elbow. "The case against my client, Jake Gleason, is being charged and tried separately."

"Not that it matters to me, counselor, but why?" the judge asked.

"I'm not using any public defender, Your Honor. I didn't do anything wrong, and I'm not a loser like the rest of these guys," Gleason said. His attorney elbowed him.

"Shut your hole," one of the orange Tic Tacs shouted.

"Hey, hey hey! I'm not a loser." Randall shuffled his feet. "You couldn't have built that still without me."

"Shut up, man!" Barrett shoved his shoulder into Randall. "Christ Almighty, you're an idiot."

Judge Hopp banged her gavel until there was silence. "For the sake of sanity, counselor, let's just get this all done. Now, most of these charges are the same." She handed the paper work off to her clerk.

"In respect to the charges of trespassing, operating a still without a license, trafficking and producing mass quantities of moonshine, Federal and State Tax evasion, how do you each plead?"

Each of the men took their turn and said not guilty when their name was called.

"Additionally, the charge of public intoxication filed against Mr. Barrett and Mr. Randall. How do you each plead?"

"Your Honor, we would like to formally enter a plea of no contest to the charge of public intoxication for Bart Barrett and Ollie Randall," the attorney said.

"Accepted," the Judge said.

I was so engrossed in the legal process, I had forgotten to take notes or at least write down key phrases. In one quick jerk, I tugged my notepad from my tote along with my wallet. My wallet bounced out and flopped against Rudy's loafer.

Both our heads bent down between the seats and his

hand bumped mine out of the way. His thumb flicked open my wallet clasp, exposing my license.

In the background, the attorneys argued back and forth over bail amount and whether any of the men posed a flight risk. Rudy glanced at me then at my driver's license. "Good picture, Kate," he said.

Bail had been argued down to a hundred thousand each.

"Do you mind?" I said. "That's mine."

"Yeah, I know." He flipped my wallet shut after reading my address aloud. With a flick of his wrist, he dropped it in my hand. "I don't live in Winter Haven Condos. You do."

I grabbed my belongings and slid over one chair, plopping my tote in the vacant seat between us like a fence.

"Officer Jake Gleason, how do you plead to the charges against you?"

Gleason stood with shoulders squared. "Not guilty, Your Honor, on all charges."

The ADA spoke up. "The people would like to amend the charges from accidental discharge of a firearm to attempted murder."

Rudy stretched his arm across the empty seat and leaned toward me. "Gleason never killed nobody. That's a fact. But I know people who have."

The hair on my arms prickled, a cold draft spread down my spine, and I shivered. What I *thought* was Rudy had delivered a subtle threat. After all, I'd have to testify to the attempted murder charge and so would Luanne. Suddenly, I was scared, but more angry. And because I was in court, because Michael was ten rows in front of me, and because the four bailiffs in the room carried weapons, my stupidly fearless mama voice growled.

"I think, one, you shouldn't eat salami for breakfast, and two, he may not have killed anybody, but he sure did try. And three, you should find a better group of people to associate with if you know actual killers."

Rudy blinked then chuckled. He slapped his big, meaty hand against my knee and said, "I like you, Kate. You could be my sister."

"I've got a brother, a *big* brother. I don't need another." I swiped his hand off my knee. Who was I bluffing? Matt was the master of debate in the courtroom. If it came to an actual confrontation between the two of them, the most that Matt could do was talk Rudy Santora into a coma.

"Quiet in the court." Judge Hopp banged her gavel and pointed at us. "Take it outside or I will throw you out of my courtroom!"

Rudy stood up. "No problem, I'll excuse myself." The attorneys continued their arguments. Rudy turned to leave and smiled down at me. "Just so you know, Kate. I associate with good people. Real good people. Some that are good at their jobs."

The door puffed closed behind him. What did that mean? Did that mean that he had assassins that didn't miss? Why was he even here anyway? Were Gleason and the others tied to Rudy Santora? And had I busted up one of Yardman's mobs businesses and, and, and...oh boy, I didn't just borrow trouble, I owned it.

"...a member of the community in good standing," Gleason's attorney said. "The charges against Officer Jake Gleason are completely unfounded. He has issued a statement that he was responding to numerous complaints as a member of law enforcement."

"Save it for the trial, counselor. The court remands Officer Jake Gleason into custody. Charges of attempted murder by an officer of the law is a serious matter, and therefore, bail is denied." Judge Hopp banged her gavel.

The front row gasped. The bailiffs shuffled the men through a side exit. Gleason turned and scanned the courtroom on his way out. He stopped long enough to mouth two words at me, and they weren't "love you."

Michael jogged after me as I exited the courtroom. I needed to get out of the building, get into fresh air, find somewhere to breathe, think, and hide.

"Hey, are you okay?" Michael slid his hand into mine and slowed me down to a stop.

"Yes, no, I don't really know, actually," I said. "I'm confused and not feeling very popular around here."

"Gleason can't hurt you, Kate. What was Santora saying?"

"Uhm, words that sounded like threats, but maybe just banter, you know." I shivered again.

"Earl!" Bonzie called.

I looked over my shoulder. Bonzie waved furiously for

Michael to report front and center. "Your boss is bellowing," I said.

"Yeah, yeah, he can wait. What did Santora say, Kate?"

His threats sounded silly as I repeated them to Michael.

"I'll speak to him. Don't worry." Michael squeezed my hand. "You going to be okay?"

I nodded, but I wasn't sure.

"Where are you headed now?"

"Back to *City Scope*," I said.

"I'll call you later to see if you want me to stop by."

CHAPTER 28

I had just cleared the first row of parked cars when a female voice yelled, "Kate."

I spun around in circles looking for a familiar face.

Helen Beck waved and said, "Hold up, Kate." She waddled like a duck through mud across the asphalt in her tweed pencil skirt and high heels.

"I wasn't in your courtroom," I said to her when she reached me.

"I know. But why are you here?" She peered over her rimless glasses with her arms folded, her usual intimidating stance. Which wasn't so bad after having Rudy threaten me.

"Didn't you hear about the cemetery upheaval on Saturday night?" I asked.

"Yes. I heard one of Yardman's finest was arrested for cooking moonshine."

"Remember my stench in Yardman story?"

She nodded.

"Well, that's what it was all about, and Gleason tried to shoot me. So I was here for the rest of the story, and he is being held without bond for attempted murder."

"Did you press charges?"

"No."

"Then how did he get charged with attempted murder?"

Huh, I wasn't sure, but it was probably Michael that did that. Even though he wasn't right on site to see it, he had heard the shot and caught me in his arms as I stumbled out of the shed.

"I guess the detective on scene reported that. Why? Do you see a problem with that?" I asked. I did, but I wanted to discuss it with Michael first before I mentioned anything about Rudy's threats.

She rested her hand on my shoulder. I flinched. Beck wasn't the type to reach out and touch someone with empathy. I appreciated it, but didn't want to accept it, nor did I like it, and changed the subject.

"So, uhm what happened in your courtroom?"

"Do you have the portrait yet?" she asked.

"It's a lost cause." I hated to admit it.

"Dammit." She slapped the side of my Jeep with her fist. "Do you have any idea where it could be?"

"Other than Bobbie Rumfield having it, no."

"We have twenty-four hours to turn over our source to the court, if not the portrait, once you find it."

"Seriously? They can't make us do that!" I was so over the whole portrait chase and didn't really care one way or the other. But it disturbed me that some unnamed person could control the freedom of the press. And it was such small stuff that I wasn't about to go to jail to protect my source.

Just then the flood of jurors I had jogged past up the stairs exited the building. Some milled around lighting cigarettes while others walked in circles looking for where they parked. Two rows in front of me and behind Helen, I spotted Fisher. His white head glistened in the sunshine. I literally turned Helen around to look in same direction I faced. "Was that the unnamed plaintiff?" I asked, and crouched behind her.

"Yes, that's him. Sylvester Fisher. And we cannot write anything about him."

"And...he has been following me and he already knows the source. What the hell is going on?" I punched the side of my Jeep.

I explained about the plane ride from Phoenix to Boston, thinking I had been followed home from the airport, the library and Terri, and the eyeglass lens in my driveway. Although, I didn't mention who had found it.

Her hands flew to her hips. "That could have helped us if I'd known."

"If I'd known it was him who filed the cease and desist order, I would have told you. If you hadn't barred me from the courtroom, I could have told you an hour ago." It was my turn to hip my hands.

"True. I see. My mistake," she said.

Did Helen Beck just admit to a mistake? That was so unlike her. First, the empathy touch, and now confessions.

"What's going on with you?" I asked before I realized I had said it. I wanted to know, but at the same time, the last thing I needed in my life was another person with issues to wade through.

She shook her head and said, "He claims the portrait is his."

"That doesn't make any sense. How is Albert Wolf's grandmother Fisher's grandmother also? Unless they are brothers or cousins."

"That is a possibility, Kate."

"I'm sure he was my mystery caller who swore at me."

"But why continue with this court appearance if he already knows your source?" she asked.

"Because he didn't know till after the court date was set. And he may not be a hundred percent sure." I wasn't sure that was possible. My thoughts were too cluttered with the arraignment and Rudy's threat to process yet another mystery. "I don't know yet," I said. "I need to go. I need to write up the arraignment outcome and then I'll go talk to Terri. See if she knows anything."

"Do you have another short piece for the *In Sight* column?" she asked.

I did. I had a file folder filled with odd requests, and Sadie's most recent one jumped to mind. The jumbled email where she claimed to know where the portrait hung and asking what happened to the stars and stripes on the flag at the Governor's mansion. I doubted she knew the portrait's whereabouts. That was just Sadie wanting to stay involved and helpful, or get my attention. I had put her off more than once since she followed me home. It was time I gave back to her. Her concern over the flag was genuine, and I could color it up with humor. Sadie would feel important. I'd feel better about avoiding her. It would be an easy piece.

"Well I do, but that will put me over word count with the cemetery piece."

"No, no, no. The cemetery piece is front page, Kate."

Front page! My breath caught in my throat and my eyes stung as tears blurred my vision. Front page! I'd never been on the front page. My emotions swung on a pendulum, striking the opposite ends, ecstatic one second, sad the next. Sad because I had no one at home to celebrate my success with me. I was sure Michael would share my joy and Luanne would congratulate me, but it was Emma that I wanted to tell most. She'd been there through my entire journalist career. I hugged Helen Beck. Besides family, who else but another reporter could understand such elations?

She patted my shoulder before waddling back toward Fisher, who was backing out of the parking space.

I stared after him until he had cleared the exit.

"I knew it," I said aloud, but I didn't know the why.

CHAPTER 29

Even though I couldn't officially print any details about the portrait story, I had more to document now—now that I knew Fisher was the person who issued the cease and desist. Ha, just like the Tarot cards predicted, "don't let anyone pull the wool over" my eyes. Beck had said we had twenty-four hours to release the name of our source to the court or face jail time. Fisher's suit didn't make any sense, because he had already met Terri. And neither of us, Terri nor I, had the portrait. I had some fast-tracking to do. But I had no direction to track unless I went back to Rumfield and pleaded with her. While I thought that through, I typed up the arraignment outcome. I left out Santora's threats and contemplated leaving town for Mexico, a good place to hide. And quiet too, just like the office, except for pounding keyboards.

At least until Joyce hollered, "Oh my stars!" and hammered her desk. It echoed through the office like a sonic boom piercing the silence.

"Whoa! You trying to give us all a heart attack?" Dan hollered back.

Habitually, we'd forget we weren't alone as we zoned in on our work.

"Yeah, really, Joyce, a little warning next time," Ondrea said.

I had to agree as I sat dead still, clutching my pounding chest. Images of Rudy standing at Mia's desk with a sawed-off shotgun blurred my vision.

"Who died now?" Dan asked.

"No one. Not this time," Joyce said.

I pushed my chair out and frowned at Dan. "Shame on you." I spun his chair around.

"Oh, oh, oh, oh, oh," Joyce hooted.

By the flurry of her chiming bracelets, she was flapping her arms. Any moment, press-on-nail shrapnel would fly around the room.

"Are you going to have that baby soon or just shout about it?" Ondrea said.

"I already did! I found it!"

"What did you find?" I popped out of my chair.

"Well congratulations, then," Ondrea interrupted. "Maybe you could do it a little quieter. I still have notes to transcribe." She pounded her keyboard as if she was hammering nails into a coffin.

"Oh you hush," Joyce said, "and write your little hoo-hah. C'mere, Kate. Come see Grandmother Petra!"

Ondrea and Dan both sighed. The entire room expanded by the sheer volume of spent air. Joyce scooted aside, and I peered over her shoulder at her monitor.

"Is that...?" My eyes bugged out, and I'm pretty sure my bottom jaw hit my chest.

"Yes indeedy." Joyce clapped.

"How did you..."

"Research." She smiled so wide her cheeks puffed out.

"Wow." I shoved her arm and sent her chair in a half spin. "You are amazing, Joyce!"

"Ha." Ondrea snorted. "Maybe Joyce should just write your column for you too, Kate."

"Hey." I sidestepped around Joyce. It was time to pull the pedestal out from underneath Ondrea's butt. "I wasn't going to brag," I said, "but for your information, my cemetery piece landed front page."

Ondrea glared at me. Joyce hugged me in a death squeeze, and Dan hooted and clapped. "Soon you'll have an office upstairs with the rest of the front page big boys!" Dan said.

I smiled so long and hard my cheeks hurt and my lips stuck to my gums. By the time Joyce unclenched her bear hug, I felt like I had been awarded the crown to the Miss America Pageant.

Ondrea had one perfectly plucked brow arched and gave me a golfer's clap. The smile pasted to her lips was the same forced smile on the picture for her byline. The practiced perfect one that had no humor to it.

I tried, but I couldn't let it go. "Oh, Ondrea, you're look-ing a little green around the edges," I said. "Are you feeling a little grounded?" I shouldn't have said it, but I did. I wanted to slam dunk a basketball in the trashcan and waggle my knees like a football player after a touchdown. I wanted to shout, "Take that," and spear my index finger into her shoul-der and knock her ego to the ground. Instead, I grinned like a mongoose and bounced on my toes.

Ondrea sniffed. "Well, the air in here is a little thick, but I understand," she said. "I owe you a sincere congratulations." She flashed her pearly whites in a true smile. "At your age, after all these years, you finally accomplished one thing on your bucket list."

"Now just a minute..."

Joyce grabbed my sleeve and tugged. "Never mind her. Go get a chair, and I'll explain what I have here."

I stomped back to my desk and dumped my tote off the chair back. I could hear Joyce scolding Ondrea on my behalf and reminding her of all the research she had also done for her. Joyce was wasting her breath. Ondrea wouldn't care. But, the next words out of Joyce's mouth were that she felt uncom-fortable coming to work because of Ondrea's constant verbal abuse toward anything we said or did. I didn't hear a reply from Ondrea, which was more uncomfortable than the banter.

I very quietly snuggled my chair in beside Joyce.

Ondrea sniffed loudly as she strolled to the break room. Neither Joyce nor I said a word to each other until she was out of sight.

"So, I ran with the name you gave me. This here is a self-portrait of Petra." She dusted the end of her troll-topped pencil across the monitor like an artist splashing color on a canvas. Joyce had a healthy collection of troll dolls littered across her desk, and each one of them stared back at me with their carbon copy trademark smirks. "And I found this article." She scrolled down the page.

The article title read, *"Immigrant Talent Woos Judges."*

"This column is from *the New York Times*, August 1907. It's a puff piece on Petra. In 1907, she entered her self-portrait into the Great New York State Fair. Although the painting wasn't for sale, it won high honors with the judges."

"Oh my gosh! Grandmother does exist!" I squealed.

Dan stood up and stretched. I could see his raised arms reaching toward the ceiling.

"Whose grandmother?" he asked.

"Portrait grandmother," I said. "Why does the article just mention her by Petra with no last name?" It was more of a rhetorical question.

"Whose last name?" Ondrea had returned from the break room and stood behind us. "Can you enlarge it?" she asked. "I can't read through Kate's head."

"I thought you had your own article to write?" I said.

"Oh it won't take me near as long as it would take you." Ondrea smiled.

I swung my chair around. "You know, I've had just about enough of you." She opened her mouth to respond, but I held up my hand. "I'm not done. I would think you would want my brother's family to like you. But at this point, when I finish highlighting your attributes to my mother and sister, they won't care to even meet you."

Joyce grabbed the arm of my chair and turned me back toward the desk.

"Kate's right, Ondrea. Now as I was saying..." Joyce continued a little more loudly. "The entire article is a standard puff piece, but it gave me a springboard to other searches."

"So what?" Dan asked. "Is she like some famous artist?"

"I've never heard of her," Ondrea said.

I rolled my eyes, but only the trolls saw. "So of course she couldn't be famous, or you would know, right?"

"I'll have you know I double majored in college. Journalism and Art."

God, help me or hold me back before I deck her.

"From everything I can find, this is the only reference of any artwork attributed to her," Joyce said.

"Told you." Ondrea tapped my shoulder.

"Well, I'm not done searching yet," Joyce said.

"Still, I don't see any mention of a last name," I said, scanning the article on the monitor.

"Maybe that's on purpose," Dan said. "You know like Cher just goes by Cher, and everyone knows who Cher is."

I nodded in agreement. It made perfect sense to me.

"We called one of my grandfathers Uly instead of Grandpa Bert," Dan said.

"Why Uly?" Ondrea asked.

"So as not to be confused with Grandpa Ski. Suenowski. Uly was short for Ulysses."

"Is that Greek?" Ondrea asked.

I buried my face in my hands and shook my head. Joyce giggled. I failed to see the relevance to Petra.

"No, why?" Dan scratched his head. "Well, I don't think so."

"Well, there were a lot of famous people and even a butterfly that share the name Ulysses," Ondrea said.

"Oh brother, please stop now," I whispered. "We don't need a history lesson."

"Is Suenowski polish or Russian?" Joyce asked, jumping on the name game wagon.

Dan joined us at Joyce's desk instead of hollering across the cubicles. If I stuck a czar hat and thigh-high boots on him, I could see him dancing with bears in the Russian circus.

"I thought we were talking about Petra?" I said.

"Both, I suppose," Dan answered. "My grandfather on my mother's side is Russian, but married a Pole."

"I bet you have some great family stories. I'd love to trace your genes." Joyce smiled.

I snickered. "You guys sound like your scripting a porn movie."

Dan, Joyce, and Ondrea all stared at me. "What?" I said, flicking my hair out from behind my ears.

Dan shrugged. "Nothing. I'm just amazed at how your mind weaves nouns together without subjects."

"The gutter freeway," Ondrea said. "Thank goodness it doesn't run in the family."

Huh, obviously Matt was still on good behavior with Ondrea. He could make gutter out of any subject.

"And Ulysses?" Joyce asked. "Like Grant. Descendant of a president."

Dan polished his nails on his shirt. "Maybe, if they flipped the names."

"Oh brother." Ondrea rolled her eyes. "I doubt that. Your grand poppa probably owned the Ulysses Plumbing that burned down twenty years ago. The only throne he sat on was the john."

"Wait, wait." I held up my hands. "Can we all get back on

track, please?"

"Right you are, Kate. Where were we?"

"So you found an article about the portrait. How does that help Kate find the portrait?" Dan asked.

Joyce sighed. "It doesn't."

"But," I said, "it's not so much about finding it anymore. It's about finding out what the big deal is with the cease and desist order and all."

"And I found out other things too." Joyce took back the floor. "The *New York Times* article on Petra gave me a birth date. She was born in 1882 and emigrated from Germany when she was ten years old. Oh, and get this." Joyce clicked from document to document so fast no one could focus on any of them.

"Tobias and Liesel were her parents. Says they were farmers." She clicked off that document before I even had a chance to focus on Tobias.

"Farmers? Where?"

"And," Joyce read the article aloud, "'In the late 1920s, German banks backed by provincial governments and the government of Prussia issued tens of millions of dollars in bearer bonds, ostensibly as part of a program to improve Germany's agricultural sector. The bonds were to mature in 1958 and were payable in New York, but to this day, neither the interest nor the principal has been paid.'"

"That's really hard to believe," Ondrea said.

"No, not at all," Joyce said. "Think about it. You live in Germany, but can't cash your bonds unless you make a trip to New York. You think farmers would have cash to make such an expensive trip? No. They would send something like that to family members already in the States."

"Like to Petra," Dan said. "She could have received bearer bonds from her homeland?"

I turned toward Dan. His eyes were saucers and he licked his lips. I had pings. "Tens of millions of dollars. Wow." He nodded back at me.

Within seconds, I had my custom Jeep built, painted cherry red, and riding down the road of no payments in my pipe dream, not that it was mine to diddle away.

"And those types of occupations stayed in the family. So they would have farmers still in their homeland." Joyce jumped aboard my train.

"Oh my God!" Ondrea yelled.

My Jeep crashed into a wall and splintered at the sound of her voice.

"Do you hear yourselves? Lemmings! All of you. What does any of that have to do with the portrait?"

"I dunno," Dan said.

"It's just interesting," Joyce pointed out.

"It's useless."

"Still. Petra could have had some of those bonds." I sucked in a huge a-ha moment and jumped from my chair. "That's it! *Your future is in the past.* Maybe she painted her self-portrait over her bonds," I said.

Tens of millions of dollars was hard to let go of, even if it wasn't mine.

The room fell silent. I looked at Dan who looked at Joyce, and then we reversed the order.

"Seriously?" Ondrea said. She pulled at the sides of her hair and growled at us. "Are you really entertaining that?"

"It's possible," Dan said.

"And how is that?" She planted her hands on her hips. "She painted the portrait in 1907. That article says the bonds were issued in 1920. Do the math, people."

The room fell silent. I plopped back into my chair like a fallen knight to the mighty queen.

"Good. Now maybe I can get some work done."

From behind the cubby wall, I stuck out my tongue. I hated Ondrea for being right. I hated she was the voice of reason. I hated I had to accept her not only here at the office, but in my home, and I hated that I couldn't get over not liking her. And I hated that even with all this new information, I was nowhere nearer to finding Terri's portrait.

"Hold on, I have more," Joyce said. "In February 1892, she arrived in New York, Ellis Island on board the *SS Rhynland*, a Red Star line steamship."

"Like the *Titanic*," I said.

"That was the White Star Line," Ondrea said.

"Whatever."

Joyce clicked and minimized the article and maximized another window.

"What's that?" Dan asked.

"A passenger list of the *SS Rhynland*."

I tilted my head sideways. The list was yellowed and an obvious scanned copy.

Joyce enlarged it to two hundred percent, but that just blurred the list. "Put it back to one-hundred-fifty," Dan said. "And if you print it, it might be readable."

I pressed my finger to the screen and pointed my way across the list. Joyce clicked print.

"Wait. There." I pointed. "Petra Von...what does that say? Fitchner, Fisker, Fishner? And why not Wolf?"

"Farmer," Dan laughed. "And what's with the von?"

"Von actually stands for 'from,' and hints of nobility," Joyce said.

"So like maybe she changed her name to von Farmer for artistic license so she could sound like van Gogh," Dan said.

"You're such a jock. Van Gogh wasn't a noble," Ondrea said. "And yeah, why not Wolf?"

"Maybe she remarried." Dan shrugged.

"Or someone's lying to you, Kate," Ondrea said. "You're gullible like that, you know."

Yup. Ondrea had completely already forgotten Joyce's words. Nevertheless, we just ignored her. For now.

"Maybe, maybe not, Kate," Joyce said. "Immigrant names changed a lot in the early twentieth century. People left their homelands and changed names because it was easy to change identities and leave their pasts behind them."

"It only takes about one hundred and sixty-five dollars to change your name in the state of Massachusetts," Dan said.

I palmed the air at Dan. "I'm not even going to ask why you know that." I scooted my chair back, bumping Ondrea out of my way.

"I just love digging up all this history. It's too bad no one ever asks you to find broken branches off your family tree. I could really help you with that," Joyce said to Dan. Which was exactly why Joyce was a great obit writer. She compiled family history into neat little packages that celebrated the life of the deceased.

"I appreciate the information you found, Joyce," I said. "Can you print out the other articles, and I'll grab those off the printer too."

At least I could give Terri and Albert some family history

if not their portrait.

I towed my chair back, ending our little huddle. Ondrea and Dan shuffled back to their desks. I grabbed the printed documents off the printer and sat back down. Before the air whooshed from my chair, my focus fell on the name Petra von Fischer. Not Fitchner. Not Fisker. No Farmer or Fishner. But Fischer as in Sylvester Fischer!

CHAPTER 30

I packed up my belongings and left the office. The three musketeers were still arguing over who was right and what was wrong with the newfound information. They barely noticed I left. But I heard Joyce holler after me. I kept going like a dog focused on the finish line. And before I knew it, I was driving, but I'd swear I was jogging. Huffing and puffing out of breath and headed straight to Terri's house.

My cell rang twice. The first caller ID was Dan. I ignored it. The second was Emma, and I couldn't ignore her.

"Hi, honey," I said with happy in my voice. "How are you? Everything okay?" I didn't have time to chat, but needed to hear her voice.

"We are back on land! Safe and sound, Mom. We just got off the ship, boat, cruise, whatever."

"Did you have fun?" I rattled off, wanting to rush our conversation, but feeling guilty. "Hope you took lots of pictures and you can tell me all about it when you get home."

"Probably would have had more fun with you here," she whispered.

I smiled. She was still my girl! "Can I call you back tonight when I get home from work? I'm about to crack the missing portrait story," I said. Sort of.

"Oh really? Cool. You better call me back. I want to read all about it." She laughed.

"Oh Emma, I miss you!"

"Me too, Mom."

I cringed as I hung up. Shame on me for putting her off, but I had a conundrum to figure out. Wading through all the information I now had required concentration time. The time it took to drive to Terri's without interruption.

But then Joyce called.

"You okay? You ran out of here on fire."

"Yeah, I'm good." I met my reflection in the rearview mirror and nodded. "Everything okay there?"

"Yes."

"Good. I need some time to compile all this information into some comprehensive order of reason. I'll catch up with you later."

"Call if you need to," she said, and hung up.

Joyce and I shared a quiet understanding about each other that we never needed to discuss or brag about. Like an older sister to me, at least fifteen years my senior, she accepted me and my idiosyncrasies unconditionally. She was everyone's protector, even keeping secrets for Ondrea and shielding us from each other, or trying.

I knew she'd seen my a-ha moment back at the office when all that information congealed in my head. Her eyebrows rose another two inches if that was possible, but she kept quiet, unlike Dan and Ondrea.

I couldn't talk about it. Too many half-finished thoughts ran through my mind. I just had to leave, even though I worried about traveling alone after Rudy's threats.

But with the whole Gleason arraignment behind me, I could focus on the portrait. Knowing Fischer was the one who filed the cease and desist order now made sense.

In my mental map, Terri was in my line of sight. To my left was Fisher, or Fischer before he changed the spelling of his name. To my right was the portrait. The phrase, *your future is in the past* huddled in the middle. What did that mean? Were there un-cashed bonds hidden in the portrait? Why did Terri and Albert have Fischer's grandmother's portrait? How were these three people connected? But one thing was for sure—Terri knew exactly what she was doing and she knew the meaning behind *your future is in the past*. She'd lied, and that's why she hid it from Albert. He didn't know. Was Fischer right about the frame being worthless sticks glued together? He had to be. Of course he was. He knew all along. It was his grandmother's portrait, not Albert's as Terri led me to believe. But did Albert know? Of course he had to know that Petra wasn't his grandmother. But I bet he didn't know about the hidden bonds, if that was even probable. That meek round-eyed old lady used me to find her mistakenly misplaced fortune.

Once again, I was the rolling stone shoved down a hill to bulldoze a trail to the truth. Just like how Abby had used me.

But what the hell was the truth? Terri found something, but then hid it from Albert. Then she lost it. I had announced it to the world, which surfaced Fischer. He tailed me to learn what I knew, which wasn't much. He tried to steal Terri's letter off my lap. That would have told him who my source was. And when that didn't work, he slapped me with the cease and desist order. And in the meantime, he kept tabs on me and found my source. Terri. Oh my God, was Terri in danger? But that would serve her right. Oh my God, or were they in this together? Or was Terri also lying when she told me that Fischer asked her for a date?

I sat gripping my steering wheel to death, staring into my open field. A car horn blared, shattering my daydream or day-mare. The light was green. Go. Damn. I didn't even remember stopping at a red light. Crap. I didn't even recognize the street I was on. I pulled over into the bike lane and let the cars behind me pass. I wasn't lost, just disoriented from auto pilot syndrome.

My cell phone rang again and vibrated in my coffee cup holder. I didn't recognize the caller ID, and instead of answering by announcing my name as always, I just said, "Hello?"

"Katie?"

I rolled my eyes. It was Sadie Arnold. "Hi, Sadie."

"Listen, Katie, I know you're just avoiding me with this trip you're not on because you think I'm a cuckoo. And I forgive you. After all, that's what friends do. Are you in your car driving?"

"What?" I understood her question, but it was out of sync with what I thought she planned to say next. "Yes, I'm in my car, but not moving." I looked in my rearview mirror and out my side windows, expecting to see her running toward me.

"Are you all right?" she asked.

"Yes." At least I thought I was. Unless she knew something I didn't. "Why?" I asked.

"Don't want to distract you while you're driving is all."

If she only knew. I didn't need her help with distractions.

"Anyway, I got good news for you about your missing portrait," she said.

Good news would be that it had burst into flames.

"Like I said, well, told you in an email, I know where it is! And I'm looking at it, Katie. Swear to God, I am. I can even reach out and touch it! See."

"Where?" I asked.

"See that's the thing. I didn't know exactly where it ended up until now. I had my suspicions because when my aunt Sambria, and you know her..."

I didn't, but...

"She's a bit eccentric for our family, yah know." Sadie laughed.

Really? I thought. Isn't that the kettle calling the sheep black? That didn't sound correct. I frowned at my reflection off the windshield.

"Sadie, Sadie—what does Sam.bri.a have to do with all this? And where are you?"

"Well, I'm getting to that, Kate. The other day when she drove me to the optometrist to replace my lost eyeglass lens—"

"Wait." I held up my hand to stop her. "What lens?" I asked. "When?"

"Oh, you forgot." Sadie sighed. "My eyeglass lens fell out of my glasses. Told you that in one of my emails. I asked you to look around your house."

I forgot? No. It was worse than that. I never bothered to finish reading her email. Some great reporter I was. I couldn't even take the time to read all the facts. And If I had, I would have known the lens that Michael found belonged to Sadie. Then I wouldn't have had a meltdown, or a fire in my oven, or a fire truck stuck in my yard! Could I even trust what I thought was the truth about Terri? Oh my God, I was a loser. I banged my head on the steering wheel.

"Sadie, I'm sorry. I need to slow down and learn to listen, I guess." The sorry was for her. The rest of the comment was for me, mistakenly spoken out loud.

"You're right, Katie. That's a good jive for you. And seeing as how we're being honest, I'm a bit disappointed in your friendship."

Slam. Yet another person to put in my disappointment box, busting at the seams.

"Where are you?" I asked again, hoping to shuffle the

crap away and get to the point.

"I'm at Aunt Sambria's house right now. And we's on our way to Camella's, Sambria's sister. She's staying there for a week to take care of baby Ramon while Camella's husband, Lamar, has heart surgery."

Yikes! Lamar, Ramon, Camella, Sambria, Sadie. I prayed she wouldn't throw any more names at me, because if I was to be a good friend, I'd need to remember all these names.

"I'll be back here to the house at...I don't know. An hour or more maybe. You can come by then." She rattled off the address. I knew where Clover Court was, so all I had to remember was the house number. Twenty-five.

"Thanks Sadie, and I am sorry."

"Uh huh," she hummed and hung up.

I glided off the bike lane and back onto Branch Street. Sadie had given me a new perspective whether she knew it or not. Shame on me for believing that Fischer had followed me. And shame on me for allowing Matt to fuel my paranoia with mud prints on my deck. Let the dominos roll. And the lens found in my driveway never belonged to Fischer. It was Sadie's all along, and I had thrown it away. I was humble-ized, or maybe it was more humility-ized.

Either way, I no longer intended to barge in on Terri, stamping my feet demanding the answers. The truth, yes, but with a little coy mixed in.

CHAPTER 31

I parked along the curb in front of Terri's house and crossed the front lawn, snapping the scrolled Petra papers against my thigh. The "For Sale" sign had been taken down. I probably wouldn't have noticed if I hadn't stumbled in the ruts left behind in the grass from the stakes. Damn, I hadn't kept track of Terri's moving progress either. I vowed right then and there that I'd get my life together and pay attention.

The window shutters on both stories of the house were drawn closed while the garage door remained open just wide enough for a pet to scoot through. The city-loaned trash and recyclable barrels were filled to the brim with lids yawning wide. On her front porch, deconstructed boxes leaned against the railing. An Avon plastic bag hung over the door-knob, and a Pizza House leaflet lay across the welcome mat.

I stuffed my Petra papers in my tote and rang the door-bell. Until I sorted out the truth, I'd keep my information se-cret, not only from Terri, but from Sylvester Fischer as well. At least I'd keep it from him until a court order demanded otherwise, if it ever came to that.

Huh. How had Terri and Albert Wolf come to possess Sly Fischer's grandmother's portrait in the first place? Who kept pictures of other people's dead relatives anyway? Then again, it wasn't just a picture. It was an oil painting. I was neither an art enthusiast nor art collector. Even if I had had the Mona Lisa in my possession, it probably would have just taken up space in my garage. I certainly wouldn't have kept Petra front and center on my living room wall unless she meant some-thing to me. And then if she did, I don't think I would have accidentally thrown her out.

I pulled the Avon bag off the door. Either Terri and Albert Wolf didn't get much company, or they didn't use this entrance often—or they had moved out altogether already. I gave the brass doorknocker a hard one-two rap and tried to peer through the stained glass window. A silhouette passed. I called out Terri's name and the shadow grew larger from behind the opaque window as she came to the door.

She opened the door just far enough to squeeze her face in the space. A red bandana was wrapped around her head. Pink sponge curlers peeked out from underneath the edge. Her coiled hair was no longer a frosted blond, but muddy red.

"Hi, Terri," I said.

"Oh, Kate. Oh dear. Was I expecting you?" Her hand fluttered up to her collar, and she clutched the gap of her blouse closed.

"No. But I suppose you should be." I may not always pay attention, but I understood body language. I smiled wide. "I have news about the portrait." I handed the Avon bag to her and picked up the Pizza House leaflet.

She opened the bag, pulled out the order book, and fanned through the pages.

"Aren't you excited to hear what I found out?"

"What? Yes, yes, of course," she said, but still hugged the doorjamb. "You could have called, though, unless the news you have has something to do with Avon calling."

I took a step forward, but she didn't budge from the door. "Can I come in?"

Her head titled sideways and her eyes slid hard left then right, like a nervous bird caged in her coop. "I'm sorry, of course you can. I was uh...just napping." She stepped aside and her hand smoothed the wrinkles on her cheek as it slid up to pat her bundled hair.

I supposed a nap was probable, with the house shuttered as it was. Although I didn't expect an award or even highflying praise over my newly found portrait intel, I also didn't expect to have to barge my way in. I'd bet her sudden noninterest had something to do with Sylvester Fischer.

As I stepped into the entryway, stale cigarette smoke assaulted my nose. She swung the door shut behind me and led me through the house. The dark wood paneling and sudden loss of backlight had me blinking like a strobe light. I held my hands out to either side of me while my eyes adjusted, and I did a slow walking spin. My sneakers squeaked on the freshly waxed hardwood floor.

We passed through the living room and I paused at the whitened spot where Grandmother's portrait had hung. Stacked boxes shored up the wall on both sides of the couch like skyscraper end tables. All the knick-knacks and family baggage that a house collects over the years had long ago been packed.

"I was just about to make a cup of tea." Terri detoured left around the staircase, heading straight toward her kitchen. "Would you like one?"

Napping and now tea. Huh, which was it? "That would be nice."

She set a blue kettle on the stovetop. The burner ignited with a *woomph*. The kitchen was lit better than the rest of the house. The light streamed through shadeless windows and a small patio slider. I surveyed the yard, looking for the white fluff ball that was pictured in the snapshot she gave me when she first requested I take charge of her ornate treasure chase. "Don't you have a dog? Poppy, right?"

"Yes. He's at the groomer's. It's hair day for the two of us." A whisper of dimples punctuated the corner of her lips.

I didn't buy her feigned old lady embarrassment for one minute.

"Napping, tea, and beauty makeovers, but no questions about your portrait?" I asked, and took a seat at the kitchen table where I could watch her movements. I may not have had a coy bone in my body, but I'd spent enough time in the office with Ondrea as a mentor. I wouldn't pat myself on the back just yet.

My question had some stun power to it. Her hand holding the yellow box of Bigelow Lemon Lift tea paused before she set it down on the table with a snap. "What? Of course I have questions." Her gaze latched onto mine.

"Shoot. Like what?"

"Like where is it?" she asked.

"An avid reader claims they have it. So we can go by and see if it is the correct portrait."

She fetched some teacups and saucers from the cupboard and placed them down on the table. "Oh? So you haven't seen it yet. I mean, not only see with your eyes, but haven't held it in your very own hands?"

The whistling kettle broke the Mexican standoff stare at each other. My inside intuition grew more certain that my ornate treasure chase had more secrets than Tut's tomb.

"Well, I haven't yet, but I will. We can pick it up today."

She spun around from the stove, eyes wide and water sloshing in the kettle. "Really? Today?"

"Yes."

"So this isn't like the 'hurry, come meet me at the library' thing?" She poured water into our cups and set down the kettle on a potholder before sitting across from me.

"No." I left it at that.

Terri glanced at her watch while she tapped the fingers of her other hand against her lips.

"We could do it on Monday if you have something else to do?" I offered.

"Oh no." Her eyes snapped back to mine. "We should go right now if you want." She tore at the knot of her bandana. When it didn't come undone, she pulled the whole thing off her head.

"What about Poppy? Don't you have to pick him up at the groomer's?"

"The dam dog can wait."

"Damn dog?"

"What?" Her eyes widened again. "Oh. Wait." Her one-sided smirk twitched her cheek. "Did you think I meant damn like swearing damn? Because I meant dam, like pregnant dog."

"Huh. Yes, I did." I backtracked through our conversation in my mind. I was sure she mentioned Poppy with a male pronoun. I borrowed an Emma phrase. "But whatever. The lady who has the portrait isn't home yet. It's not like we could just break in." After Rumfield, I never intended to enter someone's house again without an invitation.

Nevertheless, Terri started unsnapping rollers and fluffing her hair. "I suppose you're right, Kate. But is it far? Will it take long to get there? I'm not feeling very well."

For someone who wanted the portrait and frame, she was giving mixed signals. And with the Petra papers safe in my tote, I knew why.

"No. Actually, it's just around the corner on Clover

Street," I said.

"Really? How interesting. I have a friend that lives on the same street. Doris. It's a really cute, small neighborhood." She bundled all her curlers into the bandana and knotted the ends together. "Why, I could go by myself, Kate. After all, I know how busy you are. I was planning to stop by anyway. Doris is a widow and likes me to have dessert with her in the evening."

I frowned at her as I swirled my teabag in my cup. "I wouldn't dream of sending you alone, especially if you are not feeling well. I can go by myself."

Her small hand reached across the table and snatched my wrist. "But it's *my portrait*, Kate."

I looked from her face to the bony grip she had on me. "So you have said."

"What does that mean?" She released me.

As a journalist, I knew when not to spill the scoop, and shrugged.

She relaxed back in her seat and sipped her tea. "So this friend of yours really has my portrait? I thought for sure it was a lost cause."

"I'm pretty sure."

"Oh, was it the lady that picked up the boxes?" she asked.

"No, someone different."

"My portrait." She smiled then repeated it again. Her eyes got the same glittery sparkle that Emma got when she talked about boys.

"How was your date with Mr. Fischer? Did you have fun?"

"Who?" Whatever daydream she had crash-landed in reality. "Oh, him."

"Well?"

"It didn't work out. I think he was interested in my antique shop." She sighed. "At least, that was all he talked about." She talked with a heavy sigh after every word. I couldn't tell if she was disgusted with herself or gasping for air.

"So, is the frame really an antique?" I asked.

"Oh please, not you too. You are just as bad as that Fischer man. Of course it's antique. Anything made long ago that has an interest to collectors, or has a characteristic of a period is an antique. I know my business."

Just because the frame was old didn't mean it had value.

And I'd bet Fischer was testing her knowledge about antiques as a way to verify if the portrait was his.

"Why was Fischer asking about your portrait?" I asked.

"He was asking about the frame we were looking at when we were at the library. Why?"

"And did you tell him about your missing portrait?"

"Yes, why?" Terri squinted at me.

"How much did you say the frame was worth?"

She shrugged. "Between five and ten thousand."

"Wow." Huh. If she had it in her possession for any length of time, as an antique dealer, she should have an exact value. The Wolfs didn't seem to live on the poor side. The amount wasn't a fortune, but the interest in Petra's portrait seemed greater.

Her hands flew to her face. "Oh, dear. The portrait and frame. It's still intact right? I mean, whoever has it didn't take it apart, did they?"

"I don't know. Why would that matter? Isn't that what you planned to do anyway?" I asked.

"Of course, but if you're not careful, you can damage the frame beyond repair."

"Right," I said. "It's antique, not just four sticks glued together." Over my teacup, I met her eyes.

She set her cup down with a sharp tap against the saucer. "Exactly."

"I've been meaning to ask you, how long have you had the portrait anyway?"

"It came with Albert. So probably close to forty years, I'd guess. He insisted on hanging it in the living room, and I really wanted it nowhere in sight."

"So you never met Petra?"

"Who?"

Hell, she didn't even know the name of the woman that graced her walls all those years. And it was becoming clearer and clearer that Albert was the one who first took possession of Grandmother. But how and when?

"Albert's grandmother, Petra."

"Oh that's right, I had forgotten. Whatever happened to names like Jane and Mary?" She ducked her head and laughed into her teacup. "No. She passed years back."

"Where is Albert these days?" I asked, and looked around

as if he was about to jump out of a kitchen cabinet. For all I knew, she had him pickled and fermenting in some mason jar in her cellar. I had never seen the man.

"I would guess he is settled into his new condo, and as soon as I finish packing, I'll be on my way. The house sold, did I tell you that?"

"No, but I noticed the For Sale sign was gone from out front."

"Yes, it is a blessing. A nice young couple bought this old house. They have three children."

"That's nice. So, did Albert live with his grandmother much when he was a boy?"

"I don't know. He never wanted to talk about her much. Why?"

"I was thinking that he would know what the phrase on the backing meant. *Your future is in the past.* Don't you think that's mysterious? I do. Almost makes me wonder if there is a hidden message somewhere under the portrait."

"What? No. I don't think so. I mean, I don't recall seeing any message on or under the portrait." She giggled.

"Do you think you could call him and ask? I'd really like to know."

She stared at me. Her lips quivered in a perfectly round O.

Just then, my phone rang. Luanne.

"Hello? What's going on?" I asked.

"You need to come pick me up. Pleaseeeee. I had a problem with Sporty, so it's back here at the dealers and they can't look at it until tomorrow."

"So take it there tomorrow."

"I'm not going to get up at six to have it here by seven when you can drive me around."

Terri waved her hand at me. "Is that a call about my portrait?"

I shook my head no and continued to talk to Luanne. "I'm at Terri's house waiting for Sadie to call—so we can go view the portrait." I wasn't waiting for a call from Sadie, but Terri didn't need to know that.

"You found it!"

"Oh boy did I."

"Tell, tell, tell. I want to hear." Luanne then changed her mind in the same breath. "No. Tell me when you pick me up."

I looked at the kitchen clock. I had only been here twenty minutes. Sadie had said an hour or more before she even got back to her aunt's house.

"Okay, fine. I'm on my way."

I focused my attention back at Terri. "I have to run," I said. She looked surprised and maybe a little relieved. "Don't worry." I was a terrible liar, and since the next words were anything but true, I busied myself rinsing the teacups in the sink. "As soon as my avid reader calls me, I'll phone you and we can pick up your portrait."

What I didn't say was that I'd call her from Sadie's house. I wanted to be there first.

"Of course, Kate. Thank you," she said. "I'm so excited."

I bet she was excited. I doubted she would go further than five feet away from the phone waiting on my call. That suited me fine. I wasn't about to let the portrait out of my sight.

CHAPTER 32

Luanne and I were halfway to Sadie's aunt's house when I finally shut up and gave Luanne a chance to speak. In my mind's memory, I only told her about the front page story one time. But she assured me I'd told her five times in between all that I knew about Fischer, Terri, and the portrait.

"I can't wait to see this damn portrait," Luanne said. "And get this over with. It's getting boring."

I had to agree. At least after the cemetery adventure, a portrait was boring. Which had me hoping I had some interesting requests in my mail pile waiting on my desk or in my email. Something worthy for another *City Scope* front page.

Just then my cell rang. "Kate Lambrose," I answered with newfound importance. "Hello?" I asked after a few moments of silence.

"Yes, Ms. Lambrose."

It was Sadie's voice, but never had she called me Ms. anything.

"Sadie? What's with the Ms. Lambrose?" I laughed. From the moment I had met Sadie, she had made herself my very best friend.

"Now ya listen to me and listen closely, honey," she said.

"*Honey?* Sadie, what's up?"

"The aliens have landed and I don't need no CSN reporter breathing down my neck. If ya think for one minute ya'll gonna be taking anything out of my uncle's house, ya best be gett'n ya a warrant."

"Uncle's house?" I frowned at Luanne. "I thought it was Aunt Sambria's house?"

"Yes indeed, missy, ya best cry uncle," Sadie said, and hung up.

I pulled over to the side of the road, slammed the gearshift into park, and turned sideways to face Luanne.

"That was the strangest call. From Sadie," I said.

"So we're not going?"

"Oh, I think we're still going, but we might be calling the police to meet us there."

I told Luanne every word that Sadie said, verbatim.

Luanne agreed that Sadie was giving us some sort of warning by saying uncle's house, warrant, and that the aliens had landed. I dialed Terri's number next, but she didn't answer and that didn't surprise me.

I pulled back out into traffic and took my next left, then right on to Clover Court. The street was deserted of people. I pulled over and parked just past 25 Clover. Luanne and I turned around and looked back toward the house. Terri's Ford Escort was parked in the driveway behind Sadie's vintage Cadillac.

"Terri's here!" I said. "That's her car. How did she know where Sadie's aunt lived?"

"She's the alien," Luanne said.

"That doesn't make any sense. But Sadie did sound panicked. How could one little old lady be threatening?"

"Huh, remember Nora?" Luanne said.

How could I forget Nora or Abby? But I didn't mention Abby. And yes, both of them were lethal little old ladies. Just my luck Terri was another conniver.

"Kate." Luanne punched me in the arm. "Look." She pointed up the street. A silver Mercedes hugged the curb.

"Are you kidding me?" I swung the Jeep door open. "How did he get here?"

"He followed Terri?" Luanne asked.

"Maybe. Well, he had to have followed her, not us. He didn't just drive past us, did he?"

"I don't know. I didn't see. Where are you going?" She grabbed my t-shirt and pulled. The V-neck dipped dangerously low. Another two inches and my right breast would pop out.

I tugged my shirt back in place. "We need to look inside, see if Fischer is in there. Coming?"

She let me loose and shook her head. Her double loop earrings tinkled like chimes. After the cemetery upheaval, Luanne wasn't looking forward to any more adventures for a while.

I walked up the sidewalk, past the silver Mercedes, and stopped when I didn't see Fischer inside. I made a u-turn and circled the car, peering in the windows. There was nothing inside to indicate the car belonged to Fischer, but it was the same Mercedes I'd seen at the library. I turned to head back to the Jeep when a man's voice asked, "You looking for someone?"

I spun around expecting to see Fischer, but instead, encountered a tall, skinny guy walking his dog. A dog that weighed less than the leash attached to the studded collar around its neck. Both skinny guy and dog stood on the sidewalk staring at me. Tall Skinny had his white tube socks pulled up to his knees, nearly meeting his khaki shorts. And his long-sleeve white dress shirt hung off his boney shoulders.

I ran my finger along my stretched out V-neck, making sure I wasn't exposed.

"Uhm yes," I said. "Did you see a white-haired guy get out of this car?"

"Yup, he walked down that way." He pointed toward Sadie's aunt's house. I thanked him and he click-clacked his tongue. The dog started walking again. I trotted back to the Jeep.

"What'd he say?" Luanne asked.

"He said yes, that a white-haired guy walked that way." I turned and looked out the back window just in time to see Tall Skinny guy stop at Terri's car and peer inside. Next, he picked up the rat dog and ran back up the street and into the house he apparently came from.

Luanne and I looked at each other. "What the hell was that all about?"

I shrugged. "I'm calling Sadie back," I said. While I listened to the phone just ring, Tall Skinny exited the house, minus the dog, ran down the street, and disappeared around the side of Sadie's aunt's house.

"Okay, this is just weird," Luanne said. "And getting weirder by the minute."

"Let's go," I said. "Sadie's not answering."

"Call the police." Luanne begged.

"And tell them what? That there is a Tupperware party in the neighborhood?"

"Okay, good point, but at least let's look in the windows

before we go barging in."

"Good plan, then the rest of the neighbors will call the police to report Peeping Sallys."

"What rest of the neighbors? There are only three houses on this street, and that one," Luanne pointed, "doesn't look occupied."

Huh, I hadn't noticed, and now Terri's comment about it being a cute, small neighborhood made sense. No wonder she knew where to go.

"And I guess Terri's friend isn't a widow after all."

"Who?"

I explained what Terri had said about dessert with her friend.

"Could be a boyfriend," Luanne said.

"Or Albert." I laughed.

"Who is Albert?"

"Terri's ex-husband."

"Oh jeez, Kate, this is a friggin' soap opera."

"Come on, let's go see what's going on at the neighbors'." I pulled her along with me to number 25 Clover Court, despite her complaints that her three-inch spike Jimmy Choos weren't broken in yet and not meant for espionage.

The narrow house was painted country blue with a black front door. No walkway led to the front cement steps that abruptly stopped at the front door. The windowsills were near head height to me, so getting a clear view inside was impossible. And Luanne didn't have much luck either, as layers of curtains covered the windows. Even the picture window that faced the street was cluttered with sheers, shades, and curtains.

"So much for that idea," Luanne said. She dusted off her bare arms one at a time and inspected her hands for dirt.

We crept around the side where Tall Skinny had gone. There, a dilapidated back porch led to a back door. Each wooden riser creaked as we stepped on them. The screen in the storm door was ripped from the corners, and the inside door was open enough to hear voices. I dialed Sadie again.

"Who are you calling?" Luanne whispered.

"Shh." I pointed into the house. We could hear the phone ringing. I hung up and the ringing stopped. A woman's voice grumbled about the damn ringing phone. I was sure it was

Terri, but where were Sadie, Fischer, and Tall Skinny?

"What are you going to do now?" a man's voice asked.

"I don't know. I didn't expect to have to shoot anyone," she said.

"Well you haven't yet, so just go, leave," he said.

Luanne and I stared at each other, wide-eyed.

"Call the police now?" Luanne said.

I nodded and dialed Michael.

He answered immediately. "Hey, sweetie."

Sweetie? Oh hell, now I'd have to come up with a nickname for him too? Just ducky.

"I'm glad you called," he said. "Listen, I talked to Rudy, and he assured me that he wasn't threatening you. He was just teasing. Not funny, I know, and I told him he'd have to deal with me—"

"Okay, okay, but listen." I interrupted him. Rudy's threats were the furthest thing from my mind.

After I explained where we were, the strange call from Sadie, what we just heard, whom we expected was here and why, Michael said, "I know this is probably a waste of words, but would you please hang up your cape and go wait in your car? Don't go in there."

"I hear you," I said, and hung up.

"What'd he say?" Luanne asked.

"Go wait in the car." I rolled my eyes.

"Good plan." Luanne headed back down the steps.

I grabbed her arm and shook my head.

"Oh, Kate, do we have to?"

I nodded.

CHAPTER 33

I wrapped my hand around the screen door handle, yanked it open as fast as I could, and stepped in over the threshold.

Tall Skinny spun around toward me and jumped back. The portrait dangled from his hand. Terri stood behind him against the kitchen counter in front of the sink. A gun shook in her hand and she pointed it at Tall Skinny. Two sets of bug eyes glared at me.

A small, round kitchen table lay flipped over on its top. Two chairs were toppled on their sides and Terri held onto a third as if it were a cane.

"Oh no, not another gun," Luanne said as she slid in behind me.

"Terri." I held up my hands. "Put the gun down before you shoot someone by accident."

"I think it would be more on purpose at this point, Kate," Luanne whispered.

I elbowed her. "Terri, it's just a portrait. It's not worth all this."

"Oh yes it is." Her voice quivered. Her round eyes were even larger and full of fright. A scared person with a gun—not a good combination, and that alarmed the hell out of me.

"Kate," Luanne whispered. "Look to your right. The chair under the doorknob."

A wooden tall-back chair, the fourth one, had been wedged under the doorknob to keep the door shut.

"Who's in the closet, Terri?" I was sure Sadie and Fischer were the only two in the closet because Sadie dropped her aunt off at her sister's house. I shuffled toward the closet. Luanne followed close behind. Either I was her shield or she was my drop cloth.

The doorknob rattled, and the chair bucked and creaked

but didn't give.

"Kate, Kate," Sadie yelled through the door.

With my hands still held up, shoulder height, I said, "Terri, let me open the door, okay?"

Her lips moved, but she was mute, and Luanne didn't wait for an answer. She kicked the chair leg, toggling it to the floor. Sadie punched the door open. A naked light bulb hung over her head and shelves of canned goods lined the walls. "Gosh darnit, I haven't hid in that damn pantry since I was a—" She stopped mid-sentence when she saw Terri and slid along the wall behind Luanne.

"What's with the can of corn and peas?" Luanne whispered. Sadie fisted a can of each.

"Weapons against him," she said.

Fischer stuck his head out around the open door, but stayed shielded behind it.

"Don't you glare at me with that look, mister," Luanne said. "I just let you out of the closet."

I couldn't see Luanne or Sadie, but could feel them fidgeting behind me. Fischer was in my right peripheral sight. Terri moved in close behind Tall Skinny and shoved the gun in his side. Flecks of rust from the gun barrel smeared Tall Skinny's white shirt. I frowned and wondered if it was even loaded or when it was last used or cleaned. And had Terri pulled it off some shelf in her antique store?

"Terri, just drop the gun and we can all just leave. Take the portrait and go." I nodded toward the front door down the hall behind her. "We'll all just stay here while you leave."

She looked over her shoulder and back to the damn portrait.

"She's not going any place with my portrait," Fischer hollered from the pantry.

"Seriously?" Luanne said. "You really want to debate that right now? Stupid man."

"Did she call the police?" Sadie whispered. Luanne must have nodded as her earrings chimed. I'd swear an hour had passed since I called Michael and I worried that I had given him the wrong address. He should have arrived by now.

Terri teetered from foot to foot. Her eyes were glued to me and full of fear. I didn't know what she was doing, and worse than that, neither did she. We had a hostage situation.

The ransom was Grandmother Petra. I just wanted to get her to either drop the gun or leave. Someone was going to get shot and with my luck with guns lately, it would be me.

"Terri, talk to me," I said. "Tell me what you want to do." TV cop shows always tried to keep communications open with the hostage keeper. I could do that, talk and uncover the truth along the way.

"Are you Albert?" I asked Tall Skinny. He nodded several times. "Albert Wolf?" I asked, and looked toward Fischer, hoping for some sort of recognition.

"Yes," Albert said.

Fischer frowned at Albert and cocked his head.

"Do you two know each other?" I asked Fischer.

Albert answered yes for both of them. Terri frowned.

Maybe Beck was right about them being related after all. The puzzled look on Terri's face told me she didn't know.

"Is Albert your brother?" I asked Fischer.

"Hell no. He's obviously a thief. That's my grandmother's portrait, and I want to know how he got it."

"Shut up, all of you." Terri waved the gun in a circle. We all flinched and hissed.

"Oh, Terri," I said. "Just take the portrait and go out the front door. We'll all just stay here and wait while you drive away."

"Liar," she yelled at me.

"Hey, lady, you're the liar," Luanne yelled back. Sadie hummed in agreement.

I looked back at them. "You're not helping, be quiet."

"She's not leaving here with that." Fischer pointed around the door.

"You're no help either. How is that painting more important than a life? What is wrong with all of you?" I asked.

"I took it," Albert said. "After your house fire, I took it. She was like a grandmother to me too," he said to Fischer.

Fischer shook his finger at Albert. "You. You were that obnoxious brat neighbor. Now I know who you are."

What I wanted to know was if the house burned down, how did the portrait survive? But now wasn't the best situation to ask.

"Terri, please put the gun down. Nothing good will happen if you don't," I begged with my hands clasped together.

"I'm sure Fischer here would be more than happy to let you take the frame and leave him with the canvas."

"The frame," he bellowed, "is nothing but worthless sticks glued together, Ms. Lambrose, and I'd bet she knows that!"

If I wasn't sure before that Fischer was my mystery caller, I was now.

"Is that true?" I asked Terri. "Do you know the frame is worthless?"

"Yes, yes," she yelled. "What does it matter? Yes, I lied. Would you have bothered to look for a damn old portrait otherwise?"

Probably not, but I didn't say that. "And the future is in the past?" I asked, and looked from Fischer to Terri.

They stared at each other, each knowing the other knew what I didn't. Dammit.

"What does that mean?" Sadie asked.

"That's the million dollar question we all want to know," Luanne added.

"What? What do you know?" Albert asked Terri.

"I know this isn't your grandmother. Liar," Terri said.

"You're all a bunch of friggin' liars," Fischer yelled from the pantry. "She belongs to me. Petra von Fischer is *my grandmother*, my ancestor, and it's my future that's she's guarding."

"Oh lordy, I'm getting the willies here," Sadie said. "Don't be waking no ghost in my auntie's house."

I heard the clink of chains behind me. Luanne must have been squeezing Izzy's charm in her palm.

"How can Petra von Fischer guard your future?" I asked. My eyes zeroed in on the portrait. Conversation with Joyce, Dan, and Ondrea repeated in my head. "What did she paint on that is so valuable?"

"You are all idiots," Fischer said. "And I'm betting you"— he pointed at Albert—"are the biggest idiot in the bunch."

"I find that quite offensive," Albert said, squaring his shoulders.

Terri and Fischer both yelled "shut up" in unison. His mouth snapped closed, and I swore he shrank before my eyes.

"I'll have you know Grandmother Petra held a place of honor in my house. You would have left her in the ashes,"

Albert said.

"Are your fucking kidding me?" Fischer stepped out of the pantry and faced Terri and Albert. He scratched his head with both hands just to the sides of his temples like his brain itched something fierce. "You don't know, do you?"

"She loved me like a grandson."

"Oh for crying out loud." Fischer's fingers flew apart like he was exploding his brain. "She thought every young boy in the neighborhood was her grandson. She was already senile by the time you moved in next door to us."

Albert frowned. Terri twitched next to him.

"What the hell is going on?" Luanne asked.

"You sure do get mixed up with a bunch of whackos," Sadie added.

"She loved me." Albert's lips trembled.

"Idiot," Terri said. "If only I had known twenty years ago, I'd have divorced you sooner."

I glared at Terri. She not only lied to me about the frame's worth, but about Albert being the one to divorce her. And poor Albert was far meeker than she led me to believe. What a fool I was to believe yet another sweet old lady. Never again.

"If you had known what, Terri? I'm not following," I said. Perhaps I shouldn't have spoken because now all eyes were centered back on me.

"Yo, my nephew's got a computer. He can scan that picture. And I got a cousin that is pretty good with a paintbrush. We can all get a picture of Petra von ho-ha and call it a day so long as nobody gets shot," Sadie offered.

"It's not the damn picture, it's what's behind the picture," Fischer said.

"For heaven sakes!" Luanne screamed in her high octave voice. "What's behind the picture?"

The room was silent. Eyes swiveled from person to person.

"I know," I whispered. I took a deep breath. "Bearer bonds?"

"And they are mine," Fischer yelled, and beat his chest.

"No, they're mine," Terri spit back.

The gun was obviously getting heavy in her hand as it was drooping toward the floor.

"Terri, it doesn't matter. Let's just all get out of here

without having to call for an ambulance," I said.

As if on cue, sirens squealed in the distance. Terri's eyes widened and she glanced out the window and behind her. Fischer stepped from behind the pantry door. Luanne and Sadie breathed "uh oh" in unison. Fischer dove toward Albert and Terri. Like domino number one, Fischer hit Albert; Albert wobbled back against Terri. Terri fell on her ass, Albert on top of her, and Fischer on top of Albert. Luanne and Sadie screamed and hit the floor. I ducked to my knees. Fischer scrambled to his feet and twisted the portrait out of Albert's hands.

"No!" I screamed as I saw Terri raise and point the gun at Fischer.

An explosion echoed through the air. Fischer hit the floor and the portrait sailed across the room. I did a face plant, covering my head with my arms. Nothing but four wooden sticks glued together splintered into chopsticks from the bullet hitting Grandmother Petra.

The sirens wailed one last time just outside and stopped.

"Oh my God!" Terri screamed. She rocked back and forth and cradled her hand against her chest. Blood dripped through her fingers. I didn't have to wonder any more about the condition of the gun. But never would I have expected a gun to explode in someone's hand.

Sadie was the first to move, and crawled back in the pantry. Luanne went after the portrait, and I grabbed a towel off the counter and wrapped it around Terri's hand.

Albert kicked the smoking gun, what was left of it, across the room. Fischer sat stunned, not dead, against the tipped over kitchen table.

Three uniformed police barged in the back door with guns drawn. Two more and Michael raced in from the front.

He gave me a quick down and dirty scan. "Ah jeez, Kate. You're wounded. Next time I tell you to take your cape off, stay out of sight." He squinted at me and pointed to the splinter protruding from my shoulder. "What am I gonna do with you?"

I shrugged. "I got a couple of ideas." I puckered my lips and blew him a kiss.

He shook his head, grinned, and I'd swear he blushed before he turned around and looked toward Fischer.

"Who did the shooting?" he asked.

All fingers, even Albert's, pointed to Terri Wolf. And I had another front page story. Wahoo!

Grandmother Framed

By: Kate Lambrose of *City Scope News*

The Ornate Treasure Chase came to a snapshot end. Petra von Fischer's self-painted portrait is more than a pretty face captured in time.

The Yardman police department's coffer is temporarily a million dollars richer this week while the investigation wraps up.

The mystery of the curious phrase handwritten on the portrait's backing board, *your future is in the past,* was uncovered just days ago.

Sylvester Fischer, grandson to Petra von Fischer, assumed the portrait perished in a house fire that took the lives of his family forty years ago.

Although the fire had gutted the home, Albert Wolf, a neighbor of Fischer's at the time, had salvaged the smoke-stained, waterlogged portrait. Fischer and Wolf, never true friends, shared one common denominator, the love of a grandmother, and that woman was Petra von Fischer. Albert Wolf claimed the portrait as his grandmother and displayed it in his home for years.

But only one man could claim Petra as true family. And only one man knew the true meaning of *your future is in the past.* That man is Sylvester Fischer.

Fischer believed he had lost all connection with his past until a few weeks back when Mrs. Terri Wolf sent a cry for help to the *City Scope "In Sight"* columnist.

Wolf had accidentally donated what she believed to be her husband's Grandmother's portrait to Goodwill.

In an act of greed and self-interest, Terri attempted to remove the portrait from the frame to sell the frame at her antique store. And in doing so, she discovered the secret to the phrase.

Wanting to keep her newfound knowledge to herself and hidden from

Albert, she had tucked the "family heirloom" inside a box and out of sight from Albert, who later set that box curbside. Because of the Wolf's pending divorce, Terri would keep the frame and pass along the portrait to Albert, as she truly did believe it was his grandmother.

After having seen Grandmother Petra von Fischer alive and well—on canvas and thumb-nailed in the "*In Sight*" column—Sylvester Fischer filed a cease and desist order against *City Scope*. He did not want any further information printed about the portrait and he demanded to know the source.

Who claimed his grandmother and his secret as their own?

While the courtroom battle waged on, the ornate treasure chase continued quietly behind the scenes, except now two people knew the meaning of the phrase—Terri Wolf and Sylvester Fischer.

Furthermore, they both knew it promised security to whoever became the holder of Petra von Fischer's painting.

The portrait had traveled quite a distance over the years, honored in the Great New York State Fair, then holding a place of honor in Fischer's home before hanging for forty years in the Wolfs' den.

Grandmother was on the move again. This time headed to Goodwill in a van with poor suspension and an unsecured side door. The portrait tumbled out along the sidewalk and was picked up by a passerby. Sambria Arnold rescued the portrait and took Grandmother to another wall of honor in a small nondescript cape on Clover Court.

In hot pursuit of Grandmother were Terri Wolf and Sylvester Fischer.

And in pursuit of Terri Wolf, Albert Wolf joined the trail. After a carefully coded phone call provided by Sadie Arnold, a self-described "*In Sight*" fan and budding sleuth, this reporter joined the action and called for backup.

Terri Wolf had taken two hostages, Sadie Arnold and Sylvester Fischer. With a gun taken from her antique shop, Terri ordered Albert to confine them inside the kitchen pantry. They wouldn't starve, but without assistance, they weren't getting out until the chair that barred their exit was kicked aside.

All the while Albert Wolf held Grandmother carefully in his hand while his wife held him at gunpoint.

Sylvester Fischer, freed from the pantry, refused to let Terri Wolf flee with Grandmother in tow. Why the portrait meant more than his life became the bonus question to all except for Terri Wolf and Fischer.

Albert Wolf, betrayed one last time by his soon-to-be ex-wife, pleaded to keep the portrait of the woman who treated him as her own grandson.

However, neither Terri Wolf nor Fischer was ready to give up the prize.

As sirens wailed in the background, Fischer made a grab for possession of Grandmother, diving into Albert, who teeter-tottered into Terri Wolf, knocking her to the floor. In a last ditch effort to keep Fischer from his legacy, Terri Wolf fired the gun.

The bullet tore through Grandmother Petra's parted ebony hair, and frac-tured the frame into splinters. Splinters the size of chopsticks speared through the room. This reporter took one in the arm!

Terri Wolf is currently an inpatient at an undisclosed location, where she will undergo extensive physical therapy after the antique gun exploded in her hand. Albert Wolf, Sadie Arnold, and Fischer declined to press charges against Terri Wolf. A missing finger was just punishment [said Wolf].

Fischer found his lucky charm on Clover Court not in the shape of a shamrock but in a framed portrait of his grandmother.

Some families leave us knick-knacks, dust catchers of remembrance; some leave us a small parcels of land, but Petra von Fischer made sure her grandson would have security with an inheritance that had matured long ago on his thirteenth birthday. Hidden in the gift of her self-portrait, buried beneath the canvas, and pressed against the backing board were bearer bonds that had matured quietly nowhere in sight.

ABOUT THE AUTHORS

Elaine

Margarete

Collaborating from opposite coastlines is no obstacle for authors Elaine Braman and Margarete Johl. They share the passion for writing a witty mystery, heat waves, hot flashes, and Palm trees but beyond that, they couldn't be further apart than Florida and California. They met one time several years ago by chance and became fast friends, mixing like paper and pen. Although they have not seen each other since, they continue to write cozy mysteries, and thought provoking sci-fi. Right in Sight, their first cozy mystery, placed as a finalist in the 2012 Royal Palm Literary Awards.

Born in Pennsylvania to parents whose native language was German, Margarete started writing early in life perfecting English grammar. Some of the first stories she wrote were notes excusing her absence from gym class. Those believable tales spiraled her imagination into short stories she tapped out on an old Smith Corona typewriter. Having lived in Pennsylvania and Montana, she has chosen California as her home and resides near Palm Springs where anything under 80 degrees is sweater weather. She is an avid reader, occasional poet, and if there was a degree to be had for stage fright, she'd have a Master, but give her a keyboard or stubby pencil, and she'll create a world.

Originally from Massachusetts, Elaine grew up in a small town in a huge house that bordered a cow farm. Growing up in a small town is the original social media—every family knew every family's story. Her background in technical writing provides skills to organize a logical plot. In addition to winning place in the 10th annual Writers Digest short short story competition she has written instructional articles for career professionals, contributed proofing and editing for such publications as The Florida Writer, RPLA, Connections Magazine and the johnyraygun Comic Book by Rich Woodall. Elaine's philosophy is, teach what you know to learn what you don't know.

Both Margarete and Elaine juggle full time careers, family, and pets while they continue to perfect their writing craft.

To read more about Margarete and Elaine and how they writer together, visit: www.coast2coastpenpals.com

www.ingramcontent.com/pod-product-compliance
Lightning Source LLC
Chambersburg PA
CBHW031952170626
46807CB00006B/2456